Eric Malpass was born in Derby in 1910 and worked in a bank after leaving school, but his firm ambition was to become a novelist and he wrote in his spare time for many years. His first book, *Morning's at Seven*, was published to wide acclaim. With an intuitive eye for the quirkiness of family life, his novels are full of wry comments and perceptive observations. This exquisite sense of detail has led to the filming of three of his books. His most engaging character is Gaylord Pentecost – a charming seven-year-old who observes the strange adult world with utter incredulity.

Eric Malpass also wrote biographical novels, carefully researched and highly evocative of the period. Among these is *Of Human Frailty*, the moving story of Thomas Cranmer.

With his amusing and lovingly drawn details of life in rural England, Malpass' books typify a certain whimsical Englishness – a fact which undoubtedly contributes to his popularity in Europe. Married with a family, Eric Malpass lived in Long Eaton, near Nottingham, until his death in 1996.

AT THE HEIGHT OF THE MOON
BEEFY JONES
THE CLEOPATRA BOY
FORTINBRAS HAS ESCAPED
THE LAMPLIGHT AND THE STARS
THE LONG LONG DANCES
MORNING'S AT SEVEN
OF HUMAN FRAILTY
OH, MY DARLING DAUGHTER
PIG-IN-THE-MIDDLE
THE RAISING OF LAZARUS PIKE
SUMMER AWAKENING
SWEET WILL
THE WIND BRINGS UP THE RAIN

ERIC MALPASS

A House of Women

HOUSE OF
STRATUS

This edition published in 2001 by House of Stratus, an imprint of
Stratus Holdings plc, 24c Old Burlington Street, London, W1X 1RL, UK.

www.houseofstratus.com

Typeset, printed and bound by House of Stratus.

A catalogue record for this book is available from the British Library.

ISBN 0-7551-0196-0

TO ROSEMARY MALPASS
WITH MY LOVE

CONTENTS

CONTENTS

AUTHOR'S NOTE

William Shakespeare spent most of his working life in London. His world was the rough and tumble of the theatre, the Courts of Elizabeth and of James, cheerless lodgings. His circle included the players of his own Company, of whom Richard Burbage, John Heminge and Henry Condell are the most famous, the Earls of Southampton, Essex and Pembroke; the cunning Philip Henslowe, who owned a rival theatre, and the great actor Edward Alleyn, Henslowe's leading man.

But Will Shakespeare always remained true to little Stratford. As soon as he was moderately successful, he bought a fine house in Stratford against his retirement, settled his wife and two daughters in it, and went to live there when he was about forty-six.

But when a man suddenly returns to a house of women, things are not always easy. His wife, however loving, has her own way of running an establishment; to his daughters he may even be an intrusion.

This book is about Will's return to Stratford; and about Anne, for whom there was no living when William was away. It is also about his daughters, and the men they married...

PROLOGUE

The effigy lay in the darkness, unseen. It was hidden in the folds of a kirtle, which in turn was buried under gloves and stockings and bodices.

It was the effigy of a woman, and was made from the wax of candles. A piece of fine lace was draped about its loins.

The white wax was smutched by kneading fingers, legs and arms were stuck crudely to the body, the face was grotesque.

A nail had been driven into the abdomen, and protruded an inch from the back. A needle pierced each eye and each breast.

The hair was made of fine silk. It hung down to the creature's waist. It was the colour of ripe corn.

CHAPTER 1

GIVE ME TO DRINK MANDRAGORA…
THAT I MIGHT SLEEP OUT THIS GREAT GAP OF TIME.

When the woman goes out of a house, the house dies.

There may still be flowers in the rooms, sunlight like a golden carpet on the floor. But the spirit has fled.

When the man goes out of a house, it does not die. A cold, a greyness may settle upon it, as on a nunnery where faith has died. But the house does not die.

So it was with New Place, Will Shakespeare's grand house in Stratford-upon-Avon. Will was in London, as usual. So New Place was a household of women – his mother, his wife, his two daughters, and their servants.

To old Mary Shakespeare, it was less real than the house and shop in Henley Street; it was little more than a background for memories. Memories of the inevitably recurring agonies of childbirth, child mortality: Joan, Margaret, Anne, their sweet days of childhood frozen by death. All the others, except for Richard and the second Joan, in London, as far away as Tartary it seemed: her strange, loved, firstborn son, Will; Gilbert (though why he needed to go to London to be a haberdasher she would never understand); even Edmund, her baby, gone to be an actor like his brother, but not doing so well out of it, belike. Memories of them all; and of poor John, her husband, who must, she thought wryly, be finding Heaven a dry place if God and His holy angels cared not for sack and sugar.

She sat in her tall chair, straight, erect; and her needle poised and darted, poised and darted, like a heron at a pool. But often her eyes would leave her tapestry and fall upon her granddaughters, and upon her daughter-in-law. Upon nineteen-year-old Judith, hunched over her needlework, pecking away at it like a black, nervous bird. Upon golden-haired Susanna, more interested in what went on outside the window than in her tapestry. Upon her daughter-in-law Mistress Anne Shakespeare, whom she herself had helped to create out of a shy, country creature of long ago called Anne Hathaway.

To Judith the house was a refuge from the world; but it was too big. Judith would have preferred a cottage, a cupboard even – best of all a womb. But to Susanna, at twenty-one, it was a place of beauty and laughter. It was her Court, where the young men of Stratford flocked to worship and flatter. For Susanna was one of those rare women who know they have only to wait for all the world's apples to fall into their laps.

And to Anne Shakespeare, who had been born, more than forty-seven years ago, Anne Hathaway? To Anne it was an empty shell when Will was in London, a place magical with firelight and candlelight and music and love when Will was at home. For Anne, Will transformed everything by his mere presence. When he was away, the big house, her own busy life were for her, too, less real than her memories: childhood, and the rain dripping, endlessly it seemed, from the leaves of Shottery; her father's death, spinsterhood; then young Will

Shakespeare skipping on to the scene, eight years her junior, sweeping her off her feet, giving her in no time at all a green gown under a harvest moon. She glanced at Susanna of the corn-coloured hair; Susanna, conceived in a moon-drenched cornfield while a jealous God, watching, made a careful note of such unchastity, and the Devil, also watching, gleefully gave instructions for the pincers to be heated, the fires to be stoked. Two more sinners would be arriving in due course.

And now, nearly a quarter of a century later, the fires of Hell were that much nearer. Anne had no illusions. God had punished her in this world by taking Will off to London. But even that cruelty was nothing to what He would do in the next. Anne had sinned; she knew she had sinned. There would be a place in Hell ready and prepared for her. She would not be kept waiting.

But today even thoughts of Hell fire did not disturb her. Will was coming home! He had written, weeks ago, to say so. And she had been cleaning, scrubbing (oh, she had servants, but whoever met a servant who could scrub properly?), baking, cooking; encouraging Judith by giving her the simple chares of which the girl was capable, even persuading Susanna to perform a few of the more ladylike tasks. And old Mary Shakespeare had been bustling the servants about with her tongue while, in her great chair, she strove to finish her tapestry of the Shakespeares' coat of arms, the speare hedded argent and the Falcon, with the wynges displayed, and the Helmet with mantelles and tasselles.

There was a knocking at the door, loud and insistent.

Anne Shakespeare, laying lavender-scented sheets on the beds, would have like to run downstairs and answer it. But her mother-in-law had taught her that she must not open her own front door. That was for servants. One did not keep a dog and bark oneself, Mary Shakespeare had pointed out drily.

So Anne listened impatiently.

The knocking came again. Would no one answer it? Then she heard footsteps, the drawing of bolts, muttered conversation. Then the door being slammed, footsteps going away. She ran to the window, saw the back of Johnnie Cross, who sometimes earned a penny by bringing a letter from the carrier, not being capable of earning a groat any other way, poor lad.

And today was Tuesday! Carrier's day. A letter from Will? But Will had written only last month, to say he was coming to spend August in Stratford; he wasn't one to write twice in a year. But then, Anne thought charitably, he probably had other things to write.

Footsteps were coming up the stairs. The servant with the letter.

It behoved the mistress of New Place to wait and have the letter brought to her. But Anne was a woman first, a lady afterwards. Her patience had run out. She threw down the sheets, and hurried to meet the messenger.

She took the letter, and waited for the servant to go downstairs. Reading did not come easy to her. She wanted to take her own time.

She read the address. 'Mistress Anne Shakespeare, of New Place, Stratford upon Avon, in the County of Warwickshire.' She broke the seal. She read, slowly running her finger under the words, speaking them aloud. It simply said that Will would not be coming this year after all. He had to be about the King's business. The letter was brief, almost curt. She sensed that Will had been put out when he wrote it, and that some of his ill-humour had been cruelly used on her.

She went back into the bedroom. She had received a blow, but as yet she had not felt it. She needed to stay quietly, alone, and savour the pain, get it into her system; she needed to feel the poison running along her veins. Only thus could she absorb the blow, only thus could she prepare herself to tell the others, bravely, in a voice that would not falter.

She stood with her elbows on the window ledge, and re-read the letter. She would not see him now for another year. And in another year she would be forty-eight. Life was flowing away from her, without the one man who for her could turn sorrow to joy, loneliness to comfort. Life was flowing away. And the terrors of death were stealing all about her, like the fogs of November about the river lands. Another year! Could there *be* another year, when one was nearing fifty, and God was impatient for his vengeance?

This was the same room from which she and Will had gazed out at that wild February sunset, in the days before the old Queen died. How happy she had been then! And now? Another year. The wearisome procession of summer days would pass, the leaves of Warwickshire would fall like tears, like the winter rain, the fields would be white to the harvest, white with winter snows, they would gleam at the turn of the hissing plough; yet again the trees would be clothed, the birds bring forth their young in the leafy depths: all this before Will came again to Stratford. She could not bear it. She had borne too much of loneliness and heartache and parting.

Yet she knew in her heart she *would* bear it, as she had borne everything. Frail-seeming humanity, when it *had* to, could shoulder the sky.

They were at meat. And she had not told them.

Old Mary Shakespeare, delicately wiping chicken grease from her fingers with a linen napkin, said, 'Anne, those new fangled forks must be a great help with eating. In London, they say, many even among the common sort now use them.'

Susanna said, 'Oh Mother, do let us buy forks. When I supped at Mistress Whitaker's, some of the better sort had brought their own.'

Anne was in no mood to discuss forks. She said, 'I am too old a dog to learn new tricks, daughter. And if fingers were good enough for the old Queen, they are good enough for me.'

Judith crouched over the table. With finger and thumb she lifted a piece of chicken flesh from her trencher, carried it to her mouth. Her black, curranty eyes were fixed on the table; but every now and then they would flicker to left or right, nervously, like those of a gnawing mouse. For as a dog hears, and is troubled by, a thunder as yet too distant for the ears of man, so Judith alone was aware of a tension in her mother's voice, a stiffening in her grandmother's spine. And to Judith a quarrel was the most terrible thing that could happen, more terrifying than a thunderbolt down the chimney, or the cursings of a witch.

Susanna said, 'But the Queen has been dead over a twelve-month, Mother. King James is on the throne.'

Why could they not leave her alone with her disappointment and her sorrow. She said, 'There are no forks in Holy Writ, Susanna. When our Lord dipped the sop and passed it, He did not use a fork.' She was talking foolishly, and she knew it. But – another year! Another harvest, another seed-time. Life stretched before her like a weary road.

Her mother-in-law said gently, 'Think, Anne. No more greasy napkins to wash. Besides – ' She paused. What she had to say now must be said carefully. Always very much aware of the difference in her own and Anne's breeding, she was most anxious not to hurt her daughter-in-law's feelings. 'Besides – nowadays, people might expect the Shakespeares to use forks.'

'Then let them expect,' Anne said. Grandmother bridled.

Susanna's lovely brows arched. She regarded her mother and her grandmother with amused surprise. What had happened to them both? Grandmother was far too serene and sensible a woman to make an issue out of a social conceit like forks. Mother had always taught that life was too short for petty quarrels. Yet here they were, arching their backs at each other like two cats.

But Judith felt the storm. It was as though an icy rain already beat on her defenceless head. She sat, shoulders hunched, not a muscle stirring, her face almost hidden in her trencher.

And now it was as though something outside Anne had taken control of her voice. It seemed to her that she sat there helplessly and heard herself saying: 'And what is so important about the Shakespeares, that they should lead fashion? Are they gentry, then? I had thought the whole Shakespeare family were clothiers – Gilbert a haberdasher, Joan married to a hatter, your late husband, madam, a glover – why, Will himself could still cut you a pair of gloves as handsome as any man.'

It was Mary's turn to stay outside herself and hear her voice speaking: 'Aye, mistress. Glovers, hatters, haberdashers, then, all of us. But my husband was Bailiff of Stratford, and my son is at Court.' For one of the few times in her life, her voice broke. 'Do not take *that* from me, Mistress Daughter-in-law.'

Anne was silent. Mary said, gently now, 'Your husband, when he comes, will have supped with Kings, Anne.'

There was silence. Now Anne too, was looking down at her trencher. 'He is not coming,' she said at last. 'He is about the king's business.'

'Oh, my dear.' Mary was out of her seat, bending over her daughter-in-law, her arms about her shoulders. 'My dear, and I – goaded you so. Why did you not strike me, to still my foolish tongue?'

Anne took her hands, held them against her throat. She laughed unsteadily. 'Madam, all these years, and you have never shown me aught but love. And now – I quarrel like a green girl – about a fork!'

The storm was passing. Yet for Judith it had lasted too long. The icy rain was no longer beating on her head. It was *inside* her head, blinding and deafening. So were lightning and thunder; blasting, paralysing. She was still hunched, mouse-like, over her food. But her fingers gripped the table. And her eyes no longer flickered from side to side. They were fixed on her trencher, staring. Her hunched body was as rigid as a corpse. And suddenly she began to scream – the high, sustained scream of a trapped animal.

This was nothing new. And Anne knew how to deal with it: place the girl's own chrisom about her shoulders and recite the Lord's Prayer, and Judith would be herself again (though drained, bewildered, lost, as though she had journeyed a hundred miles). Nevertheless, Anne found herself trembling, and with a cold fear in her stomach. This was another way the Lord had chosen to punish her. Not, strangely, through Susanna, conceived in defiance of God's ordinance; but through the twins, conceived in the piety and respectability of the marriage bed; Hamnet, snatched away before he was twelve: Judith, sweet, simple Judith, whose frail body was a visiting place for devils.

Anne took command. 'Susanna! Fetch her chrisom-cloth. Mother-in-law! Pray finish your supper.'

Mary Shakespeare inclined her head, and went back to her place. She, who had carried eight children in her womb, and a drunken husband on her back, she did not find it easy *not to take command*. But this was her daughter-in-law's house. She did as she was told; but it was not *Anne's* will that made her do it – it was her own.

Susanna ran upstairs. She knew just where Judith's baptismal robe, or chrisom, was kept. She had fetched it before on these occasions. In a drawer in Judith's room. She went inside. She was calm. The animal screams followed her, but did not greatly trouble her. She was sorry Judith suffered in this way. But she – who had never felt the withering touch of illness in her body, whose mind was as serene and untroubled as her face – she could not encompass illness. It was something that happened to others, that one regretted but accepted, like the passing of summer, or another's sorrow.

She opened the drawer, and put in her hand to pick up the white chrisom. It was not there.

She glanced round the room. There were the truckle bed, the stand with basin and ewer, the looking-glass, poor Judith's homely cosmetics – the unguent for the hair, the tooth soap made of the burnt heads of mice, the hand salve – there was a doll, last relic of the childhood Judith was so loth to leave – but no chrisom. Of course, it would be in another of the drawers. She tried another. Kirtles, bodices, a jumble of girls' clothes. Really, thought Susanna, whose clothes always looked as though they had just left the smoothing iron, no wonder Judith is always so unkempt.

'Susanna!' her mother called from downstairs. 'Hurry!'

She leafed hurriedly through the clothes. There was something hard in one of the folded kirtles. It fell out and lay at the bottom of the drawer, staring upward with its needle-pierced eyes. Its left arm had come off as it fell, and lay grotesquely beside it. Its corn-coloured hair had spread behind the face like an aureole.

Susanna stared at the effigy. She did not need the hair for identification. She recognised the lace that wrapped the loins. It was from her own (recently lost) handkerchief.

She stood, her face frozen as by a stroke of apoplexy, her whole body rigid with horror. And even as she stared it was as though that nail was transfixing her own abdomen. She felt the iron, tearing through flesh and sinew. She clutched desperately at her stomach, groaned. 'Susanna!' her mother called again. 'Where are you, girl?'

Still clutching her stomach, still moaning, she tried other drawers, found the baptismal robe, went to the top of the staircase, paused to collect herself: my sister is distraught and I must take her her chrisom; I am Susanna Shakespeare who, a minute ago, was the happiest of God's creatures, and who is now a doomed wretch, condemned to waste away in agony. She put up a hand to her hair, which would soon lose all sheen and texture before it began to fall like autumn leaves; to her smooth, lovely cheeks, soon to be withered and sunken; to her small, white teeth, already, perhaps, rotting in her head.

'Susanna! For pity's sake!'

'Coming, Mother.' Dear God, already her voice had lost its bell-like clarity; it was an old woman's voice, croaking, feeble.

She came down the stairs. Once, she stumbled. Were her legs ceasing to obey her so soon? But – little Judith, who was so loving, so proud of her beautiful, accomplished elder sister, why should she seek this terrible revenge? They had always loved each other so dearly. Susanna had always passed on any clothes she thought Judith might like, sometimes even when she hadn't tired of them herself.

Why? But what did *why* matter, when Susanna, so lovely in her young womanhood, would be a twisted hag in a month, and dead in a year. Like all her contemporaries, she knew only too well the pitiful progression of the bewitched.

Judith was still screaming. Anne, with a puzzled and angry glance at Susanna, draped the tiny chrisom about Judith's shoulders. 'Our Father...' she began. 'Our Father...' muttered Mary, going down on her knees. Judith went on screaming. Anne felt the burden heavy on her. If only Will were here! But she did not dwell on that. Will had more important things to attend to.

Susanna watched the scene for a moment. But then another terrible thought struck her. When the effigy fell into the drawer, its left arm had broken off.

She tried lifting *her* left arm. She could not. She held it up before her with her right. She let it go. It fell to her side, hung there useless.

She turned, and went slowly, oh so slowly, up the stairs. The screaming was less sustained now; it was interspersed with sobs, hiccups, shuddering moans. But the voices went on, loud, insistent. She caught phrases: 'Thy Kingdom come... Give us this day... Not into temptation, but deliver us from evil...' She went on, up the oak, uncarpeted staircase, her feet shuffling from stair to stair like an old woman's, dragging herself up with her good right hand. And still the voices went on – deliver us from evil, from evil, evil, evil, the words echoing about the big house, or was it about the labyrinthine corridors of her own brain? She went into her room – oh happy room, where she had dreamt of a future of marriage and children, of laughter and music and dancing; now so soon to become her chamber of death.

She fell on to the bed, and lay where she fell. Outside the window the sun was down, the sky was daubed with pastels, the room began to fill with dusk, and peace. The house was quiet now. She lay there, empty, exhausted, unmoving, while darkness covered the little town.

Except for an occasional, racking sob, Judith was silent now. Her body, which had been as stiff as a plank, slowly relaxed. Mary Shakespeare pulled herself to her feet, and gave Anne a tired, comforting smile. Anne kissed Judith tenderly, and began to clear away the supper things. A woman's work goes on, even though the heavens fall.

But where was Susanna? The girl had looked so strange when she came in with the chrisom. Anne, suddenly uneasy, went and called up the stairs. No answer. But Susanna was only twenty-one, and biddable. She would not go out without asking permission. Anne called again. Then, her heart pounding a little, she ran upstairs.

Susanna lay on her bed, in the half darkness. She did not move. She did not speak. Anne shook her. Susanna moaned.

Will used to say that a man who had begotten two daughters had begotten a load of troubles. Well, it was easy for him to jest about it – much he'd ever done for either of them. But for her – ?

Yet, to be fair, Susanna had never given her a moment's anxiety – healthy, amiable, helpful, she had been a friend as much as a daughter. Anne was puzzled, and frightened. She put on her bonnet, and hurried off to fetch the doctor; leaving her capable mother-in-law to welcome Judith back into consciousness, and to listen for any sounds from upstairs.

CHAPTER 2

AROINT THEE, WITCH.

Dr John Hall, MA Cantab., had not been long in practice in Stratford; and he was already beginning to feel that he was wasting his time. A man of *his* talents, looks, and social standing should not be attending yokels and small tradesmen. Why, some of them, God save the mark, were not above calling him out to look at a horse with anthrax or a sow in litter.

He was a man with the ambitions of his class and profession: to make enough money to live in style; to mix with interesting people (which meant, of course, the nobility and gentry); to marry a wife who would grace his table and bear children as handsome as he; and above all, in his case, to bring help and compassion to the sick and dying.

But what could little Stratford, with its river mists and damp, ever produce except rheums and aching bones? Stratford could never produce a great physician, or a great anything else. Besides, although he had the manner, the bearing, and the birth, to reach the very top of his profession, all this could be nullified by the wrong marriage. And where in Stratford could he possibly find a woman with the right qualifications to become his wife?

He had almost made up his mind to move to London. And then – there was an urgent knocking at his door. He did not recognise it as the knocking of fate.

He went and opened: a country woman, simply dressed in grey kirtle and bonnet; cheeks like a wrinkled apple; a shy, anxious gravity; yet he sensed, to his surprise, an air of some authority. 'Sir, my daughter is suddenly stricken. She lies on her bed, moaning, almost without life.'

He was already reaching for his round, unfeathered hat, his bag. 'How old is she?'

'Twenty-one.'

Too young for an apoplexy, surely. He must seek other causes: love, a tertian fever – witchcraft? 'She is fevered?'

'No, sir. Cold, clammy cold.'

They were in the street now, hurrying. 'What is your name, madam?'

'I am Mistress Shakespeare.'

There were several Shakespeares in the neighbourhood. Some in hovels, some small farmers, some – 'Of New Place,' she said, with a quiet pride in her husband's achievement. Though she would always have preferred a cottage, she *could* now feel pleasure in saying, 'Of New Place'. Not because the house was grand, but because it was beautiful and well built and people admired it, and because Will so loved it – even enough to come home and live in it one day, she thought wryly.

So, Mistress Shakespeare of New Place! Dr Hall's long legs began to travel a little faster. Not only because New Place was one of the finest houses in Stratford, but also because a patient in New Place was likely to have a more interesting illness than a patient in a hovel, where the diseases were of a singularly monotonous and squalid kind; finally because he was intrigued. He had heard such strange things about this

Master Shakespeare: a common actor, who yet attended Court; a strolling player, who could afford New Place; it was even said that he had made money by scribbling, plays and the like, yet no gentleman wrote for money. Therefore this William Shakespeare was no gentleman. Yet his arms stood over his front door to prove him one. And his wife? He glanced again at Anne. Certainly not a lady. Yet certainly, he felt again, a woman who would expect, and receive, courtesy and obedience.

His mind came back to his patient. Not apoplexy, not fever. He said, 'Have any young men paid court to your daughter, mistress?'

She smiled up at him. It was the first time he had seen her smile; it was anxious, yet curiously sweet. 'They are like bees round the hive, sir. And one, Edward Lucy, vows he will die if she do not marry him. Yet – I do not think he will die, Doctor.'

'They will marry?'

'I think so.'

That left only witchcraft. 'Has she any enemies – especially among the common sort?'

'None. I, her mother, should not say this, but she is loved of all.'

So the only thing was to wait and see his patient, this paragon of maidenhood whose mysterious father was a man of substance, however ill he fitted into the social scheme. Now they were at the house. He had passed it, and admired it, many times, thinking it would make a good house for the sort of doctor he intended to become; but now he looked at it with greater interest: the warm, red brick, the diamond-paned windows, the many chimneys, the proud Shakespeare crest over the great door, and the motto, *Non Sans Droict*.

They went inside: oak panelling, heavy oak furniture, everything good, solid, uncomfortable. But who wanted comfort? The young were beginning to expect it, but to Mistress Anne Shakespeare's generation a three-legged stool, a flock mattress, were luxury indeed. Comfort, to the generation that had sent the Great Armada packing, was suspect; comfort had brought down the Romans, it was said.

There was an old lady, who inclined to him courteously; a girl, black eyes stuck in a pale face like currants in an uncooked bun. She looked at him nervously. She made up for her lack of prettiness with quaintness and character, and an elfish fragility; but not, he would have thought, one to bring the young men round her like bees round the hive. He bowed to them both. Anne said, 'It is my other daughter who is sick. This way, Master Hall.' She took a candle, led the way upstairs.

Susanna lay, sprawled, exactly as Anne had left her. The room was dark now. Anne lit more candles. Dr Hall picked up Susanna and laid her in the middle of the bed. Her beauty, in the soft candlelight, forced itself even on his detached, absorbed mind. She opened her eyes and stared at him. So strange and intense was his emotion that he shut his own eyes for a moment as though blinded. Then he said, almost roughly, 'Lift your right hand.'

She raised it, let it fall.

'Now your left.'

The hand lay where it was. 'Now your left,' he said again.

She did not move. Anne gave a little cry of fright. Susanna stared at him piteously, silently, demanding help. 'Your *left*,' he commanded.

She did not move. He said, more gently, 'Are you in pain?'

She nodded, her beseeching eyes never leaving his face. She laid her right hand on her abdomen.

He felt her pulse, lifted her dead left arm, let it fall. 'She has been bewitched,' he said brutally.

They were the most terrible words anyone could hear, more terrible than the solemn sentencing of a judge. Anne gave a strangled sob. He ignored her. 'Can you speak?' he asked Susanna.

She nodded, swallowed, licked her dry lips, strove to move her tongue, which was paralysed with fear.

'Who has bewitched you?'

She strove desperately, piteously, jerking up her head the better to swallow. At last, a hissing sound which Anne could not interpret. 'Your sister?' said Dr Hall.

'No, doctor. She could not have said that,' Anne said with certainty. But Susanna, to her amazement, was nodding.

The doctor ignored Anne. He stared hard at Susanna. She stared back. It was as though he was willing his strength into her, through their eyes. He said, 'How do you know?'

'An image,' she whispered. And, after a struggle, 'In a drawer. In her room.'

Anne, who had borne uncomplainingly so many burdens, felt that this one would crush her. She was near fainting. Witchcraft, in her own house! Witchcraft was something unthinkable; it happened only to others. 'She is distraught, sir,' she cried.

At last his eyes left Susanna's, and turned to Anne. 'Fetch it, mistress.'

She went, the candle trembling violently in her hand. The drawer was still open. She had to force herself to peer inside. It lay there; impaled, blinded, obscene, broken. She would rather have grasped a red hot coal than touch *that*; but much of life had consisted in doing what she dreaded to do. She found a glove, folded it round the evil thing, carried it into Susanna's room.

Susanna gave a harsh scream, and hid her eyes. Dr Hall took the effigy from Anne. 'Light the fire,' he said.

'But– ?'

'Light the fire.'

There were sticks and coal in the grate, flint and tinder in the hearth. Anne knelt down, lit the fire, wishing she could be occupied with this simple task for ever.

But soon the fire was blazing. Dr Hall gave her the effigy. Then he crossed to the bed, sat down, and raised Susanna so that she was sitting beside him, facing the fireplace. Then he put both arms around her, and held her so tight that she could scarcely breathe. Then he said to Anne, 'Lay it in the centre of the fire.'

She looked at him, terrified, foolishly shaking her head from side to side. He felt Susanna rigid in his arms. He felt himself trembling violently. For all his assurance, he had no idea of what would happen next. It could be that his patient would be shrivelled like paper held in a candle flame. It could be that the eyes, or even the minds, of all of them would be blasted forever, the moment the fire touched that creature. It could be the Devil himself would appear, and destroy their several reasons. Or it could be that this would simply make an end, and bring this lovely patient back to happiness and life. He held her even tighter. 'Do as I say, madam,' he said hoarsely.

Anne put the creature into the flames. John Hall looked at his patient. Her eyes were shut tight. 'Watch!' he commanded her fiercely.

She opened her eyes, stared.

They watched. For a few dreadful seconds he thought the wax was impervious to the flames. Then it began to melt; and drip, and splutter.

But it had been a wise instinct that had made him hold Susanna so tight against him. Suddenly she was writhing, screaming, twisting, jerking as though it were *her* body in the flames. Anne came and stood over her, holding her head tight against her breast, murmuring the age-old endearments of the mother for her child. Then, at last, it was over, the last of the wax melted, the nail clattered into the grate, Susanna was still; trembling, shuddering, but still.

They were drained, all of them. It was as though the powers of evil had been all around that candle-lit, wainscoted room – outside the door, in the chimney, beating their wings against the window. And this young doctor, with his strength and courage, had driven them away.

Susanna's pulse was steady. He laid her gently on the bed. She was already sleeping peacefully. 'Keep her warm,' he said, 'and lie with her tonight, mistress. When she wakes, she may be afeared.'

Anne said in an unsteady voice, 'Sir, you have saved my daughter from a wasting illness, perhaps from death. How can I ever thank you?'

He did not seem to hear her. He was gazing down on Susanna, and when at last he turned and looked at her, she saw a tenderness in his face that surprised her. He smiled. He, who until now had spoken only in brusque questions and commands, said in a soft, pleasant voice, 'Mistress Shakespeare, take care how you commit yourself. I may yet ask a high payment for my services: I may yet ask a pearl of very great price.' And with a last glance at his patient, and a friendly smile for Anne, he was running down the stairs.

John Hall's mind was working on several matters as he ran downstairs. His patient's welfare. Was it safe to leave her until morning? The powers of darkness, he knew, were not easily repulsed, and the night hours would find them busy. But the mother seemed a good and sensible woman. He thought he could leave things safely in her hands.

His patient, again. He could still feel her softness in his arms, still smell her fragrance, still feel the overpowering emotion he had known when their eyes first met. But if what her mother said was true, she was about to marry, apparently into the great Lucy family. A struggling young doctor could not hope to make any headway there. His remarks to the mother, about a pearl of great price, must, if understood, have seemed a gross impertinence.

Besides, how should he think of the girl? As the daughter of a strolling player, or the daughter of the owner of New Place? Did it matter, he was astonished to find himself wondering.

Of course it mattered. Among the qualities he had always considered when assessing people, wealth and social standing had been of great importance. Now, in the case of this girl, he was questioning whether they mattered. Could he be in love? But no. He had been in love before: in Cambridge, with the daughter of the Master of his College; in France, with the daughter of a Vicomte. And in both those cases the lady's social standing had been of prime importance, naturally. So it would have taken more than love to work *this* change. Surely, he, too, was not bewitched?

And that was another matter in his mind. In all cases of witchcraft, it was his most solemn duty to inform the magistrates. More than his duty, it was his desire. He had seen too much of the misery and suffering it caused not to want to stamp it out.

Now when you encountered it, as you usually did, in a hovel, everything was simple and straightforward. You just laid your information, and in a few days or weeks your witch would be hanged or burnt, and you would thank God humbly and sincerely that you had saved a community from a scourge as dreadful as any pestilence. But when the witch lived in the finest house in Stratford, and was the sister of a young, beautiful and wealthy patient whose life you have just saved? Then, he had to admit, some circumspection was called for.

He came into the living-room, set down his candle. The old lady was still there. So was the young girl who, since there were apparently no other sisters, must be the witch.

He bowed to the old lady. 'John Hall, madam, physician, at your service.'

She inclined her head. 'Sir, you attended my kinsman, John Lambert, son of my late sister, Joan Arden.'

He said, impressed, 'You are an Arden, madam?'

She smiled, nodded. He looked at her for the first time with interest: the lean, amused face, the outcurling lower lip, the intelligent eyes. So, his beautiful patient came of one of the oldest and proudest families in the district. Lambert had said they counted two Sheriffs of Warwickshire among their ancestors. He said, 'A noble family, if I may say so, Mistress Shakespeare. Master Lambert spoke proudly of his mother's lineage.'

'So he should.' But to herself she was saying: Oh, foolish old woman, still telling all whom you meet that you are an Arden. Why, the next person *you* meet may be the Recording Angel. Will you tell *him*, and will he then fling open the gates for you without further question?

He looked at the girl. She *could* be a witch, with that black hair, those black eyes, that pallor, the curious, hunched way she held her shoulders. Yet she had a friendly little face, a shy, anxious smile. But then, he had learnt from experience, Satan knows how to disguise his own. The

Devil's mark had been found on the most seemingly innocent.

He bowed. 'Good morrow, mistress.'

Judith's face was transformed with happiness. It was seldom that anyone even troubled to notice her, let alone address her as mistress. She rose hurriedly, and curtsied. In her haste, she did it clumsily; but to be spoken to by this handsome, tall creature was enough to discompose a princess, she told herself.

He looked at her with compassion. Poor, awkward little creature! And with a lovely sister about to marry into a noble family. He thought he could understand, though he could never condone, her pathetic attempt at witchcraft.

'Pray, sir, be seated,' said Mary Shakespeare.

He sat down on a three-legged stool, his long thighs stretching out before him. He gazed at the young girl. 'What is your name, child?' he asked kindly.

'Judith, sir.' Her speech was thick, as though her tongue lay rolled at the back of her mouth.

'A pretty name.' He was talking to her as to a child. Yet she must be – what? Nineteen? Marriageable, like her sister. But, though sweet and appealing when she smiled, she would not grace his table like the older girl; she would bear small, ill-shapen sons, her dowry would be less. And, as though these disadvantages were not enough, she was a witch, God have mercy.

He drew his stool a little nearer, settled himself more firmly. Judith gazed at him with adoration. She vowed to herself that she had never seen so proper a gentleman. And talking to *her*, staring at her as though he had never met so fascinating a creature. Perhaps, she thought, he is about to declare himself. Stranger things had happened. She had thought much about love. She knew it could grow slowly, like a great oak. Or it could strike like the lightning blast.

He said, sternly, 'Why did you bewitch your sister?'

Mary Shakespeare gave a choking cry. He hushed her with a gesture. He said again, 'Why did you bewitch your sister?'

She looked at him. But he could read nothing in that small, white face – neither fear, nor the silly pride so many witches showed. Only a sly, sly smile. And silence.

But Mary Shakespeare was not one to hold her tongue when she heard nonsense of this kind. She rose, shaking her shoulders angrily, rattling her stick against her chair. 'Sir, methinks it is *you* who are bewitched. What? Judith Shakespeare, daughter of *my* eldest son, do anything so vile?'

He said, crossly, 'Satan does not mix only with the common sort, madam.' He turned back to Judith 'Come, mistress. Do not force me to lay this information before the magistrates.'

'The *magistrates?*' cried Mary. 'Why, sir, you would be driven out of Stratford, a laughing stock.' And, though she fought against using the words, yet she used them. She had grown old, and was become incontinent with words: 'That girl is an Arden.'

'And has practised witchcraft,' he said coolly. But he had been watching Judith. And the word *magistrate* had broken down her confidence. She was trembling. Her face still had that sly smile. But her voice was a whisper as she said, 'I did but jest, sir.'

'*Jest?*' He was really angry now. 'Jest? It is a jest that you may pay for in the living flame, madam.'

The horror seemed to pinch her features, showing the fine, brittle bones. He cursed, as he had so often done before, his sudden flares of temper. Now he was all compassion. 'Do not be troubled, child. If you will undertake – and if your sister recovers, and is agreeable – then we may treat this as a family matter.' He rose, smiling, rejoicing in the delightful knowledge that both self-interest and Christian charity were pointing him down the same road.

Mary said tartly, 'Indeed, sir, I vow your kindness to a poor child quite overwhelms me.'

He bowed stiffly. 'Give you good day, madam.' He smiled to the white frailty that was Judith. And was gone.

Anne Shakespeare looked down at the sleeping Susanna. Then she took a candle, and went into Judith's room.

She was afraid. The powers of darkness were ever-present in all their lives. The moment the sun touched the rim of the earth they were out of their lairs, squeaking and fluttering like bats, howling in the night wind, tapping like dry branches at doors and windows.

But she had always kept them out of the house. By candlelight, and the strewing of herbs on the window ledges, and the bright burning of the fire, and by prayers at sunset, she had kept her house clean. And now, that foolish child had flung open the doors to them.

Foolish, she thought, not wicked; there was no malice in Judith. But Anne believed that Judith and her twin Hamnet, had shared a common existence; and that when Hamnet died he carried away with him a part of Judith's mind and strength. The girl had never been strong, but after Hamnet's death she had wasted a little both in her body and in her mind. She had gone about listening. It was as though she listened so hard for the voice of her dead twin that she never quite heard what was said to her by others. A strange, pitiful little creature, only half in this world – a daughter any mother, however sensible, would spoil and cosset.

She took her candle. She made sure Susanna was sleeping. She went to the top of the stairs and called quietly, 'Judith.' Then she went back into Judith's room and waited, wondering what she was going to say, what she possibly *could* say.

She heard the child's footsteps. She sat down on the stool; silent, troubled. Her mind was in abeyance; her mother's instincts, feelings, her mother's body had taken charge. When Judith came into the room like a sleep-walker, blinking after the dark of the stairs, Anne simply held out her arms and the girl came into them, and stood, half-lying sideways against her mother.

They stayed so, silent, for a long time; the candlelight, the familiar room. Peace! Outside, the ghost-ridden night. Inside, the peace of God, the love of mother for child, of child for mother.

At last Anne spoke – and it was as though the word was brought from a long way away. 'Why?'

Judith was silent; her face in the candlelight was brooding. Anne had seen just the same expression on her husband's face when he was at his writing. She said again, very sternly, 'Why, Judith?'

The girl turned now and looked at her, a gentle, sad gaze. 'I do not know, Mother.'

'But a devil entered into you, child, when we were at meat. Is it – ?' But she did not know what she wanted to ask.

'I am very tired, Mother. May I go to bed now?'

'No you may not; not till you have answered my question. Surely you love your sister?'

'No, Mother. I hate her.'

The voice was flat, weary, matter of fact. Anne had to lick her dry lips before she could say again, 'Why? Everybody loves Susanna.'

Judith nodded. 'That is why, Mother. And because she is beautiful, and I am not.'

It was a good, womanish reason. Anne, being a woman, could understand. But she was still afraid. It was one thing, she knew, to *summon* the powers of darkness; it was quite another to bid them begone.

Morning, and a brisk wind blowing away the goblins and terrors of the dark, a bright sun dispelling night fears.

The wind scurried about the narrow, overhung streets of Stratford, fluttered the market stalls, dispelled the stink of ale outside the widow Quiney's tavern (where her son Tom was unloading barrels too heavy for his puny strength); it danced along Henley Street, where Will Shakespeare's sister Joan, she that married Hart the hatter, lived in the old family home; it dusted round schoolmaster Aspinall and his usher; it tossed the smell of new bread from Allen's bakery into hungry nostrils; it whistled round the house on the corner of Sheep Street and High Street where lived Hamnet and Judith Sadler, those old friends for whom the Shakespeare twins were named.

Young Doctor Hall mounted his horse and galloped off to visit some outlying farms, his heart warm and tender and singing, this gay morning, with memories of that lovely, unavailable Shakespeare girl and her quaint sister.

Judith put on her bonnet, and went to fetch the milk. Pale, pensive, self-contained. No one would ever know what Judith was thinking, or even whether she was thinking. Of her sister's discovery, her mother's concern, the handsome Doctor Hall's frightening words? Or simply listening, listening for the long-ago voice of her dead twin?

The servants at New Place had finished their first tasks and were already at breakfast; but a breakfast with a difference. For once the mistress was not there to serve the meat and pottage. It was unheard of, and rumours were rife. She was ill. She was dead. There were even some who, snatching a fragment of news from the very air, vowed she had been bewitched.

Anne Shakespeare had slept badly. She lay beside Susanna. Two candles burned all night beside the bed. The powers of darkness should not have their way for the cost of a pair of candles.

She had seen the first greyness in the chinks of the curtains. She had heard the cock crow, the sparrows in the eaves beginning another restless day, the rush of a thousand starlings swooping in from their roosts, the clip-clop of hooves in Chapel Lane, the footsteps of sleepy servants in her own house. Normally she would be up and about now, setting this one to prepare the breakfast pottage, that one to sweep, another to grind the malt for the brewing, a fourth to dust. But today she lay as still as a mouse, scarce breathing. It was important for Susanna to sleep. New Place would rouse itself without her help she told herself, not believing it for a moment.

Susanna stirred, and opened her eyes. They were filled with fear. She shivered. But Anne's smile was filled with love, and hope, and tenderness and warmth. Anne sat up. Now at last she could do what she had fought against doing all through the long night. She took her daughter's left hand, raised it, and held it against her lips.

The hand was warm, and living. She felt it stir, press itself affectionately against her lips, her cheek. She took her own hands away. The hand stayed, touching her face. Then, suddenly, the girl looked at it in wonder. 'Mother! My hand. See, I can lift it.'

Anne said, in an unsteady voice, 'You have been ill; and now you are well again, daughter.'

'Yes.' She sighed. 'The pain is gone – and the palsy. But give me a looking-glass, Mother; quickly.'

Anne gave her a glass, and drew back the curtains. The morning flooded in, like joy after a night of weeping. Susanna sat up in bed, a girl in her loveliness artlessly admiring her beauty. She drew her fingers through her hair, watched the sleek fall of the gold in the mirror. She examined her clear, green eyes, her teeth, her brow, her cheeks, the round softness of her arms. No wasting, no corruption. Her fears could no more withstand the sunlight than the waxen image could withstand the flames. She said, astonishingly, 'Poor Judith! She was like to have killed me, but for Doctor Hall.'

Anne said, 'Yet you say "poor Judith"?'

'She frighted me sorely. But she has currants for eyes, Mother, and dough for flesh, and she will carry her maidenhead to the grave. So I say, "poor Judith".'

Anne said, 'It is good that you can say that, Susanna.' But she was not so foolish as to think that that was the end of the matter. She knew that, however calm and placid the relationship between sisters might seem, there were always strong undertows that neither girl could control or even understand.

And so it was. Judith, going warily into Susanna's room, found herself seized by the hair, pummelled, scratched; saw the normally serene face of Susanna stiff with fury; heard her sister's voice angrily shrill. 'So, little witch! You thought to make me as ugly as you with your spells and incantations.'

'No, sister. I vow – by our blessed Saviour – '

'By the Devil, rather. And call on him also when they pile the faggots about your ankles, and the flames begin to lick about your flesh.'

Judith was ashen grey. 'Sister you would not–? Mother, Dr Hall, both said – ' She ran a finger across her dry lips. ' 'Twas but in jest, Susanna,' she said pitifully.

'Jest? My arm was palsied, my voice a croak, my feet stumbled on the stairs. Had Dr Hall not destroyed my effigy – ' She still had the fingers of both hands sunk in Judith's wiry black hair, still shook her head to and fro. Judith, teeth clenched, eyes shut tight, waited for the storm to pass.

And pass it did. Susanna, in one swift movement, it seemed, let go Judith's hair and took her young sister in her arms. She was half weeping, half smiling in reproach. 'Oh, Judith, little fool, whenever now I have a toothache or a rheum, I shall think you have bewitched me.'

''Twill not be my doing, sister.'

They clung. There were tears in the eyes of both of them. The thin, sly smile was again about Judith's lips. Yet now she disengaged herself from her sister's arms, knelt demurely before her. 'Bless me, sister; and grant me forgiveness for my great wickedness.'

Susanna said tartly, 'I am not *quite* a fool, Judith. First – ' she went to the chest, picked up her Bible – 'swear on this book that you will abstain forever from all witchcraft.'

Judith took the Bible. 'I swear, sister.'

But the burning of the effigy had not wholly dispelled the terror that filled Susanna. She cried, with a sudden return of anger, 'And swear that I am absolved from all your former spells and curses, vile witch.'

'I swear it, dear sister.'

Judith was still kneeling. Susanna put her hands on the dark, bowed head, and blessed her. Judith rose from her knees. The two sisters stood close, staring at each other, the fair woman and the dark, the serene and the forlorn, the one to whom happiness was her natural element, and the other. They stood so for a long time, unsmiling, each trying to read that most intractable of all riddles, the human face. Then Judith turned and, without a word, ran from the room.

CHAPTER 3

O MISTRESS MINE, WHERE ARE YOU ROAMING?

The players were coming to town!

And no mere harlotry players, to beg the Bailiff on bended knee for his permission, or even to be driven out by the Constable like the rogues they were. No strolling company, with tumblers cartwheeling before over Clopton Bridge, with a brave show of drums and fifes and performing dogs, to bring a quick, darting life to the slow burghers of Stratford. No. This time it was the famous King's Men, with letters patent to wave in the face of any mayor or bailiff who said them nay; the King's Men, who acted at Court and before the London gallants; the King's Men, who numbered a Stratford man among their players, poor old John Shakespeare's son, he that got a woman eight years his senior with child, aye, *and* married her; and, after neglecting her shamefully, set the whole town by the ears by buying New Place for her, the finest house in Stratford; he that was a good merry fellow, those that knew him said; for though he walked with kings in London, he would walk as contentedly with a shepherd or a woodcutter in Stratford.

The players were coming to town! A Master Heminge, a very seemly gentleman, more like a clerk than an actor, had ridden into the town. He had visited Mistress Quiney at her tavern. Would she allow her yard to be used for play acting? The King's Men would pay well, though of course the extra beer sold would really pay for her trouble. And some of the players would lie at her tavern, though he understood the senior men would lodge with Master Shakespeare at his house. And where *was* Master Shakespeare's house, good mistress? What? So near and so direct? How different from London, with its maze of alleys and warrens. Give you good day, mistress. He swept a low bow, clapped his tall round hat on his head, and left Widow Quiney purring.

A servant showed him into the living-room. 'Master John Heminge.'

He was intrigued. Will Shakespeare was so much one of them; the best loved, without doubt, of all the King's Men. John Heminge had known him as hired man, botcher up of plays, writer of plays, sharer in the Company; he had known him as true friend, and good companion. Yet this open, friendly man had, surprisingly, a withdrawn quality. He had noble friends of whom he talked little; and most summers he would disappear for a month to his house at Stratford-upon-Avon.

There were rumours, of course. His house was as big as Somerset House, or Hatfield. He had married a woman twenty years his senior, a thin shrew of a woman who berated him unmercifully. His first child had been born at the wedding breakfast and, not surprisingly, had a hare lip and a mark like a devil's pitchfork in the centre of her forehead. His mother had been one of the greatest ladies in the land, who had married a scullion in her father's kitchens.

None of these rumours John Heminge believed; and one he had already scotched. New Place was a decent, sturdy house, the house of a wealthy tradesman, and John had smiled to see old Will's arms over the door. But it wasn't another Hatfield. And now he was about to see Will's secret world; to see that unknown, private life of someone in the public eye that is always so intriguing.

There was music, which died at the announcement of his name. 'In delay there lies no plenty, Then come kiss me, sweet and – ' The pleasant tenor voice fell silent, courteously; the girl's slim fingers ceased to pluck the lute. Yet it seemed that lutenist and singer finished the song with their eyes, smiling at each other as though isolated in a world of unending, sunlit afternoons.

And now a small, plump woman with apple-john cheeks had come forward· nervous, bustling, yet with a dignity and a sweetness of smile he found captivating. 'Sir, you are welcome. But – my husband has oft spoken of a Master Heminge. There is nothing – wrong? Will is not – ?'

He smiled reassuringly, swept her a London bow. 'Will is in excellent health, madam, and bids me say he hopes to be with you within the week.'

'But – ' She was confused. 'Only last month – I had a letter – he would not come this year.'

'Plague, madam, in London. It has driven us out on tour – Oxford, Stratford, Coventry, Leicester…'

Anne thought: this sudden surge of joy through my entire body, this ecstasy of happiness in my mind, is being paid for by a thousand deaths, a thousand agonies. So often it had happened: herself rejoicing yet troubled, because it took the suffering of a whole populace to give her her Will.

She said, 'This is good news indeed, sir. But you will take a glass of wine. This' – she indicated the tall young singer – 'this is Master Edward Lucy. My daughter Susanna. My mother-in-law, Mistress Shakespeare.'

Master Lucy and Master Heminge bowed, professed themselves each other's servant. Susanna rose and curtsied prettily. The old lady inclined graciously over her embroidery. Heminge had been married eighteen years and had twelve children. Yet, seeing Susanna's young, warm beauty, he would at that moment have given all he possessed to be the happy youth at whom she smiled so lovingly. No hare-shotten lip here, and the smoothest, most serene brow he had seen for many a long day.

And Will's mother – yes, she *could* be the high-born lady of the rumours. Both she and the girl had in their faces something of Will's high, brooding intelligence, he thought. And Will's wife? He liked her. No shrew this, he was certain. She had a quiet warmth of manner that made him feel at home. And now she became less formal. She drew a stool up beside her own chair, and sitting down, said, 'Sir, be seated.' Then she turned to him with that sweet, rather sad smile and said, 'Anyone is welcome who brings me news of Will. But you, Master Heminge, are *most* welcome. I know my husband loves you well.'

On his lips was a formal, 'Then I am indeed honoured, madam.' He rejected it. This woman inspired simplicity and truth. He said, suddenly moved. 'By God I love *him*, madam, unto death. And so do we all – all the King's Men.'

'Thank you,' she said quietly. She looked at his face. Dark, aquiline, a black thrust of beard, a tight, black cap of hair. She said, 'And Will is coming?'

'Yes. A week today. And he sent a message. He would think it a favour if Burbage and Condell and I might lie at this house a few days.'

Her homely face beamed with delight. 'You hear that, Susanna? You hear, madam? Will is coming, with the gentlemen players.'

Mary said, 'So. Thanks to the plague rather than to him, my first-born may yet visit me before I die – to hear my grateful nunc dimittis.'

John Heminge looked at her sharply; but love was in her face. There might, he thought, be a pleasant tartness here; but, as one would expect of the mother of Will Shakespeare, no biting acid.

Susanna clapped her hands. 'Nay, we will have dancing, and music. Edward, you must come *that* night. Oh, it will be so gay.'

John Heminge sipped his wine. How pleasant was this big room, slanted with afternoon sunlight, and with its sense of peace, and love. Will's family, it seemed, held him and one another in rare affection. He thought of his own turbulent brood, with all the clatter and creak of London outside the window; while, here – quiet voices within. And, without, the lazy clip-clop of a horse, the distant shouts of children at play. He turned courteously to the young man. 'Sir, I interrupted your song. Will you not – ?'

Edward Lucy bowed. He and Susanna exchanged smiles. She took up her lute. For a second his hand lay on hers, across the strings. Then: O *mistress mine, where are you roaming?* The sweet words floated about the room, dancing with the plangent notes of the lute. For John Heminge, the song was almost as familiar as the sound of the opening trumpet at the Globe, or the clatter of pennies as the groundlings took their places. Yet it never failed to move him. *Youth's a stuff will not endure...* The lovers smiled into each other's eyes again, their long, world-forgetting smile. The lute was silent, and the singer. Anne glanced fondly at her daughter. Old Mistress Shakespeare had let fall her tapestry, and was staring, lost, who knows where; into the mists of the future, or the bright mornings of childhood? But

John Heminge was back in the Globe, with Robert Armin's sweet voice dying, and for a few seconds the great theatre silent, unbreathing, rapt; before Sir Andrew and Sir Toby shattered the almost unbearable emotion with a great gale of laughter. Oh excellent Will, he thought, who can play upon men's hearts as upon the jacks.

The door was flung open. A girl came in. One hand swung her beribboned bonnet, the other tugged at a tall, grave gentleman. 'John, you *shall* come in,' she cried.

Anne said, 'Judith! Be more civil. See, we have a guest.'

Judith looked round the room, clapped a hand to her laughing mouth; but her eyes continued to dance. She saw Master Heminge, and gave him her clumsy but charming curtsey.

Her mother was watching her thoughtfully. She was glad to see Judith happy, even though it was with the kind of laughter which, in children anyway, soon ends in tears. But why was she happy? Because, obviously, she had met Dr John Hall and brought him home. Good. She herself liked John Hall, a man of kindness and sound common sense. But doubtless, like all his class and generation, driven by a thrusting ambition. So was he, she asked herself anxiously, the kind of man who would want to marry little Judith? And if he was not, and the poor child was already in love with him (as she obviously was), then – it would be enough to cut the slender thread that tied her to her reason.

John Hall looked enquiringly at Anne. There were strangers; he would not enter without permission from the mistress of the house. But Anne rose, and came up to him, and took his hand in both of hers, while her younger daughter jigged happily around him, like a dog around a loved master. 'Come, sir. You too will take a glass of wine, and meet an old friend of my husband's, Master Heminge. And yonder is Master Lucy, whom I think you have not met.'

There was a great flurry of bowing and vowing and protesting among the gentlemen. Judith cried, 'I met John near High Cross, Mother. And he walked with me – '

Anne said, 'Nay, child, you must not be so familiar. It is *Doctor* Hall to you.'

John Hall said, 'Thank you, mistress, but I have asked her to use my Christian name. We have become great friends, have we not, Judith.'

'Oh, *yes*, John.' She clapped her hands delightedly.

Anne sat him down next to Heminge and herself, gave him a glass of wine. 'This gentleman brings me most agreeable news, Doctor. My husband is visiting Stratford next week and will stay a few days. I hope you will meet him.' Much as she tried to hide it, she was almost as excited as Judith; and also very relieved. With two possible sons-in-law on the scene, it would be good to have Will's judgment; both the suitors were of a better sort than herself and Will. This frightened her; but it would not frighten Will, who walked with kings and who, she fancied, had some knowledge and understanding of men.

'I shall be most honoured to meet Master Shakespeare, madam.' And not so much honoured as interested, he thought. Master Shakespeare could not have come at a better time. For Doctor John Hall, MA Cantab., was in torment. He *was* in love. Nowadays, it was as though he walked into the rising sun, blinded and dazzled; but it was not in fact the sun that came between his eyes and his patients and his medicines and his case-books. It was the face of Susanna Shakespeare; and she was promised to someone else!

He went on visiting her as long as was seemly. But since Susanna was obviously one of the healthiest women in Warwickshire, this could not go on indefinitely. So now he was seizing any opportunity to visit the house; even using her younger sister's affection for him to bring him over the threshold (a despicable and dangerous game for a man of honour, he knew only too well).

But need it be despicable? Need it be dangerous? Looked at sensibly and unemotionally, as became a doctor, Judith would make him a good wife. She had a delicate charm; she was ten years younger than he, and would therefore regard him as lord and master far more wholeheartedly than the spirited Susanna. She would be amenable, and if he fed her up well on capons and venison she might yet bear worthy sons. She had in her veins the blood of one of the oldest families in Warwickshire. She would not grace his table; on the other hand, might not her nervous fragility enhance his own stature and urbanity? 'What a kind man he must be,' people would say, 'to take that poor little dabchick under his wing.'

And, quite clearly, the little dabchick was besotted with him. Yes, it could be a reasonably good match. Only – ?

She had practised witchcraft. Tush! A child's sport. He glanced across at the radiant Susanna. If there had been any potency in Judith's spells, Susanna's beauty would by now be marred, not tearing at his very heartstrings. One great question mark remained, however. Had William Shakespeare the qualities required to become father-in-law to Doctor John Hall, MA Cantab.?

Well, he would soon find out now. And if the answer was yes, then he thought he would marry in the springtime, when he would be less busy with rheums and fevers. He glanced at his potential bride with some affection. Of course, he didn't *love* her; but he felt a softness, a tenderness for the quaint creature which, though its main ingredient was perhaps pity, nevertheless warmed his heart considerably. His generation might sigh, and waste away, and even die for love; they would endlessly discuss love, write poems and songs about love, talk and dream and sing about love; but when it came to marriage, he told himself sensibly, then love was simply one of the seasonings.

But then he looked again at Susanna. And all his careful argument shrivelled like paper in the flame of her beauty.

CHAPTER 4

THE MOON SHINES BRIGHT: IN SUCH A NIGHT AS THIS.

Will Shakespeare was glad to be away from London.

It wasn't only the plague. Older men, those whose personalities had been formed in the old Queen's days, sniffed the air and smelt an odour of – decay? Corruption? Nothing one could put one's finger on, but a feeling that things were getting out of hand. Prices were soaring, the King was becoming more and more spendthrift, more and more at odds with his Parliament. (Though Will was the last man to blame the King for falling out with a Puritan Parliament that brought in an Act to 'Restrain Abuses of Players', causing Falstaff, so beloved of the groundlings, to have his best speeches censored. Why, Mistress Page wasn't even allowed to say 'what the devil?' any longer.)

Yet, outside the theatre, lewdness and drunkenness thrived; especially at Court, and in particular since the Queen's brother, Christian IV, had paid his state visit. The Court ladies had stumbled drunkenly about in those eternal masques. The Danish courtiers had taught the English to drink deep – a lesson they seemed in no hurry to forget. No. Things were not what they had been in the old Queen's day. This James, with his favourites, his lack of dignity and courage, was infecting the whole country from the top. Honour, loyalty, courage were words to scoff at. Something was rotten in the state of England.

But now, London, and a corrupt and trivial Court, were ninety miles away. He was back in the land of his boyhood, in a country of lost content. Another hour, and they would be at Clopton Bridge. Yet another, and he would be kissing his sweet Anne. For he had reached an age when even he was prepared to leave something to younger men: the unpacking; rubbing down, feeding, watering the horses; putting up the stage; sorting, ironing, repairing the costumes; setting out the wigs and greasepaint, burnishing the swords and armour. John Heminge had gone ahead of them, putting up playbills, making arrangements with the tavern-keeper, presenting their letters patent to the Bailiff, casting an eye over the Gild-hall where, by custom, their first performance must be given. Nevertheless, a thousand things needed to be done before that still-magic moment when the groundlings, hushed in silent wonder, heard the first words that would transport them, for an hour or two, to Venice, or Illyria, or Cyprus.

Tonight, after weeks of travel, he would lie in clean sheets snug (and a little acrid) from the warming pan, his wife beside him. Sitting in the cold, lurching waggon, the thought of such comfort almost brought the tears to his eyes. Yet, strangely, he was anxious.

Why? Because he had as many lives as a cat. In London he was the courtier, the actor, the writer of popular plays, the friend of noble men. In Stratford, he was still John Shakespeare's son, who not so long ago had been helping his father on the market stall, and now, thanks to some easy success in the gold-paved streets of London, was master of

New Place; a landowner; paunchy, respected, bourgeois to his finger-tips.

So far, Will had managed to keep the actor, with greasepaint in the wrinkles of his skin, separate from the bourgeois gentleman of New Place. Whenever they went on tour and a visit to Stratford was suggested, he had been able to point out that the town was well-served by small provincial touring companies whose romps would doubtless be more popular there than would be the discipline of the King's Men. But this time he had been over-ruled, perhaps because his fellow sharers had a very human desire to see Will's background.

Dick Burbage was muttering over his part. ' "It was my turquoise; I had it of Leah when I was a bachelor: I would not have given it for a wilderness of monkeys." ' He looked up at Will. He called across the creaking waggon, 'Another onion of a play, Will. Every time I play in it I peel off another skin. Why, you even make me sorry for this damned Jew.'

Will said, '*Must* I play Antonio, Dick?'

'Oh come, Will, *you* don't mind. You know I wouldn't ask you if Harry hadn't lost his voice.' He went back to brushing up his part. You could always rely on old Will. The most willing horse any company ever had.

And he was right. Will would have liked to be the genial host, to have sat with Anne through the performance and then to have introduced his player friends to his Stratford friends at New Place. For, strangely, now he was among the friends of his youth, greasepaint and dressing-up had suddenly become indignities, childish and ridiculous – something they had never seemed in a sophisticated London, even at the King's Court.

But he could not let the players down; if there was no one else to play a part, then he must play it. To Will Shakespeare, Will Shakespeare's private wishes did not come into it where the King's Men were concerned.

Will Shakespeare's wife had never seen a play performed. So she sat in the second row of benches in the Gild-hall, behind the row of furred gowns that was the Corporation of Stratford, and waited nervously for the performance to begin.

Nervous for many reasons: fear of the unknown, fear that Will might cause her intolerable embarrassment by waving to her from the stage, fear most of all that she would not understand what was toward. Of course Will had *read* his plays to her in their early married days (and oh, the happiness of those evenings beside the cottage fire, with the infants in bed and Will by her side! Success had brought other joys; but nothing ever as deep as the contentment of those fled hours). Very pleased, and surprised too, she had been in those days to find that she could understand them. But how what Will read then needed a dozen other gentlemen, and dressing-up, and a stage, was more than poor Anne could imagine.

On her right was Susanna, then Edward Lucy with his parents. On her left, Judith and Doctor Hall.

And every one of them agog to see Master Shakespeare. Anne, because he had sent a message to say he could not come home before the performance, and she was anxious to see how he looked, well or ill; and anyway she could never wait to see Will. Susanna and Judith, because a girl's natural fear that her father will make a fool of himself before her suitor is increased a hundredfold when that father is appearing on a public stage. Doctor Hall because of the important decision he had to make. Edward Lucy because he loved Susanna dearly, yet knew himself too weak to make a match his parents considered unsuitable. And Edward's parents because their son's infatuation for this Shakespeare girl had caused them considerable misgiving, and they both felt that tonight, after they had seen the glover's son capering on the stage, their minds would be made up.

The bare stage was bright with candles. The hall was crowded, in strict order of precedence, from the Bailiff in the centre of the front row to the pot boy from Widow Quiney's tavern standing on tip toe at the back. The excitement was almost unbearable. Most of those present had but the faintest idea of what they were going to see. That it was a Comedie, *The Merchant of Venice*, the play bills had informed those who could read. And it was said that it was written by old John Shakespeare's son, one of themselves. Oh, they all remembered young Will, on his market stall; never lost for a pert answer. You had to be up early to get the better of young Will, the gossips used to tell each other, chuckling. So they looked forward hopefully to a bit of a romp, and some bawdry, with one or two local jokes about Snitterfield or Hampton Lucy. It would, they thought, suit them down to the ground.

But now a silence settled on the hall. Every eye was on that bare stage. Somewhere, outside, a trumpet sounded. Silence. A second trumpet note. Silence, the silence that three hundred people can create, deeper than the silence of the wastes of eternity.

A third note. And now – not the leaping, capering, drum-banging headlong rush on to the stage that the groundlings were used to from their provincial companies, and had expected from young Shakespeare, but three dignified gentlemen strolling on, conversing. One, it seemed, was sad.

The others were trying to cheer him – without much success.

Anne was sorry for the sad gentleman. She had known too much of sadness in herself, not to pity it in others. Perhaps he was not well. She looked at him closely. He was sturdy, not very tall, and a little overweight. He had a trim auburn beard. His hair was receding from a high forehead. Anne looked at him in sudden alarm. *Could* that heavily-lined, grey face really be her fresh-complexioned Will's? No, thought Anne, who had never heard of greasepaint. Or if it was, then he was a very sick man.

Agonisedly, she listened to the voice. Gentle, exquisitely modulated, infinitely pleasant. A warm, Warwickshire burr! Will's voice, Will's form, Will's face – but not as it should have been for another twenty years.

She touched Susanna's wrist. The girl turned to her, smiling. Anne whispered: 'Your father. He is ill.'

Susanna's smile deepened. 'He is painted so, Mother.'

'Painted?'

Susanna, still smiling, touched her lips. Two aldermen turned round angrily and shushed. Anne, looking closely, now saw the paint glinting on Will's face, and was a little reassured. But she still didn't like his being sad without reason. It wasn't like Will. And she was shocked to see him with his face painted. Like a harlot! And it didn't suit him. One of the many things she loved about him was his countryman's complexion.

But this was nothing to the agitation that gripped her later. For suddenly the audience became restive, stirred like a cornfield in a sudden breeze. There were mutterings, even hissings. For a fat, oily Jew had come on to the stage, and the groundlings felt they were being cheated. They didn't pay their pennies to look at Jews; they could do that any day.

But what troubled Anne was that Will seemed prepared to give this Jew a bond. She couldn't understand it at all. Will had a most free and generous nature – too free, she often thought – but when it came to business he was shrewd and careful. *Surely* he must see that this Jew – ? She wanted to call out, 'Will, watch thyself. Remember how thy poor father ruined himself by giving bonds.' But she was the last woman to draw attention to herself in this way; so she sat and watched her foolish husband commit himself irrevocably.

But now she could hardly sit still in her seat. For Will was agreeing to give a pound of his flesh if the bond was not honoured! Naturally, one of his friends tried to discourage him; but Will pushed this on one side. He seemed bent on self-destruction. She began to think she would faint.

She felt Susanna's eyes on her, felt Susanna's hand clasping her own, looked up and saw Susanna's smile, heard her whispered, amused, ' 'Tis but a play, Mother. Father will come to no harm.'

Susanna's smile was serene as ever, her face had its usual inner radiance. Anne did not understand altogether, but she felt a little less troubled. And, sure enough, towards the end of the play, someone called Portia very cleverly saved Will from the consequences of his folly. Anne could have kissed her. She did not know when she had spent such an agonising two hours.

But the play was not over yet. The Jew, broken and ill (to everyone's intense satisfaction), crept from the stage, followed by curses and howls of execration from the groundlings and even the aldermen.

And then, suddenly, there was magic: magic for pleasant married couples, magic for old bachelors and old maids; magic most of all for young lovers, caught in the honey-sweet toils of love. 'The moon shines bright: in such a night as this – in such a night, in such a night, in such a night...' The word-music was sweeter, softer, gentler than the plucked strings of lutes, the stroked strings of viols. Unashamed alliteration tapping at the heart: in such a night Stood Dido with a willow in her hand Upon the wild sea-banks, and waved her love To come again to Carthage...

Judith Shakespeare's hand lay along the bench beside her, John Hall's along his breeches. Perhaps an inch separated them. But now, under the spell of her father's poetry, Judith's had moved half an inch to the left. John Hall's, moved perhaps less by poetry than by tonight's discovery that Master Shakespeare might well make a dignified and worthy father-in-law, moved half an inch to the right.

The hands touched, back to back, lay so, then turned. The fingers sought each other, clasped, embraced. John Hall and Judith Shakespeare both stared hard at the stage. In such a night, did young Lorenzo swear he loved her well – Judith was almost swooning with excitement – and a rare happiness. Rare, because for once she was not jealous; and jealousy and happiness cannot live in the same breast. But tonight she was not jealous even of her sister. John Hall might not be of such good family as Edward Lucy, but he was the properer man. Edward was weak, charming, ineffectual; even Susanna, laughing, had admitted as much, while vowing that these were the very qualities for which she loved him. But John Hall was a man – strong, determined, clever. John Hall had said he would rise to the top of his profession – and then pull his despised profession up after him. Why, when Susanna was visiting Charlecote as a minor relation, she, Judith, would be helping her husband entertain the most learned doctors of Europe. She gave the tough wiry hand in hers a loving squeeze, and Doctor John

Hall knew miserably that he, usually so strong, so decisive, was drifting with the tide.

In such a night did pretty Jessica… Susanna and Edward, hands clasped, gazed into each other's eyes, and let the word-music wash over them like a warm sea. But Mistress Lucy, impervious to poetry as to much else, dug her husband in the ribs, jerked her head in the direction of the lovers, and snapped, 'Husband, you must speak to Edward tonight.'

Master Lucy nodded miserably.

Then they all came out, into the summer night, a little more aware of what it meant to be a human being than when they went in; looking up, for instance, at the Stratford moon which, though it lacked the magic of the Belmont one, had a beauty some had never before noticed; lovers finding a new warmth, a new beauty in their love; all their minds touched, lightened, deepened by two hours' contact with a greater mind; all bound together, for a few brief minutes, by a common emotional experience.

Mistress Anne Shakespeare led her party across the road to New Place.

The servants had followed Anne's instructions well. The great chamber of New Place was brilliant with candles and silver, a sideboard was cheerful with wine and sack, with cold capons and syllabubs and cheese and kickshaws. Anne, coming in with her guests, felt a sudden surge of happiness. A few years ago, she would have known nothing of all this, would not have known how to leave her orders. But now, thanks to Will, and his mother, and her own practical intelligence, she had become an accomplished hostess; but a hostess whose charm still owed most to her own kindliness and sincerity.

'Now, Mistress Lucy, pray sit beside me. Master Lucy, sir, a glass of canary. Susanna, Judith, a glass of wine for the gentlemen. My husband and his friends will be here shortly, I understand. In the meantime – pray, Mistress Lucy, did you make aught of the play?'

'I thought your husband very foolish; you would not have found *me* giving such a bond to that Jew. No, nor letting my husband do so, neither.'

The implied reproach took away some of Anne's sense of well-being, even though she could not help feeling it was unmerited; but now she realised that any interest Mistress Lucy might have had in her had quickly evaporated. Those cold, watchful eyes were on her son, who was gaily handing a glass of wine to Susanna. 'Edward,' she called.

He bowed his excuses to Susanna, came across, bowed to his mother. His smile was bubbling almost into laughter. 'Mother, is not this a *splendid* evening. The play – and now, so soon, to meet the famous Master Shakespeare.'

'Dear boy, you are being impolite to Mistress Shakespeare, our hostess.'

Another smiling bow, this time to Anne. 'Madam, forgive me. Come, let us exchange pleasantries.'

Anne laughed. There was no doubting his charm. But what else had he to offer? A noble name? Was that all, was it enough, for Will Shakespeare's daughter? For tonight Anne had begun to realise something – dimly, slowly, but with certainty: that Will had created the splendour of this evening, and of a thousand such evenings in Oxford, Coventry, London, even at the King's Court. She had always known that the cheerful lad she had married possessed depths she would never understand. But now she suddenly saw him with new eyes – a friendly, dignified man who, not only by his own efforts had provided this pleasant house, and even the very food and wine, but who by some strange extension of his own personality was able to people men's minds with the rare creatures who had walked tonight's stage – even, most strange of all, with that loathsome Jew. She saw that Will towered over all the wealthy, powerful men she had met this evening higher than *they* towered over Mistress Quiney's pot boy. Why, he had even created *her*, Mistress Anne Shakespeare of New Place, out of the shy, simple creature that had been Anne Hathaway of Shottery: so she thought, failing characteristically to take into account her own strength and intelligence.

Sweet Will, sweet Will-o'-the-Wisp. Her whole body yearned for him; she worshipped him with body, mind and spirit. 'Make haste, my beloved, and be thou like to a roe or to a young hart upon the mountain of spices.' Here she was, a woman approaching fifty, moved almost to tears by words that had moved her in her lonely maidenhoood. Very soon now that door would open, and there he would be: smiling, sturdy, with a friendly word for all, a fond embrace for his daughters; and, for her – a pressure of the fingers, the special smile that only she would ever see, the smile that said, 'When the fire is dead in the hearth, and the candles burn low, and the wine bottle is empty, and the friends are gone – then, in the silent house, I will greet *you*, my beloved.'

It did not take Will Shakespeare long to change from a merchant of Venice to a citizen of Stratford. But for Richard Burbage, hung with a Jew's nose, a Jew's greasy locks, a Jew's gaberdine, it was a different matter. Besides, he must look his best tonight – lodging at Will's splendid house, meeting Will's wife, meeting two daughters one of whom, according to John Heminge, had the sun's radiance.

Carefully he removed the angry, cruel lines of the greasepaint. Will, sprawling in a chair, watched him with amusement.

Will was strangely relaxed. He, who was always so busy, if not with his body, then with his brain, was for once at peace. No characters wrestled in his mind. Tonight he was about to bring his two worlds – Stratford and the theatre – together, something he had always dreaded; yet now that the moment had come he was eager to show each to each, proud of his house and wife and daughters, proud of his London friends.

Curiously at peace. Tonight there would be music, laughter, love of friends, the three things he cherished most. He would not see the ghosts that so often at night crept between his eyes and the written page – the face of his dead son, the mocking lips of Southampton's dark whore, poor Annette Peyre's broken body. They would return, they would always return; but tonight he would be free of them.

The doors were flung open at last. Will Shakespeare came in. His hands rested in friendship on the shoulders of Dick Burbage and John Heminge.

He stood, smiling, blinking a little in the candlelight. He was a man who exuded friendliness, yet who always carried round with him, as it were, his own small withdrawing room, and his own vulnerability. Now, coming half host, half guest, into his own seldom-visited house, was he for a moment ill at ease, acknowledging the remorse for neglecting wife and daughters that was so much a part of him? If he was, he quickly recovered. Taking his hands from his friends' shoulders, he held them out to his wife, and waited for her to come to him.

He stood there, his heart brimming over with love, with joy for being home again, yet still a nervous half-guest in his own house. And all those who had been so anxious to see Master Shakespeare stared – and knew a strange disappointment. For to his country audience this warm, generous-hearted man held himself, moved, even smiled, not naturally, but with the art and grace of the actor or the courtier; and, with the quick distrust of provincials, they froze into themselves, and away from him.

With his rare sensitivity, he felt it, was saddened by it, and determined to overcome it. But first things first. Anne was coming up to him, neatly dressed, in a pretty blue gown, holding herself well. He was proud of her. He took her hands. 'How goes it with you, mistress?'

'Well, sir.' They smiled their secret smile. He said, 'John Heminge you know, Anne.'

She curtsied. John bowed. His white teeth flashed between his spade beard and his moustache. He and Mistress Shakespeare had already formed a high regard for each other.

Will said, 'And this is my old friend Dick Burbage, who will quarrel with a man thrice in a day, and yet not lose his love.'

Burbage shot Will a grateful glance. Anne saw this, and loved him for it. She saw a somewhat short, stocky man who might have been a carpenter or a bricklayer. Yet she knew Will loved him, not only as staunch friend and colleague, but also as the greatest of all actors. She curtsied deeply. 'I am honoured, sir, to meet someone of whom Will thinks so highly.'

'And I, madam, to meet the wife of London's most successful playwriter.'

They smiled. Will, leaving his friends with his wife, set off to allay the suspicions of his guests. He found his younger daughter curtseying to him. 'Father, this is John. He and I are

– good friends. John, this is my father, Master William – ' She could not finish.

She was terribly excited. Her words came in staccato rushes, with sudden silences. Then suddenly she remembered her manners, was down on her knees, head bowed. 'Bless me, Father.'

Rather absently he put his hands on the black, wiry hair. (What had he written? 'If hairs be wires, black wires grow on her head.' But no; that was about his whore, not his own chaste daughter.) 'Bless you, my child.' But he was looking at the tall man who was bowing rather arrogantly and saying, 'Doctor John Hall, sir, physician, always at your service.'

Will inclined his head. 'Honoured to meet you, sir.' But he was intrigued. He had always assumed that poor Judith would be hard put to it to find a husband. Yet here she was with an attractive, handsome doctor; a man moreover who had an air of knowing exactly where he was going. And it seemed that love suited her; she held her head higher, she was less intent on being part of the background. She could not keep still, but jigged about happily. 'I vow John is the cleverest doctor this side of London, Father.'

John Hall looked as though he would not actually deny it. Will laughed. 'I can well believe it, daughter.' He gave her a sudden fond hug and passed on. He came suddenly upon the beautiful Susanna.

Did I really have a part in this? he thought humbly, remembering the cornfield, and the leering harvest moon, and the Warwickshire clay that had been bed to her begetting. Yet now it seemed that all those things had been made manifest in one woman's flesh: the golden, sighing corn, the moon's radiance; it was as though her firm, strong limbs had first been moulded from that enduring clay.

She was laughing, holding an apple between her white teeth, teasing a young man who was also trying to bite the fruit.

'Eve! Still at your tricks,' he said with mock approach.

She looked up, snatched the apple from her mouth, stuck it in her young man's, jumped up and flung her arms round Will. 'Father! Oh, it is so good to see you. And your play! I vow it beats cockfighting, what do you say, Edward?'

'Oh yes, indeed, sir,' said Edward, having removed the apple, though it is doubtful whether he had understood one word of the play, due both to limited intelligence and the heady presence of Susanna.

'Father, this is Edward Lucy.'

So. Were they to have a Lucy in the family? That would indeed be another nail in the coffin of his humble beginnings. He heard William Shakespeare, Gent, of New Place talking casually about 'my son-in-law, Edward Lucy. Yes. One of the Warwickshire Lucys.' A glover's son, a despised actor, a man who did what no gentleman would ever do – wrote for money; somehow he had overcome all these disadvantages. He and the King's Men had made acting respectable, he himself had made playwriting almost respectable, his carefully amassed money had done the rest. This infinite creature who combined in himself supreme poet and hard business man, the most bourgeois aspirations with an incredible facility for writing one astounding play after another, an open and generous nature with a carefulness about money his own Shylock would have approved – this man stood tonight, surrounded by family and friends, at the pinnacle of his career.

And a dry, old voice said at his side, 'So, Will. You have it all. All you ever asked for.'

He turned, and gazed into the tight-lipped, amused face of Mary Shakespeare. He kissed her fondly. 'Only a fool could have that, Mother.'

'Why, what do you lack, Will?' She looked at him shrewdly. 'Quietness of heart?'

Mother and son gazed at each other. He was silent. She said, 'But tell me, about your brothers in London. How is Gilbert? And Edmund?'

'Gilbert is well. He came to see my play about King Lear. But' – he smiled – '*Gammer Gurton's Needle* is still his favourite.' He was desperately fending off his mother's next question – because Edmund was one of those about whom his conscience gave him little rest.

But he knew from long experience that Mary Shakespeare was not one to be fended off. 'And Edmund?'

'I have not seen him, Mother.'

'Not?' She looked at him sharply. 'But – you are one of the most important men in the London theatre. And Edmund – still seeking his way on the stage. I had always hoped he was in your care. Besides, you are sixteen years older than he, old enough to be his father, Will.'

'Mother!'

'You were not *so* much older, boy, when you found that fathering came *very* natural to you.'

He was silent. Then: 'He has not sought me out. So he either does not need, or does not want help, Mother.'

'It could still have been offered, Will.' But she smiled. Will was a busy man, and Edmund was a strange, shy youth. It wouldn't all be Will's fault.

He smiled back. And turned to Susanna and Edward. 'Master Lucy, I bid you welcome.' He lifted his glass and then, in his actor's voice, trained to reach the back of the

Yard, 'Friends! Tom, Richard, Mary, Harry old friend – I bid you *all* welcome.'

There were cheers, laughter. The ice that had formed at his entrance thawed. Will's natural warmth and sincerity would have melted an iceberg. He whispered to Susanna, 'Fetch your lute, girl.' She laughed, kissed his cheek, and was away, quick as a bird. Soon they were singing, laughing, slapping knees to keep time, the old songs, the good old songs he loved, 'Johnny, Come Kiss Me Now', 'Sweet Robin Is My Delight', ' 'Twas on a May Morning'. The wine passed, the eyes of lovers shone like the candles, the music, now sad, now gay, filled all their hearts. All except two. Master and Mistress Lucy sat, pursed-lipped, hating the happiness that lit the face of their son.

CHAPTER 5

POISON MORE DEADLY THAN A MAD DOG'S TOOTH.

New Place was still. The moon was westering, an owl called from the high beeches. The front door had closed behind the last visitor, the footsteps, the hoofbeats had died into a distant silence, the lights were out in the windows of the great chamber. The guests were abed. The Master of New Place sat before the kitchen fire with his homely wife, content.

On the table beside him was a bowl of nuts, which he was cracking with his strong teeth. 'So both the girls have suitors?'

She nodded. 'Yet I am not happy, Will.'

He waited. *He* had been *very* happy. A Lucy. And a physician for Judith. True, physicians until recently had been not much better than actors; but, like actors, they were beginning to pull themselves up. And this fellow had an air of being of good family. Besides, for Judith to have a suitor at all –

Anne said, 'The Lucys are a proud family, Will. Tonight I watched Mistress Lucy watching Edward and Susanna. She looked as pleased as though he were courting a tavern wench.'

Will stared at her in disbelief. 'Imagination, wife.' He knew well the quirks and fancies that one woman could entertain about another. 'Why, Susanna could grace a king's bed.'

'But not a Lucy's table. They will look higher, husband.'

'*Higher?*' He was put out, deflated. He was a successful man, whichever way you looked at it; and now, this wife of his had sat him down in the kitchen, and pricked the bubble. It was, he reflected ruefully, something at which she was adept. '*Higher?*' he said again. 'An Arden?'

'And a Hathaway. And a Shakespeare, remember.'

'What is wrong with the Shakespeares?' He was really irritated now.

'Only the smell of the glove leather, the haberdasher's shears.' She was almost weeping. *Make haste, my beloved, and be thou like to a roe or a young hart…* The moment she had looked forward to, longed for. And already she was spoiling it, angering him, driving him away from her. But when a thing had to be said, then she must say it. 'The Lucys are great people, Will.'

He smouldered. He cracked a nut, flung the shell fragments into the hearth. 'God's teeth, Anne, why do you have to wound me? Tonight of all nights?'

She slid on to her knees before him. 'Oh Will, I am not wounding *you*; only the family pride your mother has taught you.'

'Do not disparage my mother, wife,' he said.

'She has taught me all I know. I do not disparage her. But oh husband, I am anxious.' She laid her chin on his knees. 'John Hall is in love with Susanna.'

'But – I thought – Judith – ?'

'Is in love with him. And he will settle for second best, so long as Susanna is unobtainable. But – I have seen his eyes. All evening, they were on Susanna.'

'So were every man's; even her father's. She is like a ripening peach.'

'Will! John Hall is a good man; I like him. But I have seen his ruthlessness. Susanna is a splendid match; and if she were free, he would abandon Judith without a thought.' She stared up at him. 'And Judith would – do something desperate.'

He looked at her thoughtfully. 'Nonsense, wife.'

She went and stood by the table. 'Do *you* know so much more about our daughters than I – *Londoner?*' She asked sadly.

He stared into the fire. She stood, playing absently with a cup. 'Shall I tell you something, husband?'

He waited. She said, 'Judith bewitched Susanna. With a wax effigy. But for Dr Hall, Susanna had wasted and died.'

There was a long silence. 'She – did – what?' asked Will at last.

Anne told him the story. Halfway through he held out his hands to her. They were trembling. She came and took them, stood looking down at him, watching the horror that filled his eyes.

He had to moisten his lips before he could speak. 'But – but why?'

'Jealousy.'

He screwed up his eyes, as though she had struck him across the cheek. He was faced with the incomprehensible. He who could probe so deep into man's nature knew there were things in the human soul he could neither understand nor tolerate: deliberate cruelty; and the meanness of spirit (or so it seemed to him) that men called jealousy. His free and generous nature had tried to comprehend it, and failed. Sexual jealousy, yes. He had known all its torments; and, as was his way, had sought to free himself by loading one of his characters with its chains. But a jealous woman! Witchcraft! In his own house! He said, dully, 'Let me not see her. Keep her from my sight.'

She nodded. 'Aye. Then you can return to London; and, for you, it will never have happened.'

He said, 'A daughter of mine, driven by jealousy to witchcraft. Against her own sister!'

'Belike, husband, you should have stayed in Stratford, and had the upbringing of her.' (*…a roe or a young hart upon the mountain of spices*. Oh, the sweet was scattered, the frail windflower of love was trampled. Alas, that the folly of anger could poison the fleeting hour. Yet things had to be said.)

He would not be angry. Not with Anne. He said, 'You have done well, wife. And you have been sore neglected. But' – he could not leave it alone – 'I would not have let her grow up jealous. Somehow – I do not know how – somehow I would have rooted out her jealousy.'

'Then you would have had to root out her heart. Sisters are always jealous.'

'Susanna is not,' he said quickly.

'She has no cause. Yet she could be.'

Anne had sat down at the table. She took a hazel nut, rolled it half across the table, picked it up, put it back in the bowl. She said, wearily, 'So, you have nothing to offer, husband; I should not have spoken. You can write plays, and strut upon the stage, and act the courtier: all clever things. So leave me with such poor things as I can do – keep your house for you, bring up your daughters in the fear of the Lord, and love you with all my heart and mind and spirit; but do not tell me how I should do these things, husband, or where you think I have failed.'

She took up one of the side candles, lit it from another. 'I am for bed, Will.'

And so they lay: stiff, silent, apart; as one day they would lie with the cold stones of Trinity Church their only coverlet.

He walked beside the summer Avon, with Susanna, in the bright morning.

He was proud: a prosperous, well-dressed, comfortably built man walking with a daughter who, it seemed to him, gave the sunlight, the dancing water, the white swans a brighter radiance.

She said, smiling. 'Poor Judith! She will not be pleased, at home peeling rushes for candle-wicks while I sport with my handsome father.'

The flattery pleased him, yet he frowned. 'She will be jealous?' he asked sharply.

'A little. She cannot help it, Father. She is a woman, so 'tis her nature.'

He walked in silence. Then he said, 'Witchcraft. There was witchcraft.' He looked hard at her beauty. 'Yet – there is no blemish. Why – ?'

She said quickly, 'That is an old tale, Father. It is best forgotten.'

'I want to know.' It was seldom that Will Shakespeare sounded so imperious.

She sighed. 'The child made an effigy of wax, dressed it in lace from my handkerchief; 'twas mere foolishness.'

'Yet – your mother said – you were like to die.'

'My arm was palsied; my feet stumbled.' She stopped, turned and faced him in sudden fear. 'And it was as though I was riven with iron. The pain – '

'Yet now' – he looked again – 'there is no blemish.'

'Dr Hall saved me. He destroyed the image before my eyes. He is a proper man.'

'And would marry the witch,' he said in disbelief.

She was silent. He said, 'It is a strange match. I thought him a strong, ambitious, clever man; not the man to be attracted by Judith.'

'Stratford is not London, Father. There are fewer cattle in the market pens.'

Despite the unwonted sternness of his mood, he smiled. 'Yet there are fine bargains to be had.'

She was not falsely modest. She too smiled. 'John Hall and I would have been of a like metal. But Edward brings me a proud name – and a loving heart.'

'And that is enough?'

Again she turned and looked at him. 'I think so, Father.'

He was silent. Who was he to discuss the niceties of marriage? He, whose one thought had had to be to get a ring on Anne's finger before her pregnancy showed; whose marriage had been composed of neglect and absence. Yet, in spite of this, he had been curiously loving. He said, 'And what do you bring him?'

'A loving heart. And' – her voice was suddenly unsteady; she slipped her arm into his, gave him a little squeeze – 'a name that *you* have made a proud one, Father. The name of Shakespeare.'

'I?' he said. 'I? Oh, I know, a Grant of Arms. But – '

'I did not mean the Grant of Arms. I meant – the way your friends love you. I saw it last night. And that play. No one else could have written that. Not Master Marlowe, Master Jonson – '

Now he was really amused. 'Oh, Susanna, something to please the groundlings, no sooner seen than forgot. Now had you said *Venus and Adonis*,' he went on rather wistfully. No one seemed to mention that major work nowadays; all they wanted was more and more comedies to catch the groundlings' pennies.

She shook her head. 'It will be remembered, Father, when you are dust; even, perhaps, when I am dust.'

When I am dust... He glanced at her. God, that such loveliness – Yet she was right. She too. All her colour, all her softness – changed into brittle bone, under that same stone coverlet. *From fairest creatures we desire increase, That thereby beauty's rose might never die...* It was an old theme with him – the darling, dying buds of May, summer ageing into autumn, the fear that beauty, passing, might not be reborn. He said, almost roughly for him, 'You must marry. Soon. Pass on your loveliness to others.'

She laughed, a little embarrassed by his directness. 'Perhaps they will not be so beautiful. The Lucys are not a handsome family. Even Edward – '

It was true. Edward's amiable features did seem to consist mostly of teeth. He could not help thinking what a fine pair Susanna and John Hall would have made. And, according to Anne, John Hall loved her. He could, he supposed, refuse his consent to Lucy, and let nature take its course and witch Judith the consequences. But he was never one to play God. Where life was concerned, he preferred to let the characters write their own plot. Besides, 'my son-in-law Edward Lucy' would roll nicely off the tongue. And even if, as he suspected, the man was something of a fool, he was at least an amiable and good-hearted fool.

But now they had left the river. They were back in Chapel Lane. In front of them towered New Place, imposing and attractive. As they walked towards it, Will never took his eyes from it. The house of William Shakespeare, Gent, flanked by its tall trees, fronted by its little court. Susanna's white hand rested on his sleeve. *'Non Sans Droict,'* she murmured.

'Non Sans Droict,' he said. Then suddenly chuckled: 'Did you know how that rogue Ben mocked me in his *Every Man Out of His Humour?'*

'No?'

'He gave one of his characters a coat of arms: a boar's head proper. And for his motto: "Not Without Mustard".'

She threw back her head, laughed joyously. He did the same. Oh, it was good to laugh. Music, friendship, laughter, these three; and it could be that the greatest of these was laughter. He put his arm round her waist, hugged her to him. Still laughing boisterously, they entered the house and went through into the kitchen.

Where Judith was still peeling rushes for candle-wicks.

Anne, looking up from her sewing, was aware of many things at the same time.

She was aware that Judith, at her sister's entrance, had bunched herself together like a spider that senses danger in its path. She was aware of the jealousy she had always known – and hated – in herself whenever Will showed his friendliness for his elder daughter. It was, she tried to tell herself, the natural reaction of an ageing woman who had never been either very clever or very beautiful, to a young, beautiful, witty creature like Susanna; for such a creature had so much more in common with her clever husband than she could ever have. Yet she would not have it so. It was *not* natural. It was a sin, to be jealous of one's own innocent daughter and good husband.

She could not help saying angrily (though more for Judith's sake than for her own), 'So, mistress, you have deigned to return. And what about the tasks I set you this morning?'

'They will be done, Mother,' Susanna said meekly.

'And you, sir husband. Do you think your daughter has nothing better to do in the morning than strolling and laughter?'

'I am sorry, Anne; the fault was entirely mine.' He hung his head like a schoolboy.

She laughed now, rose, came and kissed him. 'Oh, Will, the fault was not so grievous. You need not be cast down.' Then she turned to Susanna. 'And you, girl, you are forgiven. After all,' she added tartly, 'your father is not *so* often in Stratford.'

Will grinned sheepishly. But now there was a sudden clatter; the tensed Judith had suddenly uncoiled like a spring, and fled from the room, uttering low, animal moans.

Her mother made to hurry after her. 'Leave her,' commanded Will.

Anne and Susanna looked at him in astonishment. Will had never commanded before. He could be cold, reproving even; but he did not command.

Nor was Anne, for all her gentleness, one to be commanded. 'Nay, but I *will* go to her; the child is distraught.'

'With jealousy. So let her be distraught.'

There had been only one other occasion in their married life when Anne had looked at her Will with contempt; but she did so now. 'Have you *no* understanding, husband?'

'Not for this,' he said, cold as ice. And now self pity was pouring in its acid. Here he had been, trailing wearily round the country in lurching waggons, putting up stages, acting to garlic-breathed yokels, rising at dawn from a flea-infested inn bed or even from the cold earth; weary, dishevelled, stinking. What were to have been a few hours of comfort in the midst of this squalor were spoilt by the news that his young daughter was a witch. And a gay, sunlit hour with Susanna now spoilt by the same jealous child. It seemed to him that Anne, with true woman's logic, was blaming him for everything. No understanding, indeed! She should ask Dick Burbage, or Lady Pembroke, whether Will Shakespeare had understanding; *they* would soon tell her. He simmered.

Anne said, 'If you had any human feeling you would now go and be as pleasant to your younger daughter as you have just been to your elder.'

'Nonsense!'

'*Please*, Father,' said Susanna.

Old Mary Shakespeare came into the room, leaning heavily on her stick. Her body might be slow, but her brain was still like quicksilver. She took in the situation immediately. A man at bay! 'Why, Will, I remember that look from when you were eleven, when I bade you come with us to Kenilworth and you wanted to swim instead.'

A flicker of amusement about Susanna's lips did not help his temper. God, he would not stay here and be baited by women. He longed, yearned for the man's world of the theatre: the tiring-rooms at the Globe, with never a woman to raise her clacking voice; even the mud-bedevilled waggons, crowded with men and boys, were better than this. Women! Without women his life would have been happy and blameless, his shoulders free of their burden of remorse for neglect and unfaithfulness.

Yet despite his anger, he would not be accused of lack of understanding. He said, with such dignity as he had left, 'I will go to her.'

'Oh, *thank* you, Will.' There was no triumph in Anne's voice, no mockery. She came and kissed him. 'If anyone can comfort her, husband, you can. *No* one can be as sweet as you.'

He grunted and left the room, a little less aggrieved. Anne gave him a loving smile; but Susanna looked thoughtfully at her mother, and Mary at her daughter-in-law. And both, strangely, were thinking the same thing: Will Shakespeare's wife may not have much book-learning, but she's a clever woman in her own simple fashion.

He went slowly upstairs. No understanding, indeed! That had hurt; but how *could* he understand an emotion he had never felt? A tongue that had never tasted wormwood –

She crouched on her bed, kneeling, compact, supporting herself on her knees and the very top of her head, arms tight across her stomach. So had she crouched, with Hamnet, her other self, her darling, before the peace of the womb was shattered by the noise and daylight of the world. And yet last night she had been so happy; had awakened so happy this morning, would have been happy now had not father taken Susanna walking, and left her to peel rushes. And when they returned – not slinking in remorseful, apologetic, but laughing, joyful, as though for Susanna to go walking and for Judith to do the chares was the most natural thing in the world. No one cared about Judith's feelings; they did not matter, because Judith was not beautiful, like Susanna. Nevertheless, one day Judith's feelings *would* matter, because *she* would be married to a famous physician, and Susanna to a penniless Lucy. *Then* she would make them dance.

A voice said, 'Judith.' Very gently.

A convulsive tremor. No other reply.

'Judith,' Will's coaxing voice said again.

There was no response.

He was exasperated by the silly creature; but he would show them whether he had no understanding. He put out a hand; but she was bunched as tight as a hedgehog. He could only touch her unresponsive back.

He sat there, feeling foolish and helpless; even afraid. If the witch had brought harm to Susanna once, she could do it again. And to others. She could destroy others. And, if she did, she would undoubtedly destroy herself. Rank had saved certain high-born witches from the fire, but not from the hangman. It would certainly not save the daughter of Will Shakespeare from either.

He shuddered, looking at the vulnerable body of his child. The thought had softened him, softened his voice. He said, 'I have brought you a present, from London, Judith. A gown of yellow taffeta. 'Twill suit you well, I think.' (And young Mark, who played Olivia, had been so looking forward to wearing his new gown. Well, a boy player was less important than his own daughter.)

No reply. No movement.

''Tis in the French mode.'

Still no movement; but a plaintive, unforgiving voice: 'Where is it?'

'In my waggon. You shall have it this afternoon.'

Her face was still buried in her chest. 'What did you bring Susanna?'

'Nothing. Nothing at all.'

With the suddenness of a wild creature she was facing him. Her face was blotched with weeping, drawn with misery. Yet now she smiled, her shy, sly smile. 'I do love you, Father.'

'Yes,' he said absently. He rose, and turned, and walked to the door. She watched him, startled, the smile fading. She said again, piteously, 'I do love you, Father.'

'Yes,' he said. He went slowly downstairs. They were waiting for him. Anne smiled. 'Well, husband, have you made your peace?'

'I have made my peace' he said.

They waited. He said, heavily, 'She has sold me her love – for a gown of yellow taffeta.'

They were silent. He said again, 'She has *sold* me her daughter's love – as a harlot sells love.'

'Will!' Anne was out of her chair, facing him, eyes flashing. 'How *dare* you? Your own chaste daughter! And you, her father! Oh, what a *monstrous* – ' She knew no word to express her disgust.

'Simile?' he said coldly.

She stared at him, not understanding the word, knowing only that by using it he had reminded her (and that deliberately) of her own ignorance, his own superiority. She said, 'You men! Oh, you are so righteous, so high above all human weaknesses, that you can look on us women only with contempt. But we have our uses, husband. I have known times when you have crept to me as a whipped schoolboy to his mother – to be comforted, to be made a big man again – ' She looked down at the floor. And said, quietly now, 'Even, God forgive me, to satisfy your lusts.'

Susanna was silent, appalled and embarrassed. She had never known her parents to quarrel openly before. And Mary, much as it went against the grain for her to keep out of an argument, knew that Will would be none the worse for a few home truths, and that Anne no longer needed any stiffening from her mother-in-law. So she sat, very straight in her high chair, her bright eyes missing nothing, and enjoyed herself as much as if she were at the play.

Anne moved a step nearer. She stared up into Will's face. Her fingers began to play with a button on his doublet. 'So remember, husband: we are not noble creatures, like men; we are small-minded and ignorant and often jealous and spiteful and envious – because that is the nature the Lord, in His wisdom, gave us.'

He said, rather desperately, '*You* are never jealous and spiteful, Anne.'

She actually laughed. 'Oh Will, how little you know me. I am a woman. There are biting, snapping, vicious creatures in my mind, as in all women's.'

He turned, helplessly, to his mother. 'Mother, this isn't true?'

'Of course it's true, Will,' she said testily. 'Oh, Anne is the sweetest of women; yet she has this sharpness, this wormwood. We all have. Otherwise you would not love us; we should be too cloying sweet.'

'Even Susanna?' he said, disbelieving.

His daughter spoke for the first time. 'Even Susanna; 'tis the mark of our femininity, Father.'

'Femininity?'

'Femininity,' said Mary. 'We are small-minded, as the eagle guarding her young is small-minded, or the vixen, caring only for her lair and her mate and the young foxes.'

Three women, lecturing William Shakespeare on the nature of women!

CHAPTER 6

FAREWELL, THE TRANQUIL MIND.

The great baggage train had dragged itself through the pleasant town of Kenilworth, struggled up Gibbet Hill ('Good morrow, Master Footpad, and are your chains to your comfort? A warm summer it has been, as I see by your burnt forehead; oh, sir, you have been too much i' the sun'). The long haul down the straight road to Coventry; and now, at last, they saw the medieval city, clustered for protection about its three noble spires like cherubs round the Trinity.

Dick, returning to the waggon, said, 'Coventry, Will. Below us in the valley. A pretty sight. Do you not wish to see?'

'I saw it as a boy, Dick.'

This flat, weary voice did not sound like Will. He was usually first out of the waggon to see a new town, interested in everything. 'See how that pretty stream –' 'The church stands well, does it not?' 'The burghers, Dick, are so full of capons and mulled wine I vow they can scarce walk.' But today: 'I saw it as a boy.'

Dick was sorry, He had liked Mistress Shakespeare well. A simple, kindly countrywoman. And he loved the friendly Will. Strange, if Will could be friendly to all except to this pleasant woman his wife. Yet he had seen little friendliness. In fact, the visit had been something of an embarrassment, and he was sure that Condell and Heminge had felt it too. Oh, they were all much too loyal to mention it to each other, but Will had been – and still was – a different person: morose, ill-at-ease, almost surly.

Dick came and sat down, spread his hands on his knees, blew out his cheeks. Will looked up from his everlasting writing. 'Dick, I want to play Iago.'

'Iago? *You*? But my dear Will, 'tis not your part.' Oh, he was used to people clamouring to play something quite unsuitable: Kempe the clown wanting to play Hamlet, slight, gentle Field wanting Antony. But he'd never had any trouble with Will. Will took any part he was asked to take, and did it well.

Will said coldly, 'Why isn't it my part?'

Honest Gentleman Will playing that cunning, hard-bitten soldier! It was absurd. If Will had ever been in the army, the last thing he'd have been was an ancient. Captain Shakespeare, yes. Even, possibly, Trooper Shakespeare. Ancient Shakespeare, never! He said, 'Dukes, kings, courtiers are for you, Will. You have not the manner for a rough, professional soldier.'

'I made him in the first place, Dick' – Will's look was cold and hard – 'and I would play him.'

This was a new Will. And Burbage was sensible enough, and generous enough, to know when to give way. 'Very well. When we are back in the Globe. But – '

'I did not mean the Globe. I mean when we come to Leicester.'

'*Leicester*? The good burghers will not want your blackamoor; his rantings would not let them sleep. And I will

not black my face again on tour, I vowed it at Guildford,
remember?'

'*Othello*, Dick. At Leicester.'

'But why?' Burbage was exasperated.

'To purge my soul, Dick.' His sigh came from his very
heart. 'To purge my soul.'

So. He had gone; with a cold kiss, and a hurt misery in his
eyes. And he would not return until the airs of a new
summer ruffled the Avon, and teased the leafy trees.
Meanwhile, this summer still lingered. Oh, if she could push
the sun down the sky, strip the elms, paint the rooftops with
frost, scatter the snow like goosefeathers. Then, at least, the
year would be helping to bring her Will back to her. But the
stately pavane of the seasons was not to be hurried. Summer
and autumn trod their slow measure.

Yet, below the crust of ice, the winter stream flows on.
And time flowed on in Stratford, and the patterns of life
formed, and broke, and re-formed, the dancers came
together, and bowed, and retreated, and set to new partners.
Master Lucy bowed and retreated, as Anne had foretold, his
parents dragging him away by his coat tails. Susanna wept;
an April shower of weeping; and Judith, almost radiant in
her yellow taffeta, smiled a sly and satisfied smile – until,
setting again to partners, she saw John Hall and Susanna
smiling and bowing to one another, and herself alone; and
knew that the dreams that sustained her were fled in the
cold light of dawning.

Will's cheeks were as leathery as his jerkin. His pate was
hidden in a wig of crisp, short hair. His neat beard had been
cropped to mere stubble. His carapace of steel and leather

gave him the stiff, plodding walk of the soldier. Now, hand stroking chin, he murmured, 'Ah! I like not that.'

A black face turned to him; asked, casually, 'What dost thou say?'

'Nothing, my lord: or if – I know not what.'

He felt a strange exultation. Now they were getting to the meat of the play. He had sown his first seed. And already the foul weed of jealousy was beginning to shoot. 'Was not that Cassio parted from my wife?' Another hour, and the acrid-green leaves, the suffocating tendrils of this loathsome plant would have dragged this sooty-visaged fool into the mud. And he, Iago, would have been both the architect and fascinated observer of this downfall.

The play went on. Othello got deeper in the toils. Such of the burghers as remained awake wondered what all the pother was about. None of them had ever met a black man; but they all knew instinctively that this was exactly how a black man (or indeed any foreigner) would behave – irresponsibly, crazily, dangerously.

The King's Men were amazed; old Will never failed to surprise you. A good actor, granted; but, tonight – he just *was* Iago. He was living the part.

He was, too. Subtle, ingratiating, sympathetic, flattering; cunning, devilish, arrogant, gloating. Above all, gloating. *Farewell, the tranquil mind; farewell, content!* He gloated. *O! blood, blood, blood!* He gloated, creeping about the stage like a blood-gorged spider. *Work on, my medicine, work!* He, sweet Will, gentle Shakespeare, most generous of friends, most great-hearted of men, had created this monster of evil. And now, he *was* the monster. He had created this cataclysm of a play. And now, with a whisper here, a glance, a quiet word there, he was pushing it towards its fearful climax.

And when that climax came, and Othello crashed, dying, upon his wife's bed, he surprised and shocked himself, and all the company, by lifting up his head and howling, long and triumphantly, like a wolf.

After the performance, he spoke to no one. They watched him, furtively, with a kind of awe, as he pulled off his soldier's trappings, shook his hair free of its wig, looked ruefully at his savaged beard. Only Burbage dared accost him. 'Will, you were magnificent.' He sprawled on the chest that held Will's mirror. 'But have you purged your soul, old friend?'

'No,' said Will, not looking up, dabbing away at his cheeks.

'I'm sorry.' Burbage had the true friend's gift of being understanding even when he understood nothing. 'So I blacked my face to no purpose?'

'We have taken two pounds,' said Will the businessman, still dabbing. 'More than we shall take at Stamford with *Julius Caesar.*'

Dick pulled himself up by putting a friendly hand on Will's shoulder. 'I'll go and get this damned black off.' He went his way. The King's Men, that band of brothers, knew all about not talking to a man who didn't want to be talked to.

Though he had still to discover why, he felt ashamed, unclean, hateful to himself.

At the inn, he even asked about the possibility of taking a bath. But the enquiry was received with such lack of enthusiasm that he apologised for making it, and consoled himself with the knowledge that by *not* taking a bath he was avoiding a well known health risk.

Instead, he set his introspective mind to answering a few questions. Why had he wanted to play Iago? Why had he played the part with such savage relish? What had the jealousy of the Moor to do with the jealousy of his daughter? Above all, why this dismal self-loathing, this feeling that he had – what? Betrayed someone? Yes, that was it. Betrayal. Of whom? Of Judith, poor, bereft half-child. In his disgust and anger he had set her up, poor creature, with a noble commander of men. And then he had used all his cunning (and his hatred of her sin, as he saw it) to bring her down, and to utter his howl of triumph over her. Oh, it was monstrous! She would never know, Anne would never know, no one would ever know. Even he himself could only vaguely comprehend the bitter workings of his mind. But if only the child were here now! What would he say to her? *Daughter, I have sinned against heaven and before thee, and am no more worthy to be called thy father.* Because I lacked the understanding a father should have for his daughter. Because my hatred of the sin made me hate the sinner, and made my soul bitter.

He smiled. He went and found Dick Burbage, who sat with a pint pot before him. He slid on to a stool beside him. 'Dick, I have news for you.'

Burbage looked at him, a little warily. Will was queer these days. Prickly! You had to be careful what you said to him. Burbage said, 'Let me fetch you some ale, honest Iago. Then tell me your news.'

They sat, in a Leicester tavern, London's greatest actor, London's most popular play writer. They sipped their ale, staring at the wall in front of them. And at last Will said, 'My news, Dick. I have purged my soul.'

Richard Burbage said not a word. He turned, looked thoughtfully at his old friend. Then, still silent, lifted his ale cup and clinked it against Will's.

They sipped, a silent toast, and went on staring at the wall.

'Swet Mistress Susanna, My parents have bid me write this letter. I may not see you more, it is my father commands. Else will he dissinheritt me. Yr devoted servant Edward Lucy.'

He had made heavy weather of her name. Otherwise, the letter was better than she would have expected.

But the content! 'Coward, poltroon, weakling!' Susanna, for all her serenity, knew how to rage. That he should dare to weigh *her* – her beauty, her wit, all her woman's tenderness and love – against a miserable inheritance, *and* find her wanting! Well, let him keep his prospects, and let his parents find some rabbit-toothed she to bed him withal. Much Susanna cared. She would find some *real* man who would match her, metal for metal, strength for strength, joy for joy. God, what a pair they would be: tall, handsome, of a gallant structure of body both. Among the fat burghers of Stratford, they would stride like king and queen.

She did not think it would take her long to find such a one.

No one could be in any doubt that Susanna was in a rage. 'Bates, saddle my horse. Bring him round in ten minutes.' The clatter of shoes up the stairs, slammed doors, then the clatter of riding boots down the stairs, my lady in the hall, in a black riding cloak, eyes flashing, swishing at the banisters with her crop. Anne was startled but tried to appear unperturbed. 'Where are you going, daughter?'

'Out.'

'I did not suppose you would don riding boots to sit at your needlework. Out where?'

'Anywhere. Nowhere.' She thrust Edward's letter into her mother's hand. 'Now you will understand, Mother.'

Poor Anne! She did not like even her daughters to see how long it took her to read a letter. So she said, 'I will read it when you are gone.' She even held open the front door. 'Take care, daughter.'

Susanna strode forth, having planted a sudden, repentant kiss on her mother's brow. Anne looked out at the great, powerful bay. The situation seemed to her fraught with danger; she herself had never ridden anything more spirited than a carthorse. She shut the door, and gave herself to deciphering the letter, though she already had a good idea of what she would read in it.

She read it, sick at heart; not so much for Susanna as for Judith.

And then: the front door was flung open. Judith burst in, followed by John Hall. 'Mother, John wishes to speak with you. In private.' She tried to sound serious, but laughter bubbled out of her like a spring of dancing water.

Anne curtsied. 'Very well, Doctor Hall. Come with me. Judith, busy yourself with stripping the lavender.'

She led the way to her own simply furnished sitting-room. Her mind seemed to her to move like an old, tired horse. She tried to flog it into action but it would have none of it. She bowed her visitor to a chair, sat down herself, Edward Lucy's letter still in her hand.

John Hall bowed, took the chair.

They looked at each other: he, well-born, young, educated; she, of humble origins, almost illiterate, ageing. Yet there was a liking, a respect between them. They had once, together, while a summer's night closed about them, withstood the assaults of the Devil. Normally they would have smiled. Today there was a constraint. He said, 'Madam, I wish to ask your leave to pay court to your daughter Judith.'

An hour ago, despite her misgivings, she would have said, 'Oh sir, I give it most freely.' Now, with that weakling's letter in her hand, she sat silent.

He misunderstood. 'I have a fine house, Mistress Shakespeare. And my practice is growing. I already count my Lord of Northampton among my patients.'

She spoke at last: 'How old are you, Master Hall?'

'Thirty-one.'

'Judith is but twenty-one.'

He said quickly, 'Does not your husband say, "Let still the woman take An elder than herself, so wears she to him, So sways she level in her husband's heart"?'

She looked at him in surprise. 'You come prepared, sir.'

'It is my custom, madam.'

'Yet you are said to be of a Puritan cast of mind. I would not have thought my husband's plays – '

'I attended the play in Mistress Quiney's yard. *Twelfth Night*. A pretty piece. And Master Shakespeare clearly shares my own interest in the human condition.'

He was being a little clever for her. She brought him back to earth. 'And you would court Judith?'

He inclined his head.

She said, watching him closely, 'You will forgive me, Doctor, but I would have expected Susanna to be your quarry.'

'But she is – ' He bit his tongue.

Anne was smiling, but sadly. 'Promised, were you going to say, Doctor?'

He was silent.

Anne made her difficult decision. Oh, if only Will were here! Why did she always have to be mother and father both? She said quietly, 'Before I grant your request about Judith, I must tell you one thing that I have no right to tell you. Susanna is no longer promised.'

She watched his face, hoping to learn much; but she learned nothing. Too many patients had searched that face for knowledge of life and death, for it to give anything away.

She gave him time. The silence in the little room was oppressive. The clock ticked heavily. At last she said. 'Judith is as vulnerable as a wounded bird, but it is better she should be hurt now than later.'

'She would not be hurt later,' he said. 'I am a man of honour, Mistress Shakespeare.'

She inclined her head to the small rebuke. 'So, it must be now?' she asked.

He said quickly, 'I did not say so. Do not put words in my mouth, mistress.'

She had learnt enough. Impassive though he tried to keep that face, hope was beginning to shine through like the sun through morning mist. She rose. 'I think you need time to consider. I also think that you are too old, sir, for my younger daughter.'

He took the point. 'If you say so, madam.' But he was a man of compassion, as well as honour. He could not bear to hurt any of God's creatures. 'But Judith? She will be so eager to learn – '

'It will be better if you do not see her. Come, this way, quietly. I am the best person to deal with her questions.' She let him out of a side door. A man of honour, as he claimed?

Yes, she supposed so. But, like any man, happy to escape and leave the women to do the clearing up. She put her head through the kitchen door. 'Judith,' she called. And went back to her small sitting-room.

Judith burst in, like an arrow towards the target. 'Well, Mother, what did you say?'

'That you were too young and he too old. A man nearly old enough to be your father, and set in his ways. A man – '

'Mother! You – you sent him away? With that answer?'

'I did. For your own good, child.'

'And – and he went? He did not – curse you, beg, revile, weep? He did not *demand* that you let him court me?'

'No. Doctor Hall is a man of the world, Judith. And a gentleman.'

'But – he loves me, Mother.'

'Did he ever say so?'

'No. But – '

Anne said, 'Bring your stool, Judith and sit beside me as you used to, and we will talk as in the old days.'

Judith, dry-eyed, dutifully brought up her stool, sat down beside her mother. Anne put her arms round the thin shoulders, drew the child to her. So had they sat, watching the daylight fade, the firelight grow, in those dark days that followed the death of Hamnet. So had Anne spent the long hours to keep the weaker of the twins this side the grave. So had she sat, talking, talking, talking, willing her own strength of mind and body into that frail form. And now she said, 'What shall we talk about, daughter? Shall I tell you of the time when goodwife Compton – ?'

Judith said, 'And he did not protest? He went away?'

Anne nodded. 'Goodwife Compton – '

'He *does* love me, Mother. At Father's play, he – took my hand. He – ' Gently she pulled herself away from her mother's arm. 'May I walk out, Mother? My head aches. A turn by the river – '

'I will come with you,' Anne said quickly.

'No, Mother. I would be alone.'

'Very well, child. But not by the river. Why do you not visit your Aunt Joan Hart in Henley Street? See, I will send her a basket of mulberries.'

'If you wish, Mother.'

Anne had feared storm, tempest, floods. Such docility made her uneasy, though she knew that the last reaction one would get from Judith would be the expected one. It also made her compassion almost unbearable. She took her daughter's hands. 'I am sorry, Judith. Did you love him very dearly?'

Just a flash of fire. 'Not *did*, Mother. Do. And always shall.' She wandered out of the room. Anne said, 'I will to the still-room for the mulberries.' She followed her daughter, curiously afraid.

But Judith returned an hour later, with an empty basket, and said that Aunt Joan Hart was well, and grateful for the mulberries, and that Uncle William Hart vowed that the hatter's trade had never been so bad, and that there would soon be nothing left for him but to join the Abraham-Men, a jest that seemed to have caused his niece considerable amusement.

CHAPTER 7

THOU THAT ART NOW THE WORLD'S
FRESH ORNAMENT.

'Father, On 5 June I shall, God in His mercy being willing, marry Doctor John Hall in Stratford Church. Your daughter begs, nay commands, that you will be present. Mother and Judith, thanks be to God, are well, and send their duty. Yr obedient and loving daughter, Susanna.'

Much had happened since Will had played Iago in Leicester. The plague had subsided. The long, weary baggage train had turned for home, dragging its way through the mire, and the shortening days, under the rain and the falling leaves of England's counties. They had reached a Globe that was cold, dark and empty under October skies. Then the long business of unpacking the sodden waggons had begun, and an urgent, desperate refurbishing to begin production again. After a tour the coffers were always empty, costumes ruined, swords rusted, the players themselves tired and often ill; the audiences had to be coaxed back to everyday living, after months when everyday living was concerned mostly with dying. It would be weeks before the audiences drifted back in any numbers, weeks before the pennies clinked as merrily as before, weeks before the groundlings really absorbed themselves again in the dramas of *Othello* or *Macbeth*. They had had bellies full of drama in their *own* lives, during that long, stinking summer, thank you very much.

But the King's Men, who had so much – brilliance, leadership, an unequalled team spirit, the writer of the most popular plays in London – had another quality: indestructibility. A few performances at Court soon put their finances in order. Their audiences came back. By Christmas they were their own men again.

But Will Shakespeare had lost – a quality, a lightness of soul. That visit to Stratford had left him troubled. As so often before, he had looked into his heart, and hated what he saw. But whereas on other occasions he had seen lust, or cowardice (expected failings), this time he had seen something that he had *not* expected: intolerance, lack of understanding, a desire to hurt. He had hurt Anne, wantonly, casually; Anne, to whom his rare visits were her Saints' Days. Why, God forgive him, he had dressed his poor little Judith in the clothes of a blackamoor general, had clawed her down into the mud, and howled like an animal at her degradation. He, sweet Will, gentle Shakespeare, the favourite of the groundlings, of the Inns of Court, of the Court itself, had bayed like a dog!

A man, he thought, does not age day by day, or even year by year. He ages step by step. An event, a felt emotion will destroy a fraction of self esteem, of gaiety, of peace of mind; and the man will be that much older. He will have gone down a step, to stay there until the next moment of ageing. And so, he thought, we go down those long, broad steps until we stand at last on the edge of the well of forgetting.

And now he had a letter that told him the end of a story, but not the story itself. When he visited Stratford, the girls had two suitors. And now it sounded as though Anne's prophecy had proved correct. Lucy was out, Hall was in, with Susanna. So what had happened to the forlorn Judith? What problems had poor Anne had to face while he, her husband, held the groundlings in the palm of his hand, or drank in their applause like nectar?

But Judith was not, apparently, forlorn. She went quietly about her chares. She walked, alone and self-contained, and gathered the autumn crocuses (frail-seeming as herself), went sticking for firewood after the October gales, gazed for hours, fascinated, at the pictures the frost etched upon the windows, bobbed courteously to Doctor Hall when he came courting Susanna, was obedient and submissive to Anne in all things. In January she gathered the first winter aconites, the first snowdrops from the gardens of New Place, and bound them into a nosegay for her sister. Her mother watched her daily, and wondered, and was troubled. But no one knew what Judith was thinking, or feeling, no one would ever know with Judith. All her mother could say was that the shy, sly smile was seldom on her lips, except when she thought herself unobserved; and that often, in the night, there would be a sound of weeping in the big house. But when Anne took her candle and crept into Judith's room, she always found her child sleeping and untroubled.

And Susanna was certainly not forlorn. She and John Hall were indeed of a metal, and their love burnished them both. He seemed to grow taller, more assured. His rather full cheeks had an air of having been polished with wax, his chestnut hair gleamed with a thousand different lights. But it was his eyes, strong, decisive, compassionate, loving, that most drew men – and women – to him.

As for Susanna: if her radiance before had been of the morning, now it was of the noonday. The sun, at the height of his glory, could teach Susanna nothing. The green pools of her eyes sparkled in this midday sun. Yet, like her lover's, they were also pools of tenderness and compassion.

Susanna laughed much; John, as became a doctor and something of a Puritan, little. But he joyed in her laughter, and she found peace in his gravity. And now they were to be married; and they would be the handsomest couple, so folk said, to walk down Trinity nave for many a long day.

They were to be married, in the sweet of the year. And to Susanna that spring had an unbelievable richness, a wonder that was beyond all telling. White clouds on blue skies, white swans on the blue Avon, sailed serenely; flowers sunned their pretty faces, the skies of April were a patchwork quilt of colour, the willows danced solemnly in frocks freshly laundered. All Stratford and its countryside sparkled and danced, with the surge of life rising, yet once again, from muddy death.

And what a pother! Shakespeares, Ardens, Hathaways, Halls, pouring into Stratford from every point of the compass. Now Uncle William Hart couldn't sell hats fast enough. Round hats, tall hats, hats with feathers, hats with plumes, hats like pancakes, hats like chamber pots, hats for all gentlemen from Puritans to rakes, to deck themselves withal.

And here came the gentlemen: John Lambert, old Mary Shakespeare's nephew, at odds with his aunt over a piece of land these many years, but a wedding was a wedding; and Dive Hall, between whom and his bridegroom brother was little love lost, but a wedding was a wedding; and Bartholomew Hathaway, Anne's oldest brother, who had been no more forgiving than God about Anne's early unchastity; but a wedding was too good to miss. And her other brothers, Thomas, John and William; and their wives, all eager to see New Place, all eager to see sister-in-law Anne giving herself airs like a goose in a swannery. Why, they remembered a time when that girl had been as doomed to spinsterhood as a Jew to perdition; aye, and would have stayed so, had she not snared a boy eight years her junior.

So the family came together, as families do, with laughter and chatter and kissings and embracings – and scarce a shred of charity.

Gilbert, Will's brother, left his London haberdashery, and came northward for the first time for years. No one, not even his lady mother, showed much enthusiasm when he walked in. 'Well, Gilbert,' Mary said, putting up her face to be kissed, 'so the marriage tables have drawn you where your mother could not.'

He guffawed loudly. He was one of those who will laugh, suddenly and immoderately, for no apparent reason. And his laughter, like his voice, had a corncrake quality. Mary looked at him, all knees, elbows, wrists and knuckles; ill-chiselled of features, a man who had only to enter a room to fill its occupants with a strange unease. No, she thought, Gilbert was not a son to be proud of. When the good Lord first mixed Gilbert's blood in her womb, He must have been very sparing with the Arden blood. Strange. But no doubt, she thought, He had used too much of it when He made her firstborn son. For Will was Arden through and through. Clever, courteous, gentle, he could make a leg as well as any Arden forebear; all Will had taken from the jumped-up Shakespeares was his name.

Oh, Will had his faults, of course. Who hadn't? No one could say he'd been a particularly good son, or a good husband, or a good father. In fact, he should have been here days ago. Why, poor Anne didn't even know for sure that he was coming. It was a pity, she thought, that out of all the thousands of words Will must write, he couldn't sometimes spare a handful to put in a letter to Anne. She said, 'I thought you might have brought William and Edmund with you, Gilbert.'

'Edmund? *He* could not pay the carrier to St Albans, let alone Stratford.'

'Oh, poor Edmund. I would have paid – '

'And Will is too grand for haberdashers. 'Tis said he will speak to no one now below the rank of Gentleman.' He laughed hugely. And suddenly lifted his voice in a raucous line of song: 'But belly God send thee good ale enough.' He grabbed a handful of raisins from the sideboard, flung them into his open mouth like hailstones, and gave his mother a grin in which silliness and defiance were pretty evenly mixed.

Mary was not surprised that Will had chosen not to face the journey's tedium with Gilbert; but she did wish he would come. Poor Anne had too much on her shoulders. New Place was beginning to seethe like a noble house on which the Court had descended, and Mary knew it was not so much the work and the planning that troubled Anne. It was the grand, and not so grand, visitors; all of whom were watching Will Shakespeare's homely wife with the cold eyes of vultures.

Anne was indeed terrified. A gathering of friends was one thing, an embattled family another. A family gathering never relaxed; each person was alert for any slight. The allotment of bedrooms, and of places at table, was a source of endless bitterness and resentment. And though each individual member was interested only in his own position, there could be sudden fierce alignments, powerful factions could form quick as a thunder cloud, and this collection of individuals could in a moment become a single animal, fretting its spines like an affronted porcupine.

There was too much for any one person to deal with. The food: even those lying at Mistress Quiney's tavern came to New Place for their meals. And snipe and pheasant and partridge, larks, quails and blackbirds would disappear from the table as quickly as, in life, they soared from the fields at sight of the fowler. Great mounds of artichokes and turnips went with them; followed by quince pies and cheese and kickshaws. Beds to be made, fires to be laid and tended upstairs and down, hot water and hot towels to be carried to the bedrooms morning and evening, lamps and candles to be tended, prayers to be said, privies to be emptied, soap balls and unguents to be distributed; even, God save the mark, the occasional bath to be prepared, and all the precautions taken to avoid the chills and fevers that this foolhardy operation was attended withal.

And, as well as all this, to design her own and her daughters' wardrobes; to ensure that Susanna lost no tittle of happiness in these her own special days; to watch Judith with care and kindness; to ensure the comfort of all her guests. And, when she could be anxious no longer, to remember with a wry smile her own perfunctory wedding in a bleak November, her own shy return to a house of strangers, her own and Will's sad knowledge that all she had to offer on her wedding night was an already unwrapped parcel.

To Judith, frail child, that spring was a torment. The house filling with noisy strangers; the men licking their lips at sight of Susanna like hungry men at an eel pie; the women clucking and exclaiming over the bride's clothes; her mother, grandmother, everyone far too busy to spare Judith a word or even, it seemed to her, a thought; her father, who had last departed from her with contempt in his eyes, about to return and treat her with equal contempt. If only she could say: this is Susanna's summer, but next year, or the year after, the summer will be mine; then she could perhaps have been patient.

She could not. Next year, too, would be Susanna's, married to a handsome husband, and perhaps with a child at her breast. And the year after, and all the years. No year would be Judith's. The furthest seat from the fire would be hers. She would be flung scraps of affection, as a dog is fed scraps from the table. And she did not want scraps. She wanted, longed for, yearned for love, love abundant, love overflowing. And this she would never have, now that Susanna had stolen her John. It was not fair; it was grossly unfair. But it was the way of the world. Those who are born to happiness will be happy. To others, the bitterness in their souls will be always on their lips. In her strange, withdrawn way Judith knew this. And stole away in solitude to hug her misery, as a woman steals into the dusk with her lover.

'If I might suggest, Master Shakespeare, this *yellow* velvet for our breeches, and the *blue* brocade for our doublet. And I suggest' – the tailor whinnied like a horse – 'nay, sir, I *command*, the *short* cloak with the upstanding collar, worn over *one* shoulder. And, since we are not *over* tall, I vow we shall be able to wear the hat with the *peacock* feathers.'

'And you will make a peacock out of *me*, sir,' Will said pleasantly. He was interested in clothes. But there had been so much talk of pickadils and wings, of French-hose and trunk-hose, of panes and points and canions and netherstocks and Venetians, that he was becoming weary. And he did weary nowadays; the zest for living was still there, but sometimes there had to be a quietness, a withdrawing. Still, he *was* in his early forties. One could not go on forever; his sun, inevitably, was westering.

'But for our daughter's *wedding*, Master Shakespeare.' The tailor sounded hurt. 'It is meet we should be dressed seemly.'

'Seemly, yes. But – '

There was a knocking at the door. Mistress Mountjoy, Will's landlady, came in. She eyed the bales of cloth, the rolls of silks and brocades, the feathers, buckles, ribbons, tapes, all the items needed to clothe a gentleman, with interest and envy. Then she remembered herself, bobbed: 'Sir there is a fellow would speak with you.'

'What kind of fellow, mistress?'

'One of the common sort, I would have said. Yet – ?'

'Yes, mistress?'

'There is something in his manner – '

Will looked about his gaunt room, enriched for once with the tailor's costly stock-in-trade. This was a part of that other life, his Stratford life, which since his last unhappy visit, he was more careful than ever to keep separate. He would not wish one of the Company's hired men, or some importunate fellow seeking work, to see this splendour. 'I will come down,' he said. He bowed courteously to the tradesman. 'Master tailor, you will forgive me?'

The tailor's bow was so exquisite, so ornamented with twirls of palms and wrists and fingers and knees and elbows, that Will was halfway downstairs before he had finished. But he was not over-pleased: a *Gentleman*, breaking off a fascinating discussion about *clothes*, to go and speak to one of the common sort!

The man was waiting patiently on the doorstep. He was of slim build, pale, with thin, sensitive features. A young man. His clothes were as poor as Will's were rich. Will had seen these lady's hands, the thoughtful face, the poverty and hunger, in too many men not to recognise them. The fellow was a destitute actor, anxious for such security as a hired man's six shillings a week could give, and he was not the first who had had the temerity to seek out the friendly Master Shakespeare at his lodging.

Will was tired; but he'd been a hired man himself. He'd worn those soul-destroying clothes. And he'd known hunger; not, in his case, of the belly; but the hunger to strut and shout and weep upon the stage.

Nevertheless, humane feelings must never be allowed to interfere with business. He said, 'I will bid my landlady find you meat. And tomorrow you may go to the Globe Theatre to ask Master Heminge for work. But I warn you, our ranks are full. You would be better advised to save your shoe leather.'

'Will,' said the young man. 'Do you not know me?'

Will peered. Friendliest of men he might be, but he did not take kindly to 'Will' from an unemployed hired man. Yet he said with his usual courtesy. '*Should* I know you sir?'

The hungry face was transformed by a smile of great sweetness. 'I am told I attended your wedding, sir. In my mother's arms.'

Will went on staring. 'You are from Stratford?'

The young man said, quietly, 'I should have said "in *our* mother's arms", Will.'

He was still staring. Then: 'Edmund!' he said, unbelieving.

'Your young brother whom you have scarce met since he came to manhood.'

Edmund! Who had made a rather embarrassing entrance on this earthly stage sixteen years after his eldest brother, six years after his youngest, in the twenty-third year of his parent's marriage. Edmund, his brother, who was scarce older than his daughter Susanna! Will threw his arms round the young man, his eyes filled with tears. 'Edmund! Why have you not sought me out before?'

The gentlest of reproaches. 'Was it not your place to seek *me* out, brother?'

It was true; and he had always intended to. His own brother, a poor player in London, and Will had not lifted a finger to help, or even to find him, telling himself that if Edmund needed help he would soon come to Will; that young men were often touchy; that he, Will, worked usually an eighteen hour day; even that Will Shakespeare, of the King's Men, was a great deal easier to find in teeming London than an actor who, it seemed, could not even find work as a hired man. Oh, he knew how to talk to his conscience, did Will; he'd had so much practice. The trouble was that conscience so seldom listened.

'Oh, Edmund.' He steered the young man towards the stairs. 'Come up to my lodgings. You will not have eaten? Mistress Mountjoy shall find – ' Then he remembered that damned tailor, the silks and satins and jewels; hardly what he would have chosen to show a brother he had allowed to starve!

But Edmund hung back. 'No, Will. I simply – Gilbert said Susanna was to marry – a present, nothing of any worth, I am afraid.' He pushed a small cloth into Will's hand.

It was not even wrapped. Will, who needed time to compose himself, unfolded it. A tapestry, beautifully and exquisitely made. This, from a brother he had never lifted a finger to help! Tears were almost choking him. 'Edmund, you should not – '

'It is nothing.'

'It is everything. Oh, Edmund, you must come to the wedding. Mother, especially, will be so pleased – And Susanna – '

The young man shook his head, smiled. 'I have no money, no clothes. No, Will, I am not wedding company.'

'You are coming. My tailor is ready, and waiting at your command.' He half dragged his brother up the stairs and into his room. 'Now, master tailor, doublet and hose and cloak for this gentleman. And shoes, fit for a wedding guest.'

The tailor was outraged. *He* did not make clothes for the common sort. But now, to his relief, this fellow was saying 'No, Will. I cannot – '

But there was a most unusual glint in Master Shakespeare's eye. Will was learning at last to command. 'Come, sir, your measure, and your shears.'

The tailor bowed, and set about his distasteful work with a smile.

CHAPTER 8

FOR THIS AFFLICTION HAS A TASTE AS SWEET
AS ANY CORDIAL COMFORT.

Now they could see the spire of Trinity, clean and sharp in the still evening.

Peace, everywhere. Peace in the quiet meadows, the tunnelled lanes; in Avon, muttering like an old woman at her orisons; peace in the clip-clopping of their tired horses, peace in the setting of the sun, and the blackbird's nunc dimittis. Peace in the clear heaven, peace in the restless hearts of men, peace in the heart of William Shakespeare.

Peace, and love; love for the wife he was so soon to see again; love for Susana whom, tomorrow, he would escort so proudly; love for this fair, slim brother, young enough to be his son, who rode so pleasantly beside him; love for dark Judith now that he, Iago, had destroyed her, jealous Othello. Judith, dark like the blackamoor, pale and dark like Southampton's wanton, pitch balls for eyes, black wires for hairs. Judith, who had (unforgivably?) gone on living when her twin Hamnet died. Judith, my daughter, my windflower of a child, I would bear you in my arms as tenderly as my Lear the dead Cordelia – when you are absent; but we shall not be together ten minutes before you anger me. I, the most patient of men, treat the whole world with courtesy and gentleness – the whole world, but not my own poor daughter. 'God forgive me' he murmured on the quiet air.

'Brother?' Edmund turned and looked at him solicitously.

Will laughed. 'I did but ask forgiveness; I need it more than most men.'

'*You*, Will?' Edmund was amused.

'I, Will Shakespeare. I am not what the world sees, brother. But we will not speak of that tonight. The world is at peace, and I would be at peace with it. See, the swallows are flying high. Tomorrow will be a good day.'

Tomorrow. Yes, he was pleased with himself. Not only had he come home for his daughter's wedding; he had come home in good time, well before sunset on the day before the marriage. But that was only right, of course. There would be much to be done. Anne would doubtless welcome a hand with the preparations.

And then at last they were there, in the courtyard of New Place; the sun gilding the chimney pots and sparkling in the diamond panes of the windows, and the lawns mysterious and still under the long shadows of the poplars.

Bates led away the horses. And on this balmy evening, with the heat of the sun tempered by its setting, everyone felt it was reasonably safe to venture outside. And out they came, wisely donning hats and shawls and cloaks – Shakespeares and Ardens and Hathaways and Halls; the rich, the thrusting, the handsome laughing at the front; the poor, the shrinking, the unhandsome in the background, smiling anxiously at jests they could not even hear.

Anne was in the house, too busy even to greet her lord. But now there was the imperious tapping of a stick. Mary Shakespeare wished to advance; and the crowd parted before her like the Red Sea before the Israelites.

She and Will embraced fondly. Then her eyes fell on Edmund.

For a few moments she could not believe it. Then: 'Edmund!'

She, who had wept but seldom in a long life, wept now. It was the suddenness, she thought. She had never hoped again to have all her surviving children about her. And now, here they all were: dear Will, her favourite; Gilbert, sunny Joan; old bachelor Richard; and now, the child of her old age, her babe, shy, gentle, smiling Edmund. Why, she had scarce recognised him. She gave him her hands. He took them in both of his, bowed over them, kissed them. 'Mother!' Despite her tears, her fine-drawn features took on their accustomed smile. 'So! You have learnt London ways, boy, since you left my breast – so short a time ago.' She took his arm. 'Come, my babe, and tell me how you came by those fine clothes.'

'From Will, Mother. And he hired fast horses. He – '

' – is your brother. And could well have done much more.'

'I did not wish more,' he said, flushing. 'Even this – '

' – sticks in your craw. I know. You have the Arden pride. But it will not hurt Will. He may – I do not know, but I suspect – he may have done much for his country; more, perhaps, than his country realises – but so far precious little for his family.'

'Mother! Will is much thought of in London.'

'And little in Stratford. Getting a woman with child, deserting her for years – '

Edmund was silent. Then he took his mother's hand, let her to a garden seat. When they were both seated he said, in a voice that was almost a whisper, 'I, too, have got a woman with child, Mother. And the child is like to die.'

She gazed at him, silent. Oh men, men, men! Was the human race so noble, so splendid, that there must always be this urgency to renew it? Herself, eight cruel births; Will, getting Susanna so fast he had scarce time to marry before she was mewling in her cradle; now gentle Edmund, defying God and Hell fire and the Church to add to the human ant heap; and tomorrow night, God help us, Susanna would begin the work of generation. But Edmund, her babe, her last-born! She said, 'Who is the woman?'

'One who was kind to me.'

'So I would gather,' she said tartly.

'No. I mean – she gave me shelter, food.'

'And you repaid her by planting a bastard in her womb. Oh, Edmund.'

He said nothing. The sun was going now. Only the tower of the Gild Chapel kept its honey-glow. The garden was chill. To stay out of doors any longer would be the height of folly. They rose. Mary pulled her shawl about her. She laid a hand on her son's arm, looked at him with the detached sadness of age. 'So the child will die?'

He nodded.

They began to walk towards the house. 'Is he baptised, Edmund?'

'Yes.'

'I am glad. He has, after all, the Arden blood. It would not be right that such a soul should blow forever down the winds of eternity.'

June the fifth. Susanna's wedding day.

The shrouded moon sank, oh so slowly, in the mists. The star-fire paled. A lightness touched the east, Avon glinted coldly. Swans lifted heads from downy backs, scratched tentatively, nobly launched themselves. The unsleeping cattle viewed the day without surprise, without emotion. Young horses shook themselves, whinnied, galloped for joy; then, as though ashamed of such an undignified display, fell quietly to grazing. Ten thousand birds began their day-long agitation. Smoke stood up from cottage chimneys. And men, waking, faced the day with fear, or resignation, or weariness; some few, even – those who did not suffer from the stone, or the scurvy, or the face-ache or the belly-ache, or a dreaded master, or God's displeasure – with hope.

John Hall awoke, to the incredible, astonishing thought that next time he entered this room the firm body of Susanna Shakespeare would be his, to have and to hold: at which thought his Puritan conscience, always a light sleeper, woke with a startled cry.

Will Shakespeare rose, crossed to the window, looked out. The sun was up, casting a brilliant light on a lake of morning mist, on which floated the tops of trees, the tops of houses, the chimneys of cottages, and, far away, the tower and spire of Trinity Parish Church where, this morning, he would walk so proudly with his Susanna. And he also remembered his own hasty wedding. Poor Anne! What had he ever brought her? A fine house, which she didn't really want. Himself to love? But she could have found worthier men than William Shakespeare to give her overflowing love to. He turned to speak to her, with a great outpouring of tenderness. But Anne was downstairs. On this wedding morn, she had been up before sunrise.

Susanna lay, her hands clasped behind her head, and pondered. She had been free as air. And today she was giving herself into bondage; a sweet bondage, she hoped. But none the less she was about to give her body, and all her worldly goods, into the hands of another. She, who had laughed and danced with half the young men of Stratford, who had ridden her bay and swum deliciously in sweet Avon, must now give herself to housekeeping and childbearing and child rearing and solemnity. She must wear a badge of ownership on her finger, even change her name. The maid is dead, long live the matron! Susanna Shakespeare is dead, and all her maiden joys. Vivat Mistress Hall, and all her long content – and care!

Judith was awake, her curtains drawn tight against the hateful day.

Even the sun shone for Susanna. Susanna and the sunlight were, in some strange way, one.

Judith was one with the night. The dying moon, the shrieking owl, the darting mouse were Judith's familiars.

She lay on her back, legs tight together, hands crossed on chest, eyes closed. And willed herself to die.

Her limbs were rigid. But her mind – her mind would not die.

Outside, on the landing, she heard the quiet scuffle of feet, a stifled laugh, whisperings. Then, suddenly, singing, the clear, soaring voices of women, the strong, deep voices of men, in sweetest harmony. 'Now join we with the dainty lark, To greet thy wedding morn – '

Judith no longer lay like a corpse. At the sound of the music she had flung herself on to her front, buried her face in the pillow, covered her ears. But she could still hear the singing: 'Come forth, O bride, and greet – ' And then a great commotion of shouting and laughter as a door was flung open, and Susanna's clear voice cried, 'Fie, gentlemen! Would you disturb the last maiden slumbers of my life?'

It pleased them well. Judith heard them clattering downstairs, chuckling, chattering. What sound is so hateful as laughter from which one is barred? Her hands were still covering her ears, her eyes were screwed up tight, so that she was not aware her door had opened. Until she felt a hand about her shoulders, another stroking her hair. And a gentle voice said, 'I shall always remember, Judith. When my sister married she was younger than I. I had not met your father, then. And I was already – no longer young. I shall always remember, Judith.'

The girl was silent. But, almost imperceptibly, her head turned and she looked at her mother.

Anne said, 'My heart did not break. But it was as though' – she touched her breast – 'as though it had turned to heavy stone, here.'

Judith went on staring.

Anne said, 'I saw my whole life before me – without love, or comfort, or purpose.' She held Judith yet more closely. 'As you see yours now, daughter.'

A slow nod. Anne smiled, and pressed her cheek to Judith's. 'That very same evening, I met your father. So, you see – '

'My father. Who got you with child, and went to London straight.'

'And returned to marry me.'

'You had ensnared him well, Mother.'

The hand, still stroking the black hair, faltered. But Anne said, quietly and sadly, 'No, child, I did not ensnare.' She sat, staring at the bright needles in the chinks of the curtains. 'Your father is a good man, Judith. And I – I did not act the harlot. What I did, I did in love. Yet you hate him, I think; and you despise me.'

'Oh, Mother, I do not.' Almost for the first time, the shy smile: 'But it is as though there were wormwood on my tongue. I must say things I hate myself for saying.'

Anne smiled. 'And you will dress, and make yourself pretty, and go gladly to see your sister wed?'

'I will go to see my sister wed, Mother. Never fear.'

Anne looked at her anxiously. But she had already given Judith too much time. She kissed her daughter fondly, and hurried downstairs.

On the right, a scattering of Halls. On the left, a solid phalanx of Shakespeares and Ardens and Hathaways. Everyone in his or her best, the church smelling of new linen, new velvet, new leather – and *money*. A few furred aldermen. Everyone stiff, formal, on his dignity. In the back pews, half Stratford. The wedding of the Shakespeare girl was proving the biggest event since Jack Yardley was hanged for purse-stealing. It was as bourgeois and provincial an occasion as one could imagine.

Enter, at the great west door, a poet, a Groom of the Chamber to his most Christian Majesty James the First, a man who was as much at home in these provincial surroundings as he was at Court or on a stage set up in some inn yard, a man who was at home anywhere on this green earth (for did he not love it all as few men have loved it – the flowers and the sunlight and the waving corn, the wind and the rain, the quirks and follies and nobility of his fellow men; the loveliness, the darting minds of women?). And talking of women, by his side came one of the fairest of them, tall, slim, but with her beauty whitely veiled. And behind, bearing her sister's train, dark Judith, her quick, nervous eyes seeing nothing but the cold stone floor of Holy Trinity.

Will smiled at Susanna, smiled at Judith, though even now the child was irritating him, simply by the hunched way she was holding herself, and by her obvious misery. He, a professional actor, was about to make one of the most important entrances of his life. He knew Susanna would play her part. He also knew how one poor player could ruin a scene.

But to his relief Judith looked up, gave him her shy, anxious smile, and nodded to show that she was ready. They began the long procession to the altar.

He walked with an actor's grace, a father's pride, his own sturdy carriage. Yet his tears were almost blinding him. A sudden, overwhelming love of home and family was almost choking him. Beneath his feet, long-dead Stratfordians lay and did not hear the bride's light steps. Yet they too had married here, and brought their children to be christened here; had walked beneath the churchyard limes in happiness and sorrow and despair; had known carking care and sweet content. And now –? There, on his left, the Cloptons slept in gilded glory. Sir Hugh, Lord Mayor of London, had come home to lie in Stratford. He, Will Shakespeare, would do the same. But he would not wait for death to bring him. He wanted more of Stratford than a cold sunless tomb. He wanted the swans, and the proud sweep of Avon – and a wife to whom he could, at last, bring happiness.

And there was his wife, quietly dignified among all these resplendent peacocks. As they approached she half turned her head, and gazed: not, and perhaps for the only time in her life, first at her Will; not even at the bride. But at Judith.

She willed the child to look at her. But Judith's eyes were firmly on the floor. Judith dared not look at anybody.

The girl had made an almost superhuman effort. Her sister was marrying the man she, Judith, loved. Demons of jealousy tormented her mind – would have done so even had Susanna been marrying a stranger. And she had fought the demons, tried to drive them out; because her pathetic attempt at witchcraft, and the danger in which it had placed her, had frightened her sorely; more, had helped her better self to see quite clearly, and with loathing, her worse self.

But there were other devils, and these tormented her body: devils that stiffened her limbs, as though with cunning poisons; that could cast her, screaming, to the floor; that could bring foam to her lips, a wild clawing to her finger-nails. And over these devils she had no control. 'John, wilt thou have this woman – ?' And it was as though waves of fire washed over Judith, so that she was blind and dumb. 'I, John, take thee Susanna…With this ring I thee wed, with my body I thee worship…' And it was as though the stone flags of Trinity heaved like the living ocean, and a great cloud of blackness covered the whole earth. Yet, despite the buffeting of the storm, she was still on her two trembling legs, still fighting, as she had never fought before, the powers that sought to drag her down. 'Those whom God hath joined together let no man put asunder.' And now, it seemed, the devils were tugging at her hair, tearing at her cheeks, pinching her black and blue, so that she would have cried out in pain, yet she made no sound. And suddenly there was a peace in her heart, and in her whole body. The floor ceased its heaving. She looked up. John and Susanna and the priest were far away, at the altar. She and her father stood alone, at the entrance to the chancel. He looked down at her; and, in his charged emotional state, saw a face, drained and pale, yet of a strange, fragile beauty. She smiled. And there was such sadness, such love, such *triumph* in her smile that he moved across the nave, and stood beside her, put his arm about her shoulders, and held her to him, protective and strong.

And Anne, turning her eyes from the immemorial group at the altar, saw her husband and her younger daughter standing together, for the first time in their lives, in love and trust. And suddenly she wept, as a woman will always weep at a wedding. (For, strangely, more tears are shed at weddings than at funerals. The human race, in its rare moments of communal happiness, is a moving sight.)

And then: they were coming out into the sunshine and the cheerful breezes. And the breezes merrily tossed the bride's veil and the feathered hats and the aldermen's gowns; so that suddenly they all forgot their dignity and pomposity and position, and laughed and chattered, blinking in the sunlight, unashamedly drying their eyes, freed from their tensions like prisoners freed of their gyves. A hail of wheat grains, flung by laughing maidens, added to the cheerful confusion. Then they gathered themselves together; and Doctor Hall, grave and proud, and Susanna, loving everyone there but most of all her dear John, led them gaily back to New Place where the servants had prepared such a wedding breakfast – capons and rabbits and blackbirds and pheasants, kickshaws and syllabubs and pies, Rhenish and sack and ale and canary – as never was.

But even 5 June 1607, that happiest of days, could not go on forever. Other days were waiting impatiently to put on their little shows, their comedies and tragedies. The sun went down behind the poplars, a breeze of evening stirred in the knot garden where Edmund Shakespeare and his niece Judith, those shy, quiet creatures, had found a refuge from the uproar, and a sweet companionship. They rose to go indoors.

The doorway was crowded. The bride and groom were about to leave for Hall's Croft.

John Hall was anxious to get away; not with a bridegroom's natural desire to be alone with his bride (as a learned doctor, a man of thirty-one, and something of a Puritan, he would never have acknowledged such urgency); but because a certain lewdness was beginning to creep into the conversation, and this embarrassed him deeply. It also, it seemed to him, embarrassed his new mother-in-law, but not, surprisingly, old Mistress Shakespeare who, as an Arden, could never be accused of vulgarity; and not, even more surprisingly, his own lovely bride. In fact, he could almost have imagined that Susanna was the flint from which these lewd fellows struck their spark.

He grasped his father-in-law's hand in both of his. 'Thank you, sir.' He kissed Anne's cheek. 'And you, mistress, for' – he remembered a less happy day, when it had all begun – 'for a pearl of very great price.'

Her smile showed that she too remembered. 'Bless you, John.' Then she turned away, so that he would not see the smile fade – he who was robbing her of daughter, sister, friend.

Susanna embraced them both. 'Father. Mother.' Her smile was radiant with happiness. She waved to the cheering, laughing Ardens and Shakespeares and Hathaways. They cheered the more. John Hall smiled and waved. Laughter and happiness filled that moment as the sparkling drops of water fill a cascade. A servant threw open the door. Bride and groom stepped out, and came face to face with a nervously smiling Judith.

Susanna was furious with herself. She would have gone away without giving her sister a thought! Gone to her marriage bed without a thought for Judith's loneliness. Impulsively she took her in her arms. 'Judith! We had looked everywhere for you.' (And forgive me, Heaven, that was kindness, not the sin of untruth.)

Judith said meekly, 'God give you all happiness, sister, and make your marriage fruitful.' She turned bravely to Dr Hall. 'And you, sir; I wish you every good.'

He kissed her hand, suddenly moved. 'I thank you – sister.'

She smiled, without nervousness now. But Susanna, still troubled, said, 'I had sought you to give you my bride favour, that you may sleep with it under your pillow, and dream of him that will come a-wooing.'

'None will come a-wooing, sister.' But she still smiled as she took the favour of rosemary bound with ribbons. And then, suddenly, 'Give you good even, sister, brother,' a quick curtsey, and she was gone among the crowd.

CHAPTER 9

MY BROTHER HE IS IN ELYSIUM.

Sometime before sunrise the clouds crept up, rain spattered on the roofs of Stratford, and there was a single, violent clap of thunder.

It woke John Hall and his bride; they turned, and smiled in drowsy wonder, and drifted back into sleep.

It woke Will Shakespeare who said, 'Are you awake, wife?'

'Yes.' She had been awake a long time, thinking of many things; of her daughters; of Susanna, pretty babe, now already (and unbelievably) lying in a man's arms with all the blessings of Church and State; of Judith, facing without hope the long years of spinsterhood; of the fires of Hell; of the success of the wedding arrangements; wondering, above all, how long Will would be able to stay. Another twelve hours, and the last of the guests would have departed. How wonderful if Will could stay for a few days!

He said, 'Susanna. It is strange. It seems so little time – '

'That she was innocent? Innocency is short lived as a flower, husband.'

They were silent. He said, 'I think the dawn is not far off. I must to London early.'

A longer silence. She would not risk speaking until she could be sure her voice would be steady. 'So soon, Will? I had hoped –'

He sighed deeply, took her in his arms. 'I am sorry, wife. But soon, now I am determined' – his voice broke – 'I will return and make up to you, Anne, for the lost years.'

She lay, stiff and unresponsive. 'The years are lost for ever, husband.'

He sighed again. And then she would have cradled his head against her breast, but she was too late. He was out of bed, thinking sadly that she was right, and that no talking or pleading or loving would bring back to Anne the years he had stolen from her.

It was still dark outside the window. But then the cock crew.

Mary Shakespeare did not need the thunder to wake her. Nowadays, more and more, dream and waking were merging into one.

And this troubled her. She could accept the pains of age in her limbs, the dimming vision; but that her keen, clear mind should become clouded – no! This was monstrous. For surely this was a part of her immortal self. She could shed her ailing flesh, but she did not want to go among the bright angels, mindless and wandering.

But this morning, thanks be to God, she knew just what was what. The wedding was over; Susanna had already gone. Today the rest would go – her sons, her friends, would turn and troop away, as men turn away from a grave. Belike she had looked her last upon them, and they on her. Lord, now lettest thou thy servant... Outside, the cock crew.

The thunder's sharp clap did not awaken Judith. She slept on, serene, untroubled.

For Judith had conquered – or anyway had come to terms with – her ghostly enemies.

She had, by a conscious and tremendous effort, cast off jealousy. And this act had filled her with a peace that passed all understanding. Susanna was gone. Now Judith could see her life stretching before her – a maiden, spinster life, untouched by the tensions and conflicts of love, the pains of childbearing: life with mother and grandmother, then life with mother, then life alone. A house of women, untroubled by those tormenting creatures, men! A lonely life, a sad uneventful life; but she could face it, now. From somewhere inside herself she had dredged up a wonderful, an unexpected courage.

The bride favour, the sprig of rosemary tied with ribbons, lay under her pillow. But no bridegroom came to haunt her dreams. Only, strangely, young Tom Quiney, small and monkey-faced, running from the Grammar School as she had seen him do, so often, from the windows of New Place.

The cock crew. A day of glorious summer, of happiness, of achievement, was already superseded. And the hour glass ran, the clock ticked, the earth spun, the blood flowed and slowed and thinned. The sweet summer wasted, the year wasted to its end. Pale Edmund died even as the child in Susanna's womb was kicking and stirring with life.

On the last day of the old year Will Shakespeare sat alone in the gaunt cold of St Saviour's Church, in Southwark, and watched a sour priest consign his brother to the sour London earth. His youngest brother, whom he had let starve in life, and had recompensed with twenty shillings for a forenoon knell and burial in the chancel.

He shivered. A dying year, a dead brother. Sweet Will, gentle Shakespeare, loved by all, unbelievably successful, sat alone in a cold church, yet not alone. Guilt, remorse and death sat beside him.

Edmund, little older than Susanna! A golden lad. Golden lads and girls all must like – what? chimney-sweepers? Oh, that was good. Like chimney-sweepers, come to dust. Fear no more, my brother Edmund. Fear no more the heat o' the sun...

He cheered up. There was something to work on here.

And the old lady who had, in her middle age, given Edmund birth was still alive, he thought. Tough, sinewy, resilient. This would be a heavy blow to her. Not a thing to put in a letter. He must wait until Twelfth Night, for then they were commanded to Court. After that, if the weather stayed open, he would take horses, bring the news himself.

But the weather did not stay open. On 6 January a blizzard began that raged on and off for days. Then came a frost that sealed the drifts into ice mountains. These did not melt until February; but when they did they brought floods that drowned the roads. And then in March he became caught up in the long negotiations to take over the Blackfriars Theatre for their winter performances. It was August before the lease was finally made over to himself and others of the King's Men. He signed his name – and then, the theatres being closed again by plague, he took horses for Stratford.

The last fourteen months had made no great change in Mary Shakespeare. She had, as it were, no more than weathered. A year older, a year frailer; more forgetful of yesterday, but with events of fifty, sixty years ago bathed in a clear brilliance.

Susanna had wasted no time in making her a great-grandmother, a fact at which she evinced little pleasure. There was not much point in being erect, elegant, fashionable, when you had a great-grandchild to advertise your age to one and all. Not that she stopped being erect, elegant and fashionable. Mary Shakespeare, born Arden, would defy age as she had defied all life's annoyances, as she would, as a matter of course, defy death himself when the time came.

Nevertheless, she had to admit that life was taking on, more and more, a dream-like quality. People would appear beside her, and talk, and then suddenly they would no longer be there and the candles would be lit and the curtains drawn, when she had thought it was still noonday. The dead now visited her as often as the living. The babe she held in her arms was sometimes her great-grandchild Elizabeth, sometimes her own daughter Joan who had been born when Queen Mary, she who burned the martyrs, lay dying, two reigns ago. Life was sometimes a thing of shifting shadows, and dreams, and changing mists; sometimes, of awful clarity.

Her hands lay in her lap. Another hand, warm, strong, masculine, clasped them both. A voice said, 'Edmund is dead, Mother.'

'Why, Will. What are you doing here?'

'I bring ill tidings, Mother. Edmund is dead.'

Edmund. Who was Edmund? She knew the name. Edmund my son. Now it was the moment for awful clarity. 'Oh, Will; tell me.'

Now *two* hands clasped hers – comforting, strengthening. 'After Susanna's wedding, Mother. I took him into my lodgings. Oh, it was good to have him. I had never realised before – how lonely… Good to have a young brother, almost like a son. And then – he wasted, and died.'

'When?'

'December.'

She looked at him, long and thoughtfully. 'And now 'tis nearly autumn. Your horses were slow, belike.'

'I – tried to come, Mother. But – '

'Or perhaps Will Shakespeare finds difficulty in writing a letter, in putting words together. He would not be the first.'

'It was ill news to put in a letter, Mother.'

'Oh, Will,' she said. 'I know. Your brother – wife, daughters, mother – what are they, compared with your King James, your Lord of Southampton, your Lady Pembroke?'

He said, quietly, not looking at her, 'That is unfair, Mother.' Yet he knew that if, instead of the King and courtiers, she had said, 'Your Hamlet, your Malvolio, your Cordelia,' she would have been most fair.

She said, 'His bastard. What happened to his bastard?'

'Dead. These twelve months.'

She was silent. Then she said, 'I did not want Edmund. I was weary. I did not want the nine months' weariness, the agony, the long caring. But I bore him, and cared for him, and loved him. And he is dead. And his bastard is dead. Save for my travail, it is as though he had never been conceived. Where was God's purpose, Will?'

'Edmund did know happiness, Mother.'

'With his whore?'

'With his whore. She was a good woman, Mother.'

'Then the Lord bless her and keep her, amen. Have you seen your granddaughter?'

'Not yet. I came straight – '

'A tiresome little creature. Yet she carries the last of the Arden blood. But oh, Will, Will. Edmund, my babe. Did you say dead?'

'Aye. Dead, Mother.'

'I do not think – ' But she fell silent. The mists were beginning to roll up from the valleys. The clear, sunlit view was obscured. 'You have dealt me a heavy blow, Will. Did you say – Edmund? What o'clock is it?'

'Bedtime, Mother.'

She rose, straightened herself painfully and carefully: knees, back, shoulders, chin. Then, erect, proud, independent, she walked slowly to her room.

That night, they fetched Doctor Hall to her. She was delirious. Or, rather, it was as though her mind had slipped out of the present, run backwards, and fallen into a groove of thirty years ago, when she had been mistress both of herself and of those about her; it was as though she had rejected the present, when both her old body and her old mind refused to obey her, and when she dwelt in the house of another.

Will Shakespeare sat beside her, holding the limp, or sometimes jerking, hand, and was filled with a great sadness. That clear brain, that decisive mind, that strong will, all her serene womanhood, reduced to a babbling and a whimpering. 'Mary Shakespeare, my lord. But you knew me once as Mary Arden.' Dear God, she was back at Kenilworth, at the Princely Revels, greeting Lord Leicester. And then: 'Oh, my dear. Welcome to Henley Street. Welcome to our family.' She was welcoming Will's bride, her new daughter-in-law, to *her* home. And now *she* lived in *Anne's* home. Time's whirligig!

And that voice? Plaintive, thin, that had once been so firm and assured. He put up a hand, touched a thin, grey temple. Bare ruined choirs, where late the sweet birds sang!

Doctor Hall gave her a concoction of mallows, violets, borage and cucumbers; then a syrup of red poppies, rose water and oil of vitriol. He bled her a little, but her response was minimal. So he commanded a hen to be cut in two, and applied to her head; and radishes, bruised with salt and vinegar, to her feet.

This, though it did not cure her, held the degeneration at bay. She continued in her same sad state until early in September. And then, suddenly, the mists rolled away. It was the time once more for clarity. She found herself gazing at the smiling, compassionate face of her eldest son. 'Will,' she said cheerfully, 'I am going to die.'

'Nonsense, Mother.'

'I am going to die.'

He tried to match her cheerfulness. 'Then you must make an oration, Mother. Prophesy!' He smiled ruefully. 'All my characters do, the groundlings insist on't.'

'But I am not one of your characters, boy. *You* are one of *mine*.'

They smiled delightedly at each other; he had always relished her wit, and she his appreciation. He said, 'So. What will you tell Saint Peter? That you created Will Shakespeare, who created Lucrece, and Adonis?'

Her smile faded. 'Oh, Will. The best of my sons. 'Tis good that you are here to see my dying.'

And die she did, fading into forgetfulness even as the summer faded into autumn, unafraid, in dying as in living. Mary Shakespeare, daughter of Robert Arden, Gent, wife of John Shakespeare, Gent, mother of William Shakespeare, Gent, went serenely to meet the Trinity, the Angelic Host, and the Communion of Saints. Unafraid, knowing that an Arden was certain to receive the usual courtesies.

Two deaths, in less than a year. Will was sad, and troubled. He had written so much about dying: defiant, noble dying in a splendour of words. But these deaths were different: a quiet slipping away into a lonely shadow-land. Here was no enemy to be defied, challenged, beaten down; only an ebbing tide, a falling dusk. Oh, proud brave Mother who shaped and bore me, you, even you, bowed your head and went in silence where he bade you. O Tyrant Death, who leave your victims no pride, no will, must you humiliate even in the hour of your triumph?

He went back to London. And once again New Place became the house of women it had always been. But now there were only two. Mother and daughter. And no young men swarming like flies round a honey pot. A house of women.
    Quiet. Joyless. Waiting. Waiting without any sure hope.

Next April, he would be forty-five.
    He was growing tired, diminished by two deaths, wearied by four plague years. Success was a wild, tireless, unbridled horse to which he desperately clung, to which he *must* cling; for his only choice was to go where the wild horse took him, or be thrown to the muddy ground. But he was tired – and the work grew; now they had the Blackfriars Theatre as well as the Globe, they were more and more in demand at Court; over the Christmas period they were summoned there twelve times. The horse plunged onwards, through brakes, through forests, ever climbing towards broad, shining uplands, nostrils flaring, hooves thudding; and the rider clung to the heaving beast, and gazed with even greater longing at the beds of bracken, the banks of wild thyme.
    He had another cause for weariness, one which he dared not admit even to himself. He was like a woman, worn out by much child bearing who, after her latest travail, holds a puny, sickly creature in her arms. *Pericles!* Oh, it was popular. It brought in more money than *Lear*. But if this was the best

he could do then he was failing. He would never again – and this thought filled him with a great and heavy weariness – never again know the high excitement of a *Hamlet*, an *Othello*, even a *Twelfth Night*. Laughter, high tragedy, no longer flowed down his arm into his writing hand. The work of creation had become conscious and laboured. Will Shakespeare's occupation's gone! Consign, consign, and come to dust!

He was so very weary. He wanted only one thing, and that was impossible: to feel again in his mind, his brain, his hand the mighty clash of conflict, to soar with his genius but once again among the star-fire.

As always seemed to happen now, spring, which brought the primroses to Warwickshire, brought only plague to London. The buboes, the stink, the terror. The giving up of the things of life to attend to the affairs of death. Children, young lovers, rubbing shoulders with hideous death. And, in the cool mornings, the hot noondays, the drowsy afternoons, the doom-laden tolling of a great bell. The air vibrated with it, the scalp prickled with it, the brain burst with it, the soul sickened with it.

In Stratford there were bells. But they rant at decent intervals, their clangour was softened by trees and grass and river. He yearned for the peace of his native earth. The knell had got into his brain, he heard it now even in the infected night, it beat in his dreams. His work with the Players was finished. He would go home. He was weary. There was no more to be done.

And he owed Anne a life.

CHAPTER 10

SO, GOOD NIGHT UNTO YOU ALL.

Judith was happier than she had ever been before. She had, for the first time in her life, someone's undivided love and attention. She adored and clung to Anne, walking with her to the market, or to visit relatives. And in the evenings the two women would sit contentedly with their embroidery, while the sunlight climbed the panelled walls; and there were few sounds, only the settling of a log in the hearth, the murmur of conversation, a dray rattling up Chapel Lane.

There was only one interruption in Judith's happiness: every Tuesday Susanna would visit with her babe, and then she would find herself in the background once more.

Oh, Susanna and Anne were never less than loving to her – even Elizabeth would give her a windy grin – but it wasn't the same. She wanted *all* a person's love, and it stood to reason that Mother would prefer Susanna to her. Susanna had looks, charm, a splendid husband, a pretty babe. She would be a credit to any mother; while Judith, dark frail creature, was a credit to no one.

Susanna came at two, and left at five. Judith would sit on the edge of her chair, and smile, and speak when spoken to, as uneasy as an ill-sitting hen. But five o'clock on a Tuesday was the happiest moment of all. She and her mother would stand in the doorway, waving farewell. Susanna would round the corner. Her mother would close the door, turn and smile at Judith. Judith would smile back, slip her arm comfortably into her mother's. They would return to the living-room. Susanna would have brought the gossip. Together they would mull over it till bedtime. And then sweet sleep, and another gentle, quiet day tomorrow. The sheep in the fields, the rose on the brier, were not more content than Judith Shakespeare on a Tuesday evening.

Not so Anne. She was happy to see Judith free from the devils that had so long tormented her; but for herself she was sad. She was fifty-four, and life had passed her by. The only thing she had ever asked – to have her husband by her side – had been denied her. Now she was an old woman. Even if he came now, their sun was setting. There could not be much time left. In her dreams the flames of Hell were growing brighter, closer. It was said that to dream of Hell twice in a month was a sure sign of death. She often dreamed of it twice in a week.

Often she imagined what life would have been like, had Will stayed a glover. The two of them, together. Will coming home in the evening, eating the food she had prepared for him. *Will coming home at evening*. The very words brought tears to her eyes. Heaven, she thought in her loneliness, *heaven* is a man coming home at evening.

Twenty years ago he had left Stratford by carrier's cart. Now he was returning; the same cart, the same carrier (his features darkened with twenty years of grime and weather); even, Will could have sworn, the same joyless horse.

A box of clothes, a bundle of books, a gown for Anne, a marmoset in a cage for Judith. Not much to show for twenty years of busy life. But he carried other things the carter did not see, made no charge for: the love of friends, achievement, the proud title of Gentleman; a deep contentment that he was coming home, and this time for good.

And recent memories: Richard Burbage, John Heminge and himself perched glumly round a tavern table (as once they had sat, glumly, nine years before, on the eve of Essex's rebellion). And Richard saying, incredulously, 'But, Will, we need you.'

And himself: 'So does my wife, Dick. Oh, you will find better actors than I.'

'But not a better playwriter,' said Heminge.

'Even that, John. Young Fletcher can do better than I' – he sighed heavily – 'now.'

'Nonsense. Even with his friend Beaumont to help him, he'll be no Shake-scene.'

They had argued, pleaded, cajoled, flattered. He could not be moved. For at last he had resolved the long dichotomy of his life – London; excitement, achievement, work. Stratford; love, peace, the things of home, the things of life's end. It was resolved.

But he had filled his friends with a great sadness.

Memories: the King. A Groom of the Chamber could not go and bury himself in Warwickshire without the King's permission.

James was not an appetising sight. He never had been. But now, after six years of ruling in God's name a people who cared not twopence about him (or, he sometimes feared, about God) his face had become a cunning, wary, obstinate mask. He was civil. 'Aye. Ye've sairved us well, Shakespeare, with your conceits and quibbles.' But some things still rankled. 'Aye. Your *Banquo* was a sair disappointment, mon. A sair disappointment.'

Will bowed his hand. 'If your Majesty could only have guided my prentice hand, sire.'

'Ye're right. But the anointing balm lays heavy burdens on a man. I could have been a bonny writer, had not the Lord called me to kingship.'

'Uneasy lies the head that wears a crown, Majesty.'

The round, credulous eyes stared in amazement. 'Master Shakespeare, ye've put it in a nutshell.' Will had a wild hope that Majesty was going to knight him on the spot for this felicitous phrase (and no man would have appreciated 'Sir William' more). But no. Majesty remained silent, motionless. Will bowed himself out.

Memories: Richard saying, 'Will, for your last day with us, you must choose the play.'

To hide his emotion he had said, smiling, 'Ben's *Every Man in his Humour*, Dick?'

'No. A play by that lewd wag Shakespeare.'

Hamlet, he had been tempted to say. *Hamlet* was himself, his agile brain, his darting thoughts, the core of him; but he put it from him. He would have *Twelfth Night*. Feste was his folly, his melancholy, his bowels of compassion. *Twelfth Night!* The gulling, the yellow stockings, the cross-garters. The wind and the rain!

Memories: the tiring-room. Burbage/Malvolio leaning on his steward's staff. Condell/Sir Andrew, Heminge/Sir Toby, all the rest, their eyes on the stage, glittering in the candlelight.

Alone on the stage, Robert Armin with his lute, the candles lighting his thin, sensitive face; the audience silent, entranced. 'A foolish thing was but a toy.' A hand fell on Will's shoulder, squeezed it. And another. Not a word said. 'Hey, ho, the wind and the rain.' Another hand. Firm, strong, loving. Another. 'But that's all one, our play is done…' The hand squeezed his shoulder, the arm was about his shoulders in strong, male affection, passing the love of women. His eyes were full of tears. Farewell, a long farewell! (He made a mental note.) The rain it raineth every day. A fitting end. The wind and the rain. A dying fall…

But it was not the end. There was still the tavern, the old songs, the catches and rounds, the ale jars clinking. The famous King's Men saying farewell to the best-loved of all the King's Men: in a tavern; to the sound of music; in a sea of ale; a fitting end.

But even this was not the end: dawn, and the carrier's cart waiting; a cold and lonely situation for a man to find himself in, doubts and fears and regrets fluttering about his ears like little winged demons. And here, materialising out of the morning mists, three sturdy, warmly-dressed men to bring him strength and comfort – and gifts. Richard Burbage with a portrait of Will as Antonio; John Heminge with a bottle of Rhenish; Harry Condell with a silver chain to hang about his neck.

He embraced them all, men with whom he had worked and argued and laughed and rejoiced these twenty years; men between whom was the highest respect and love; men who had climbed together out of sunless valleys into those shining uplands of success; men who, climbing in the foothills, had beheld undiscovered, shimmering peaks and conquered them.

He stowed his belongings. He climbed up beside the driver, the cage with that damned marmoset on his knee. The driver whipped up the horse. Will waved. He looked back. Dick Burbage, John Heminge, Harry Condell stood motionless against a backcloth of Paul's, touched now by the rising sun, and of the Thames shipping. A turn in the road, and he had seen his friends for the last time. A few more turns, and he saw his last of London, its towers and spires glinting and gleaming in the light of a new day.

London, thou art of townes A per se!

Will and the marmoset viewed each other with considerable antipathy.

He, who so loved the hares and the birds and the dappled deer of England, could not love this outlandish animal. It seemed to him a travesty of that noble creature, man – man stripped of soul and dignity and humour; man naked in his lust and greed. But perhaps his antipathy went deeper. Did it remind him of that human foetus that had so threatened his life when he was eighteen; that had shackled him with marriage and a provincial life, and clipped the wings with which he longed to soar?

With his dagger he sliced an apple, pushed a segment into the cage. An old man's hand clawed it from his fingers, carried it to an ancient face.

The creature peered at it near-sightedly, turned it over, sniffed meticulously at the whole length of it, let it drop.

Will was anxious. Ever since he had bought the marmoset from a sailor in the Exchange it had been a dainty but avid eater, the prehensile fingers skilfully feeding food in to the biting jaws. He looked at it more closely. Was there a sluggishness about those quick limbs, a glazing in those bright eyes? Could death, who had taken Othello and

Hamlet and proud Caesar, be interested in this cruel parody of them all?

But he had other things to think about. He was going home – to Anne, to Susanna; to his son-in-law, a man to whom he felt strongly drawn; to Judith.

Judith? Much of his life would now, inevitably, be spent with Judith. He did not relish the thought. He could not make himself love her. Pity her, perhaps. Even, with a great effort, be patient with her. But love? No. Perhaps, like the marmoset glaring evilly at him from its cage, she reminded him of things best forgot: of Hamnet, who died; and that dark whore, in whose arms he had lost all he had, save only the appetites he shared with this obscene manikin. Nevertheless, he would do his best. And he had made a good start; he had remembered to bring her a present. He felt pleased with himself.

The Gild Chapel clock struck five.

Susanna smiled, rose, and scooped up Elizabeth who, having made the exhilarating discovery of independent motion, now crawled and explored everywhere, inquisitive as a caterpillar on a cabbage.

Judith and Anne rose with her. The three women walked to the door of that house of women, talking: things said a hundred times before, domestically antiphonic. 'My love to John, daughter.' 'And his to you, Mother.' 'God go with you, Judith.' 'And with you, sister.' ' 'Twill rain, as like as not.' 'John prays for it, for his herb garden.' Then a protracted adoration of Elizabeth. Then Susanna was into Church Street, with a last wave at the corner. Anne shut the door, turned and smiled at Judith. Judith smiled back: the loving, radiant, *happy* smile she kept for five o'clock on Tuesdays; the door shut on a frightening and mocking world.

Mother and daughter walked towards the living-room. Outside, the wind was driving up the rain, wantonly creating a blizzard of cherry blossom. Clouds scudded before it fearfully. But inside – a peaceful evening; with the splash of rain on the window, the wind rattling the shutters, the hurried steps of homegoing travellers, to send an appreciative shiver down the spine.

They sat down, took up their tapestries again and their domestic antiphon: 'Susanna is putting on a little weight, I think.' 'Yes, Mother. It suits her well.' 'And I vow the babe grows more like her father daily.' 'Indeed yes, Mother.' 'And such a prattler. "Da-da-da," she says already. Why, her mother did not so till – '

The antiphon ceased; forever, did they but know it. A gentle, pleasant stream that had meandered through their lives ceased; stopped, dammed forever – by a peremptory, cheerful knocking at the front door.

They looked at each other, started. The servants were all out; Anne had given them leave to go to the fair. Who came knocking, on this damp evening?

Anne had always one breathtaking question to answer *that* question. Will? But no. Only a handful of times in their marriage had *that* been the answer. But ten thousand times the answer had been disappointment. So. Not Will. But who? Two women alone in a house needed to know who came knocking.

Anne went and opened the door. Judith stayed in the living-room, trembling. They had shut out the world. And the world had come knocking. The world was hammering at the door and devils were beating with their fists at the doors of her mind. She pressed clenched fists against her temples. It wasn't fair that her beloved Tuesday evening should be so shattered.

She listened intently; longing, above all, to hear the door shut and her mother, *alone*, returning along the passage.

But she listened for this in vain. The wind foraged among the eaves, the raindrops rattled; was there a murmur behind nature's turbulence, a man's voice, and her mother's? She could not be sure. She sat tense, her limbs poker-stiff, fists clenched against her temples.

CHAPTER 11

DOST THOU NOT SEE MY BABY AT MY BREAST
THAT SUCKS THE NURSE ASLEEP?

Anne opened the door.

A middle-aged man, the sturdy frame grown a little stout. The chestnut hair greying, and receding from the high forehead; the countryman's fresh complexion becoming mottled; the cheerful, boyish smile a little wary. Time, that brings down the oak and cracks the marble, could not be expected to keep his hands off her Will. The world will stain the brightest and the loveliest, given time.

She saw the trunk of clothes, the bundle of books, the cage with some kind of creature. And she knew that the thing she had prayed for every night for twenty years had come to pass. The thing she had dreamed of, imagined, acted out in her thoughts a thousand times, had happened. One day, she had thought, there will be a knocking on the door. And I shall go, and open, thinking it a beggar, a tradesman; and find Will there, with his belongings, come home for good. And it had seemed to her that her joy might well choke her; that her happiness would sweep away the floodgates of her soul.

And now, it had happened. Will had come home, and stood before her, as in the dreams and daydreams of all the years.

And she felt – nothing!

Had she had to wait too long? Was she too old? Were her emotions fading, like her blue eyes and the gold of her hair? Or had her sweet Will-o'-the-Wisp died, even as shy Anne Hathaway had died? A plump, ageing woman with apple-john cheeks; a stranger, of prosperous middle-age. What had *they* to do with a lover and his lass, the acres of the rye, a bride-couch of gossamer and moonbeams?

Her smile was troubled, her voice flat and without expression. 'You have come home,' she said.

'Yes,' he said. 'I have come home.'

She stood aside for him to enter. 'We have grown old in absence,' she said.

He looked at her in surprise. How many times had he said, 'I owe Anne a life'? And now that, at last, he had brought it her she seemed too stunned to speak. Oh, he didn't want gratitude; but he did want the pleasure of giving pleasure. He kissed her, almost shyly.

His kiss seemed to awaken her. She seized his shoulders, held him to her. 'Oh Will, is it *really* you?'

'Yes,' he said, smiling, kissing her more warmly.

'And this time – you are not going back?'

'I am not going back.'

Now she buried her head in his shoulder. 'So often – I've thought of this moment. But I was unprepared.' Almost she hated him for not writing. Had she been expecting him, there would not have been this feeling that one of the supreme moments of her life had slipped by before she could grasp it. The happiness would have been a sweetly flowing river – not a flood that she ran from lest it engulf her.

She stood away from him. 'Come. Judith will wonder – ' She began to walk towards the living-room.

He had hoped that Judith might not be at home; but apparently she was. He followed his wife, with a curious sense of being a stranger in his own New Place. He might have been in London, about to inspect some new lodgings.

He came into the living-room. It was warm, and pleasant, this grey evening. But all he saw was the white, scared face of his daughter, the stiffness of her movements as she knelt for his blessing.

He put his hands on the dark head, murmured a blessing. Then he stooped, put his hands under her armpits, raised her up (and it was as though, physically, he had to lift her). He was determined to be kind. He stood, staring into her face; then, gently, he kissed her, first on one cheek, then the other. 'You are grown beautiful, daughter,' he said, smiling.

She flushed painfully. Yet she smiled for the first time. 'Not I, Father. Beauty is not for me.' She still spoke thickly, as though her tongue was rolled back in her throat.

He shook his head. 'You are beautiful,' he said again. 'It is – a wildflower beauty.' A beauty, he thought sadly, that has no permanence in it; the delicate beauty of the violet, that can be bruised even by the wind.

She bobbed, with her clumsy charm. He said, 'But I have brought you a present, Judith.' He went into the hall, came back with the marmoset in its cage.

When he returned, Anne had disappeared – to prepare food, he very much hoped. He had not eaten since Oxford.

Judith was sitting on her stool, hands folded in her lap, demure, showing nothing of the turmoil, the pulsing of the blood, the twitching of the limbs beneath her black kirtle.

Will came in, the cage held behind his back.

To Judith, a gift was only something to be compared with gifts given to other people. If it was better than theirs, both it and the giver earned her love. If it was worse, she hated the gift, despised the giver, and envied to detestation those who received finer gifts.

But this time she was the only one to receive a gift. She couldn't wait. She jumped up, forgetting all her fear of her father, and ran to meet him.

Smiling, he brought the cage round and put it into her hands.

'Oh!' She gave a little cry that changed swiftly from fear to delight. 'Oh! But – but Father, what – ?'

He was touched by her radiant face, her sparkling eyes. He felt a warmth for this strange child such as he had never felt before. 'A marmoset. Brought from the Indies, by a sailor with a broomstick where his leg ought to be.'

She wasn't listening. She had taken the drowsing creature from its cage, and was back on her stool, cradling it in her arms, gazing at it with adoration, murmuring the universal endearments of a mother for her child. 'There, my babe. There. Sleep, sleep, pretty wanton.' She sat, crooning, rocking her child. Virgin mother, grotesque babe. A spinster of twenty-five, whom life had passed by, clutching her infant to her milkless breast.

Will, who wept easily, was deeply moved. And to think that he had once howled like a dog at his symbolical destruction of this lonely girl.

He said, almost in a whisper, 'Judith!' And held out his arms.

She looked up, startled, then undecided. Like any mother with her child, she wanted to give all her attention to the marmoset. But now she also loved Father; for had he not brought her, and her alone, a present? Carefully and tenderly she put the creature back in its cage. And came and curtsied before her father. 'Sir, it is the prettiest creature. I vow – '

Will said, 'He will eat fruit, and spiders, and flies. Feed him well, daughter.'

'Oh, I will, Father. And he shall sit on my shoulder when I visit, and I will make him a pillow of feathers, and – he shall be all my delight, Father.'

His soul ached for her. He put his hands on her shoulders. 'Judith, I have come home. We must be good friends, you and I.'

A shy, grateful look from the pitchball eyes. 'With all my heart, sir.'

They stood close, smiling. Anne, coming in with the beginnings of supper, was relieved to see them friendly. Will, man-like, had never shown as much interest in his younger daughter as in the ripe Susanna. Not that she could resist a tiny stab of jealousy. Will had never told her she was beautiful. Not that she was, of course; but a man might lie without risk of Hell fire, if it was to please his wife, surely.

Judith said, 'Mother, Father has brought me the most wonderful of gifts. See.' She said, suddenly forlorn, 'I would I could suckle you, babe.'

Anne looked at the babe, horrified. 'Fie, child! As well suckle the Devil as that ugly creature.' She was filled with a strange dread. The marmoset was one with the hobgoblins that had haunted the Shottery lanes of her youth, one with the grinning devils of her nightmares.

Judith looked hurt, and held the creature closer. 'He is not ugly, Mother. He is my pretty babe.' But the bubble of her happiness was pricked. She and her mother, so happy. Father coming home, and a new tenderness springing up between father and daughter, giving another dimension to her happiness. And now, already, a tartness on her mother's lips, a hatred for the nearest thing Judith would ever have to a child of her womb. She said pathetically, 'Can you not love him a little, Mother?'

'Faugh!' Anne made a sound of disgust. Will said, gently, 'Do not be jealous, wife.'

'*Jealous? Me?*' She glared at him; and was not pleased to see him looking amused. Yet, in her heart, she wondered; and, woman-like, changed the subject. 'Now, Will. It is a poor home-coming. The servants are all at the fair. But there is pickled herring, and good home-made bread, and cheese; and a bottle of Rhenish.'

Poor Robert Greene had died of a surfeit of pickled herrings and Rhenish. Pickled herrings and Rhenish had been Will's supper at Mistress Mountjoy's six days out of seven. Leaving London he had thought glumly: goodbye theatre, goodbye friends, goodbye the pleasures of the Court. And then, more cheerfully: goodbye, pickled herrings and Rhenish.

But he said, lightly, 'Better is a dinner of herbs where love is, than a stalled ox and hatred therewith.' He sat down, at the head of his own table, in his own grand house. His wife poured him a glass of wine. He held it out to her in greeting, then to his daughter. He sipped. He put down the glass. He had come home. William Shakespeare, London's most popular play writer, a well-known actor, a friend of the brilliant and the famous, had come home to spend the rest of his life with his country wife and his country daughter: women to whom the King was a far more remote figure than God, to whom the theatre was far less real than the joys of Heaven and the pains of Hell; who had never heard of the South Bank, Paul's, the Exchange, Paris Garden; nor, he greatly feared, would want to hear.

What in God's name, he suddenly wondered, were they going to talk about for the rest of their lives?

Soon after supper Judith rose, bobbed to her father, and begged to be allowed to go to bed.

He rose, embraced her. 'Give you good night.' He watched her fondly as she kissed her mother, picked up her precious marmoset, and went to the door, where she turned and smiled.

She had grown tall. If only she would not hunch her shoulders so, but hold her head high as befitted the daughter of William Shakespeare. Even though, he thought sadly, the bloom is off her. Already I can glimpse the dry, withered look of the spinster. When she had shut the door he said, 'Are there no young men in Stratford, wife?'

'None for Judith, I fear. None has come courting, husband.'

Husband. Wife. Two high-backed chairs, one each side of the fireplace. A bright fire. The wind in the chimney. Candle flames, flickering sideways in a sudden draught, like rapiers, like tongues. Husband. Wife. One each side of the fire, in the long evenings. As it should be, as it should have been, through the long years. But not for her and her Will. Only now, when she was old. The happiness and peace of all the lost evenings should be hers now, and were not. She still felt nothing. She slid down on to her knees, laid her head in her husband's lap, longing to say so much, to pour out what should have been the fullness of her heart. Yet all she said was, 'Oh husband, husband, husband.'

He stroked the grey hair. He, who did not usually have trouble in finding words, found none. At last he said, 'I have achieved much, Anne. My plays have brought much money to the King's Men. They have been played at Court. The

Inns of Court men liked my poems well. I have walked with princes.'

She turned her head, smiled up at him proudly; though she knew that this was not what he was seeking.

He said, 'And you have lived in Stratford, and maintained a fine house when you would have preferred a cottage. You have brought up my children, cared for my parents, while I – ' He broke off. 'I could not have had my success without you, Anne. You let me go – where I had to go.'

She was still smiling up at him. 'Could I, or anyone, have stopped you?'

He was startled. He had always imagined that he, the most amenable and good-natured of men, was clay in anyone's hands. Yet, now that Anne said this, wasn't it inevitable that he had gone to London? *Might* he still have been a Stratford glover? And, if he had been, would Othello and Hamlet and Lear have stormed forever chained in the dungeons of his mind?

But he *had* gone; and he had returned. And soon it would be as though it had never been. The plays forgotten, new young actors, perhaps even new companies, other men following him and Burbage on those voyages of discovery into the human heart. It was all very sad. But he had drunk enough Rhenish to make the sadness mellow, to gild the future; not that there would be much future. He was nearing fifty – He too slipped out of his chair, knelt on the hearthrug beside his wife, put his arm about her shoulders. So they knelt, gazing into the fire. And he said, 'Is it good to have me home, wife?'

And suddenly it *was* good. At last she could accept that all her dreams and daydreams had come true. She had found, at fifty-four, her life's happiness. They gazed into the fire, hands clasped, her head on his shoulder. He turned his head, brushed her hair with his lips. 'I owe you a life,' he said. 'I owe you a life.'

A log shifted in the fire. Flames spurted, and died, and spurted again, as the sparks flew upward.

Judith, candle in hand, crept up the stairs to the top of the house.

She went into a room crowded with lumber. She found the wooden cradle that had housed generations of infant Shakespeares. She carried it down to her bedroom, set it at the foot of her bed. She covered the bottom with an old kirtle. She lifted the marmoset from its cage, laid it in the cradle, covered it with a kerchief. It lay there quietly, staring up at her with its sharp, anxious eyes.

She sat on her bed, began to rock the cradle. She crooned an old, wordless lullaby. Her heart was full, overflowing with love. So she sat, for a long time, until the creature's eyelids drooped, opened, drooped again. Even then she stayed, lips slightly parted in wonder, watching her sleeping babe...

She must have fallen asleep; for suddenly she was awake, still dressed, sprawled on her bed. Her candle was guttering. And from the cradle came a terrifying, choking sound – the agony of a small creature in its death-throes.

Judith uttered a piteous, forlorn cry. She snatched the marmoset from its cradle. Perhaps it was cold. She held it to her, chafing its tiny hands, its feet. It clung to her, its teeth chattering, eyes starting. Perhaps it was hungry. In desperation she tore open her bodice, pressed its mouth against her breast. The animal fought with what pitiful strength was left to it, tore her flesh wildly with its claws. She did not feel it.

Mother! Mother would know what to do even if she did hate the creature. She seized her guttering candle, ran across the landing to her mother's door.

She flung open the door. 'Mother!'

She checked, appalled. The room was lit by many candles. Her mother, kneeling by the bed, looked up startled from her prayers. But that was not it. A naked man stood with his back to her, combing his beard. A naked, hairy man, a gross travesty of her pretty, dainty monkey. Fleshy. Covered with reddish hair. A monstrous parody of her furry, darling pet. And in her mother's bedroom! She felt the bile surging up into her gorge. With a choking cry she turned and ran.

When she got back to her room the marmoset was dead.

Anne left the Almighty in mid-sentence, snatched up a candle and hurried into her daughter's room.

Judith lay face down on the bed, cold, stiff, like a body that had been sealed in ice.

Her stillness frightened Anne. She ran back to her room. 'Will! Quick! Fetch John Hall.'

Will, who had just been getting into bed, looked bewildered. 'What? Now?'

'*Now*. Judith is still, as in death. But – ' She went back to her daughter.

Judith had not moved. But now Anne saw the twisted body of the marmoset, an antic death, lying in the very cradle that had held her own babes.

She gasped with horror at such defilement, snatched the creature up, wrapped it in the kerchief, groped her way down the dark stairs (forgetting the candle in her horror) and threw it down on the kitchen floor. The morning fire was the place for that thing.

Then she went back, and sat holding her daughter's cold hand until the doctor should arrive.

Will plodded along Church Street in the darkness, the wind and the rain.

God! He wasn't used to this sort of thing. He'd been in Stratford eight hours at the most, and already despatched like a servant to fetch a doctor to a silly girl! In his world *he* did the despatching. In his world Will Shakespeare, once undressed, stayed undressed. He did not put on breeches and hose and doublet, re-fasten buttons and points and tapes, and go out into the night. And of course he shouldn't have done so here. He should have told Anne to send a servant. But 'go,' she had said, and he had dressed and gone, as obedient as young Francis sent to fetch ale for Burbage. A man, in a house of women! He had been away too long. It would take time, he realised sensibly, to become master in his own house. He had left Anne in charge for twenty years. She could not be expected to remember immediately that he was not one of the servants.

Despite these understanding thoughts, he felt resentful, as well as cold and tired. Had it been a terrible mistake to exchange the love of those splendid companions, *men*, for the infinitely more complicated love of wife and daughters? He had thought, longingly, of the Warwickshire flowers. He had thought of Anne's loneliness, of the sweet haunts of his childhood. He had thought of quiet days. And already – He felt his foot slide in some filth, swore. He should have brought a lantern; but 'go quickly,' she had said, and he had dressed, and gone.

Hall's Croft was in darkness. He had hoped desperately that there would be lights; he was too kind a man to enjoy rousing others. Besides, Doctor Hall appeared somewhat arrogant; Will did not fancy a reproof from his own son-in-law.

He knocked, waited.

He heard shuffling footsteps, saw in the windows the will-o'-the-wisp dance of candlelight. Bolts were drawn, keys turned. The door opened. He glimpsed the figure of an old man. But then more candlelight floating down the stairs, a flurry and a billowing of silk and lace, a woman's' voice, clear and commanding: 'Compton, say the doctor will visit no one before morning. He is weary almost to death. Say that *I* command it.'

The old man said, 'Sir, but give me your name, and the doctor will visit in the morning.' He made to shut the door.

He, a mere man, could not go back to a house of women with *that* message; besides, Judith no doubt *was* ill. He called out, 'Susanna!'

She was already half-way upstairs again. She paused. A voice she did not recognise. And yet it called her name. So it must be a personal friend, one of the more well-to-do patients. She came slowly down the stairs, crossed the hall, peered into the darkness, while the old man still held the door ready to slam in the stranger's face.

'Susanna! It's your sister, Judith. She is – '

Susanna could see nothing. 'Judith? But who are you, sir? Come, where I may see you.'

So. His daughter had learnt to command now she was Mistress Hall. Until tonight only one man, and he the King of England, had commanded Will these many years. Now everyone was giving him orders, it seemed. He shoved the door angrily, so that the old man tottered. He stepped into the candlelight.

'Father!' she cried in amazement. But she collected herself quickly and curtsied with elegance, her gown billowing about her in the night wind. She said, 'And Judith is sick? I will fetch John at once.' She ran upstairs two at a time, holding her skirts high before her.

A daughter to be proud of, he thought. To be wakened at midnight by a father she thought in London; yet to curtsey as composedly as though she were at Court; to look as beautiful as though she had spent hours before her mirror; to grasp a situation and act on it. No 'I thought you in London'; no thinking him a phantom, a vision come to tell her of her father's death; no waste of precious moments: 'I will fetch John at once.'

The old servant grudgingly invited Will inside, gave him a chair. Very soon Doctor Hall came running down the stairs, followed by Susanna. The servant held his cloak and hat, put his bag in one hand, a lighted lantern in the other. Susanna pressed Will's hand. 'God go with you, Father.' Her smile, he noted, was as radiant as ever. 'Oh, come along,' snapped John Hall.

Will obeyed orders once more, almost running to keep up. 'Now. Tell me her symptoms,' said the doctor as soon as they were out of the door.

'I – didn't see her. But my wife said that – she lay like one dead.'

'No twitching of the eyes, the limbs?'

'She – did not say.'

John Hall grunted. He strode on. Will felt a fool. Doctor John Hall, in a windy midnight, seemed a very different character from the amiable and elegant John Hall who had married Susanna on a golden summer's day.

But suddenly he said, in a very different tone, 'I did not know you were in Stratford, sir.'

141

'I have but lately arrived.'

'For how long?'

Will said, 'For as long as you can keep me alive, Doctor.'

John Hall checked in his rapid stride so suddenly that Will almost fell into him. He held the lantern up to Will's face, stared. 'You mean you have come to live among us?'

'Yes.'

The doctor clasped a hand on each of his shoulders, banging Will with the lantern on one side and his bag on the other. 'Sir! Thank you, and thank God. I shall have a man of intelligence to talk to at last.' He strode on.

'You flatter me, son-in-law,' Will said drily.

John Hall laughed. 'You think me arrogant; but I have seen some of your plays. You are interested, as I am, in men. I in their bodies, you in their hearts and minds. We can complement each other, father-in-law.'

'My work is done,' Will said in a flat voice. But was it? Might not this man, with his knowledge of men's bodies, inspire him anew? *Canst thou not minister to a mind diseas'd? Pluck from the memory a rooted sorrow?* He had always wanted to probe more deeply into this. But there was never time. And the groundlings wouldn't have wanted it, anyway. But now, with all the time in the world, and no groundlings to please, and a doctor for a son-in-law, might he not at last write the deep, soul-searching stuff he always wanted to write? He began to feel more cheerful about the future than he had felt all evening.

John Hall examined his patient: the little witch, as he always thought of her, half tenderly; the little witch who, had things turned out differently, would now have been Mistress Hall.

She lay stiff and cold. But she was not dead. Her pulse beat thinly, her breath clouded a mirror. Clearly she was in some kind of convulsion, brought on by – what?

Uppermost in his mind was the fact that this girl had, however innocently, trafficked with the Devil; and *he* was a guest it was far easier to invite into one's house than to expel. So was this a case of demoniac possession? He would have expected frenzy, a wild delirium, but he had heard of cases where the possessed could be lifted by head and feet like a plank.

He had only just begun his examination when he found something that filled him with dread. Had he discovered the plague buboes he would have been less appalled. The girl's bodice was unfastened (clearly she had been preparing for bed) and her breast was scored with a dozen angry weals!

It was as though a clawed hand had torn at her flesh. He took a candle, and closely examined her finger-nails for fragments of skin. Nothing. Besides, Judith was evidently a confirmed nail-biter; these nails were gnawed down to the quick. *They* could not have inflicted such wounds.

Something glinted on the bed. A button, still attached to a piece of cloth. He looked again at her bodice. It had been *torn* open, he now saw.

He sank down on the side of the bed. He'd been weary enough before this discovery; now he felt helpless. What chance had his powders, his herbals, his plasters for the stomach, in a case like this? Judith did not need a doctor. She needed a minister of God.

He went downstairs. Mistress Shakespeare had roused the servants. The candles had been relit, logs thrown on to the fire, there were glasses of hot wine. His parents-in-law greeted him warmly but anxiously. Will put an arm about his shoulders, a glass of wine into his hand, led him to the fire. 'Now, John, what have you to tell us?'

He looked at them gravely. 'Nothing good,' he said abruptly.

Will said, 'She will die?'

'Her body will live.'

Anne said angrily. 'Do not speak in riddles, son-in-law.'

He said, 'First tell me what happened.'

Anne said, 'She ran into our room distraught. I went back with her to her room. Her creature was dead. I think that is why – '

He said sharply, 'Creature? What creature?'

Will said, 'The marmoset I brought her. She called it her babe. She would – an she could, poor maid – have given it suck.'

Dr Hall was looking at them both fiercely. 'Where is this – creature?'

Anne picked up a candle. 'Come.' She still sounded angry. She led John Hall into the kitchen, pointed to a white bundle on the floor.

He bent down, pulled aside the kerchief, motioned to Anne irritably for the candle. She gave it him. He examined carefully the little claws. Then he replaced the kerchief, rose, gave the candle back to Anne. 'Thank you, mistress.'

They went back to the living-room. He was still grave, but clearly more relaxed than when he left the room. He said, 'So. I am not a great believer in blood-letting, but I think – in this case – a little. And I will give you a liniment of wax, saffron, and vinegar of squills, madam, to anoint her stomach with. I will also give you a powder of coriander seeds, and some shavings of hartshorn and ivory, best taken I think in a white wine.' He turned to Will. 'If, sir, you will come to Hall's

Croft in the morning' – he saw a gleam in his father-in-law's eye – 'or better still send a servant – '

Will inclined his head. 'Your wine will be cold, son John.' He crossed to the fireplace, rang a bell.

Anne, still seeming angry, said, 'What did you mean, son-in-law, "Her body will live"?'

'Nothing, madam '

'I thought perhaps you had doubts about her soul?'

'No.'

'Then why did you say, "Her body will live"?'

He sighed. A woman was like a mastiff at a bear-baiting. Once let her get her teeth in, and the strongest bear could not shake her off. He said, 'Judith once practised witchcraft.'

'Many years ago.'

'The Devil has a long memory, mistress. He does not forget those who have once called upon him.'

'And what has this to do with Judith's illness? Have a care, Master Son-in-law. I am not disposed to link my daughter's name a second time with Satan's.'

It was no good. He said, 'This will sound foolish to you now. But – ' He paused. The girl had come in with more wine. He waited till she had set down the tray and moved to the door.

Anne could not control her impatience. 'But what, sir?'

He said quietly, 'Judith's bodice was torn. Her body was scored by nails – or claws.' Will shuddered. 'Remembering her witchcraft – ' John Hall smiled defensively. 'How foolish this must sound; but, knowing nothing of the marmoset, of course, I feared she had lain with the Evil One.'

The servant shut the door behind her. It was like a thunderclap in the silence. John Hall said, 'She would certainly not be the first maiden to do so.'

Will said, 'Now, John, *this* wine is hot, and spiced with clove and nutmeg. A glass, against your journey to Hall's Croft.' But Anne said, sadly, 'If you, her brother-in-law, can think these things, what will the world say about my little black cygnet?'

The world, alas, would very soon tell her.

CHAPTER 12

THE BABBLING GOSSIP OF THE AIR...

Doll Scattergood had a cheerful face and a splendid 17-year-old body; but nobody had thought to try to give her a mind. She had never been out of Stratford. Her world was perpendicular rather than horizontal: Heaven above, Hell beneath, and, in between, the kitchens of New Place where she worked, and the dormitory where she slept with the other maids.

There was Easter, Christmas, Mop Fair and some smaller fairs, and Church on Sunday. Apart from this, her life consisted entirely of work, food, sleep, larking with the other servants – and gossip.

The gossip was endless, highly coloured, and imaginative. It was the outlet for humour, malice, drama, imagination, hate and fear. It was the mirror of love and human relationships where there was no love, no human relationship. A new titbit of gossip was silver; but Doll Scattergood's newest piece of gossip was more than all these.

Up the stairs she went, two at a time. Then the second flight, a bit slower now, panting; it would not do to be out of breath and unable to tell her tale. She strove to prepare her tale with all the dramatic force it deserved.

The other three maids were asleep, but the sound of her shoes on the stairs, and her heavy breathing, soon had them awake. They knew the signs. Someone was coming with a tale to tell. They sprang up in bed like the sheeted dead, their white smocks glowing in a fitful moon.

Doll Scattergood burst in, jumped on to her straw pallet, sat cross-legged and gasping for breath.

The suspense was unbearable. 'What is it, Doll? What is toward?' asked one in a soft Warwickshire voice.

Doll turned and faced her. 'I'll tell thee what is toward, Rachel Grafton.' She paused, filling her lungs. Her hearers were past breathing, even past blinking. Doll said, 'Mistress Judith hath lain with the Devil.'

For a moment there was utter silence. Then one girl screamed; the others uttered long, breathy sighs, compounded of horror, fear, and satisfaction. But they had the innate courtesy to say nothing. Doll had brought them something to keep their minds and tongues busy till Mop Fair. She must be allowed to tell the story in her own way.

And tell it she did, with a simple dramatic force her master might have envied. And when at last they had mulled it over, sucking the sweetness from every seed like a man with a pomegranate, the summer dawn was not far off.

Nevertheless, Doll Scattergood was awake again early, happy in the knowledge that, though she had eaten her cake, she still had it. She had had last night's triumph, but that was not the end of the matter. Today she would have the pleasure of telling the menservants. Provided, of course, no one forestalled her.

She rose quietly from her rustling straw, dressed and went down to the pump in the yard to wash, hoping to find some of the menservants about; but the sun was still low, and, as she finished washing, the Gild Chapel clock struck five. The house would not awake for nearly an hour yet; even the mistress would be still abed.

The unaccustomed mental excitement was unsettling her. She needed some physical exercise to balance it. She was a good, conscientious servant, who did not need setting to a task. Wednesday, she knew, was her day for scrubbing the kitchen floor. For that she would need hot water, and for hot water she would need a fire.

Singing merrily, she went to an outhouse, found sticks and logs and some dry tinder. Oh, how happy she was! Scrubbing the kitchen floor was one of her favourite tasks – the hot water, on arms and hands, the smell of the soap, the hiss of the brush, the gleaming stone, the strenuous exercise – it satisfied all her being. And, folded warm in her bosom, like a pretty bird that she would soon let fly again, was her wonderful story!

She went into the kitchen. The sun had not yet reached it. It was dark and chill after the sunlit yard. She crossed to the vast, open fireplace. Something lay in the hearth, wrapped in a white kerchief.

She raked the ashes out of the big fire-basket, piled the kindlings and logs in the hearth. Then, her hands now being free, she thought she might as well satisfy her small curiosity about the bundle.

She picked it up.

It was light, but had the curious heaviness of death. She was suddenly reminded of the horrid time when her mother had given her a still-born brother (herself then ten) to bury in the midden. The same feel of stiff, tiny limbs beneath the cloth, the same sense of obscene death.

But none of the maids had been confined. And if one of the men's doxies had presented him with a little embarrassment, he would hardly have left it here for anyone to discover.

She pulled aside the kerchief. A tiny, hideous face stared up at her, showing its teeth in an everlasting grin of torment.

She imagined she screamed, yet no sound came. The creature slipped form the kerchief, fell to the floor, lay there, still staring at her; its limbs, its tiny body, still twisted in that final agony.

She stood, staring. Then, whimpering piteously, she ran, clutching her stomach, her shoulders hunched and swaying from side to side, out of the room, along the passage, up the stairs, up the second flight, still moaning and whimpering, into the bedroom, into her bed and under the coverlet where she lay, teeth chattering, shivering in all her limbs.

They could get nothing out of her. She cried 'Water!' and that was all. Yet when they held the cup against her rattling teeth she did not swallow, and the water splashed down her kirtle. They were not to know that she wanted water – all the water in Avon – to wash the touch of the Devil's bastard from her fingers. It was an hour before she was able to tell them the fearful truth: that not only had Mistress Judith lain with the Devil; she had stillborn his bastard, a creature half human, half demon; and that she, Doll Scattergood, had held the monster in her hands, and so was defiled and damned forever.

Anne came into the kitchen. It was well after six. She was late this morning, but she had sat all night with Judith, who still lay as one dead.

She was tired, and anxious, and dispirited. Though she knew that Judith's illnesses passed like summer storms, she always found them frightening. And she suspected that Will was hurt at being left alone on his first night at home. But most of all she knew that the thing she had hoped and longed and prayed for these twenty years, Will's return to Stratford, had come and gone almost unnoticed; was already in the past, its thunder stolen by Judith. It had been the same, she remembered, on Will's last visit, with the players. Could it be that the dark shadow of Judith (who seemed to want nothing but to be part of the background) would always fall across their happiness?

She stopped dead. The marmoset lay naked in the hearth. The kerchief (its grave clothes) lay apart. The ashes had been raked from the fire-basket, and kindling and logs were piled in the hearth.

She was afraid. She believed in fairies, of course. Who didn't? But though many of her friends had found their kitchens scrubbed and dusted, their fires lit and burning cleanly (and all in return for a bowl of cream left outside the back door) it had never happened to her. No. She was more inclined to suspect the dead monster, which had laid aside its grave clothes (in some hideous travesty of our blessed Saviour's Resurrection?) and then done these things. Perhaps, she thought shuddering, in an attempt to burn the house down.

She remembered how the burning of the effigy had restored Susanna to health. Fire was the great purifier, whether of witches or heretics or the Devil's lesser servants.

Trembling, she lit the tinder. The wood caught, blazed, she threw on small logs, waited impatiently till the fire had a hot, bright core. Then, calling upon every ounce of her courage, she seized the marmoset with the fire-tongs.

She lifted it towards the fire; but then she paused. It was not her creature to burn. If, when Judith recovered, she found her babe gone, her tears and reproaches would be more than Anne could bear, and might well bring on another attack.

Anne overcame her revulsion, wrapped the marmoset again in its winding-sheet, and went and laid it on a shelf in an outhouse. On one point she was certain; she would not have it in her kitchen.

Only then did she begin to wonder what had happened to the maids. She marched determinedly up the two flights of stairs. Why, it must be nearly half past six!

Doll Scattergood, a pleasant girl, she found was ill; but that was no reason for the others not to be about their duty. She dusted them downstairs, gave Doll a powder of hartshorn and a motherly talking to, and went about her business. It was time to take another look at Judith, to see about a thousand and one things, to assure her husband that he was not forgotten. And it occurred to her, perhaps for the first time, that instead of now having a man to take some of the weight from her shoulders, she had acquired another child.

Judith was coming slowly out of her grey limbo. Will was subdued, but then he'd never had much to say at breakfast. The maids were in a strange, restless mood, their minds scarce on their work at all. Well, girls were odd creatures, as full of quirks and cross-currents as the Avon in flood. Which reminded her; it was time she went and had a look at Doll Scattergood.

To her surprise, Doll was up and dressed – not in her working smock but in her own clothes. And she was busy tying the four ends of a large kerchief about her few belongings.

A strange fear gave Anne's voice a greater sharpness than she had intended. 'Doll! What are you doing?'

'*Going*,' said Doll, not looking up, pulling the kerchief tight.

'Going where?'

'Home.'

'Why?'

'Never you mind,' said Doll rudely.

There had been a time when Anne would probably have taken this. Not any more. She furiously seized Doll's chin, pulled her head up, and forced the girl to look at her. Why are you leaving?

Doll looked sulky, angry – and terrified. Anne realised the girl was trembling violently, but she looked as though neither cord nor rack would make her speak.

Anne said again, 'Why are you leaving?'

The girl tried to force her chin down. Anne let it go. The girl stared at the floor in silence, slightly rocking her shoulders.

Anne said quietly, 'Have I not treated you well, girl?'

A whispered. 'Yes. That you have, mistress.'

'Then who has not?' This, sharply; for one dreadful disloyal moment her mind turned to her husband, of whom, really, she knew so little.

Doll was silent. But she was a good-hearted girl. She felt, in her vague, instinctive way, that she owed a kind mistress an explanation. ' 'Tis witchcraft, mistress,' she mumbled.

She could have said nothing to frighten Anne more. It was a word she had lived with for too long. Her lips were suddenly dry. 'What do you mean, girl? Witchcraft?'

The girl, cornered, now had a touch of defiance. 'Best ask your daughter, mistress.'

'Judith?' It was a cry of horror.

The girl nodded. And began to weep bitterly. 'Let me go now, mistress. I do not want to talk about it.'

'But *I* do.' She had to know. 'Sit down, Doll, and tell me.'

Doll remained standing, sniffing, obstinate. 'No, mistress.'

Oh God, what had Judith done now? She had to know, but with this silly girl's obstinacy, and Judith's sly deviousness, it would not be easy. She said seriously, 'Doll, I have known girls – pleasant, foolish girls like you – whipped at a cart's tail for telling lies about their betters.'

For the first time Doll Scattergood looked at her mistress, and her eyes were frightened. ' 'Tisn't lies, mistress. Oh, let me go. I am afeared in this house, with that thing – '

'What thing?' God, don't let it be another effigy!

Doll's lips shut tight.

Anne sprang up from the bed, seized the girl's shoulders, shook her violently. 'What thing?' she screamed, as she had never screamed before.

Doll suddenly held up her hands before Anne's face, fingers outspread. 'These hands have touched it, and I am damned forever.' Her voice had been high and piercing; now it was soft as a sigh. 'Oh, mistress, mistress, mistress.'

Anne's voice was equally soft. She sat down again on the bed, pulled Doll Scattergood to sit beside her. 'What thing, girl?'

'The Devil's child,' said Doll Scattergood. She shuddered uncontrollably.

Anne held her tight. In silence. She had seen a sudden glimmer of hope. Yet she was afraid to put it to the test, in case it proved false. At last she said: 'Where did you see this thing, Doll?'

The girl wrestled with her tears, her revulsion, the shudders that tormented her body. 'In – in the kitchen hearth, mistress.'

The glimmer of hope flared, like a rising sun. Yet still she did not understand. She said, 'But why are you talking about Mistress Judith and witchcraft?'

Again that stubborn, frightened silence. Then, in a whisper, 'Doctor Hall said she had lain with the Evil One, mistress.'

The sun of hope was quenched in cloud; if this story once got out of the house, it would spread like a fire in stubble. Judith would be doomed irrevocably to the flames: either by the slow and awful process of justice, or by the terror-driven populace. She must act quickly. Yet, even now, it might all be too late.

She said quietly, 'You are a foolish, wicked girl, Doll, listening and prying and thinking you can understand the conversation of your betters.' She turned on her in sudden anger. 'Do you *want* to be whipped at the cart's tail?'

'Oh *no*, mistress.' The girl was whimpering.

'Then come with me.'

Anne marched her downstairs, through the kitchen (where Doll gave the hearth terrified glances) and into the yard. She unlocked an outhouse. It was dark inside. Anne went in, brought the bundle out into the sane morning light.

Doll screamed.

Anne said, 'Quiet girl. Now. Did you tell the other maids this nonsense?'

Doll nodded miserably.

'Very well. Fetch them.'

The girl hurried off. Anne stood holding the marmoset. It revolted her. To her, who had seen only honest English creatures, it did indeed seem like the Devil's child. But she waited patiently.

The maids arrived, nervous and tense. They saw a grim-faced mistress, a frightening bundle. They shrank away. Anne

155

ordered them to gather round. Reluctantly they did so, still clutching dusters and brooms and knives.

Anne said, 'You go to fairs, all of you. Has anyone of you seen a monkey?'

There were some nods, some puzzled frowns. Rachel Grafton said, 'Aye. At Mop Fair, mistress. A danced to a tabor. A was an evil creature.'

Anne said, 'Not evil, child. God made him, as He' – she tapped the bundle – 'made this. A monkey is an animal, like a cat or dog, but different because he comes from outlandish parts.' She wasn't very sure of her facts, but thought she would at least know more than the girls. 'And the Lord, for reasons of His own, made him something like a man. A little man.'

But their eyes were still on that bundle. If it held what they thought it held, they weren't interested in words. All they wanted was to run and hide in their beds.

But Anne went on, knowing she must appeal to reason where there was no reason. She chose her words with desperate care; she, to whom words had never come easy. She said, 'Your master brought Mistress Judith such a monkey for a present.'

She looked at their faces. They were not listening. They were staring, every one of them, at the bundle she held in her hands.

She stamped her foot in anger. '*Listen* to me. The creature, this monkey, died. And in his death agony scratched your young mistress on the breast. So that Doctor Hall thought – for a moment – the Devil had ravished her.'

There was a horrified intake of breath. Perhaps she had not been wise to refer again to this matter? 'But it was not the Devil.' She smiled sadly. 'It was only this poor little monkey.' And very gently and slowly she began to unwrap the kerchief.

There were screams. The girls shrank back.

'Touch it!' commanded Anne. 'Every one of you.'

They just stared at her. She put forward every effort of her will. Her eyes flashed. 'Touch it!'

They still shrank away, but among a group of women there is always one whose curiosity will overcome both fear and revulsion. Rachel Grafton edged forward a hand, drew it back, put it forward again.

Anne held her breath. A finger touched the soft fur. Jerked back as though burnt. 'Oh, Oh, Oh,' cried Rachel, hopping on one foot. 'I am burnt, God help me.'

There was pandemonium. Another moment, and the girls would scatter, never to return. O God, prayed Anne, help me to save Judith from torment.

And God, it seemed, heard her. For here came Judith, pale, fragile, but composed. The maids fell away before her, staring awestruck. Judith, without a word, took the marmoset gently from her mother. She held it fondly, rubbed her face in its fur. 'See, girls,' she said, 'my babe. See, touch his fur. Is it not soft? See, his pretty teeth, his little ears. Is he not beautiful, my babe?'

There were tears in her eyes. 'My father had him of a one-legged sailor. But, alas, he died.'

The girls had drawn imperceptibly nearer. A hand reached out, touched the fur. Another. Soon they were all touching, aaah-ing in pity. 'My father meant it kindly,' explained Judith. 'He did not mean to break my heart.'

There was a compassionate sigh. Another. The girls had always been sorry for Mistress Judith. Rachel Grafton actually guffawed. Slightly intoxicated with released tension she said, 'There, mistress. And we thought you had lain with the Devil and borne his child.'

There were titters, shocked giggles. Judith smiled her shy, sly smile. To have been thought worthy of the Prince of Darkness! She could not help feeling flattered.

Anne had remained wisely silent. Now she said sternly, 'Has any of you mentioned this to the menservants?'

A vague shaking of heads, murmurs of 'No, mistress.'

'Or to any outside of this house?'

'No, mistress.'

Anne said, 'If I find that these slanders about my daughter *are* common knowledge, I shall know who has spread them. You will all suffer. The justices deal harshly with any servant who maligns a gentlewoman.'

And with these threats, which were so unlike her, she let them go. They dispersed, slowly, chastened, wanting to show their remorse and loyalty, anxious even to go on stroking the poor, shrunken little corpse. But in the end they went, with their brooms and pails and dusters, back to their work. The pretty bubble of gossip, that was to keep them going to Mop Fair, had burst before their eyes. Well, there would be others. But it would be a long time, they felt, before they found a morsel half so delicious.

Anne and Judith looked at each other in silence. 'I shall bury him,' Judith said, 'under the mulberry tree.'

CHAPTER 13

RIPENESS IS ALL.

Gradually, Will's mind had ceased to whirr like a striking clock. The peace of Stratford began to seep into his bones. He began to think less of what he had left behind, and more about what he had gained: the glory of an English May; time to stand back and look at his life and what he had made of it, time to prepare himself for that loneliest of all journeys on which, soon or late, he must set out. Not that he would waste much time on that; life was too crowded with sweets to spend much thought on dying. Ripeness was all, as he fancied he had remarked on some occasion. And there was an end on 't. There was time to give Anne something of the happiness he owed her; time to win the love of Judith.

But that, he feared, might take more time than he had left to him. He had made such a good beginning. But was it *his* fault that the creature died? And this question reminded him of a sad and bitter period in his life, when he had cried to a railing Anne: 'It is not my fault that Hamnet died.' Oh, why must Judith always remind him of that loss; always come between him and the happiness to which surely he was entitled? He had brought her a gift that turned, in a few hours, to dust. Did she *have* to punish him by turning the household upside down with her vapours and faintings?

But this morning she had gone cheerfully off to market. And the day was perfect: a day for a man to stroll in his gardens, to hear nothing but the bees busy in his flowers, the bubbling wood pigeon, the Gild Chapel clock's gentle disposing of a man's life. He said, 'Put on your bonnet, wife, and let us walk in the garden.'

She said, 'A woman, leave her tasks to idle a morning away? Nay, husband, I am not one of your Court ladies.' But she looked pleased, nonetheless, and decided she could spare ten minutes, just let her set the girls to their tasks...

The sun, warm on hand and cheek; the smell of earth and growing things and flowers; the play of sun and shadow. Peace. He looked at the trees, the house and barns, the miniature beauties of the knot garden. All his. He and Anne spoke little, their voices soft as the murmur of bees. Peace. This was what he had come home for. To find peace, and to see the happiness that filled Anne's homely face. He squeezed her arm. 'Is it as you hoped, wife?'

She smiled up at him, her face filled with that sweetness that was hers alone. 'It is as I hoped, husband.' They were passing a seat. A yew hedge sheltered it from all the dangers of the English sun. It looked on to a sweep of lawn, backed by herbaceous borders and some fine elms. She led him towards it. He sat down, sighed with content. He said, 'I suppose, had I stayed a glover, we could still, perhaps, have had all this. And had it ten, fifteen years ago.' He sighed again. 'Can you forgive me, Anne?'

She was silent. Then she said, 'Had you stayed a glover, and had we still been in the cottage in Chapel Lane, I should have been content, Will. But I think you would have suffocated.' She wrinkled her brow in a way she had when her country intelligence tried to wrestle with something outside its limits. Then: 'This is something I cannot understand, but must accept: that any other man might be a glover, or a baker, or a blacksmith, all his days; depending on how he was prenticed. But that you, alone, had to be what you are.' And though I could not understand, I accepted.' She put her hand on his. 'I knew that it was not wilfulness, husband; but it was my cross.'

They were silent. A blackbird sang in the elms. He said, 'How I look forward to working in this garden, Anne. Oh, James and Hubert will not welcome me, but I want to work with my hands, by the sweat of my brow.' He laughed. 'I want to wield a tool that is not feather-light.'

She hoped he would not see the sudden tears in her eyes. It was one of the things she had imagined: herself, calling Will to come to dinner. Will, his doublet over his arm, earth on his hands, tramping up the path, washing at the pump, sitting down at table with the appetite of a hunter. Countryman Will! It still was, she knew, a part of him; overlaid, perhaps, by the arts of the actor and the courtier. But still there, like the strong oak behind the panel carving. To overcome her tears she said, 'Do you not want to hear news of your friends?'

Friends! The players: stout old Burbage, Harry and John and Augustine; my Lord of Southampton, my Lord of Pembroke; some dead, some estranged; but all, at one time, friends. But Anne spoke of other friends: shopkeepers, tradesmen, farmers, salt of the earth. But would his words and theirs now be of different currencies? Would there be aught left to talk about?

Anne said, 'Judith Sadler has but poor health these days. And oh, I met John Combe in the market, and he asked after you kindly. And poor Widow Quiney – things have gone hard with her since Richard died. A tavern is no occupation for a woman without a man.'

'Has she not sons?'

'Only one in Stratford, and he a ne'er-do-well. A pleasant lad, do not misunderstand me – not an ounce of malice in him – but he is like a leaf blown by the wind.'

Will listened – half to the Stratford gossip, half to the toiling bees. Both were equally soothing. And the blue sky, and the blackbird song, the sounds, the scents, the colour of a May morning. So would he wish to sit, with his Anne, until his sun dipped behind the poplars.

And so, for a time, it came to pass. The turbulent stream of life runs smooth on occasion. And so it was. A man worked in his garden. And returned to the house at dinner time, his doublet over his arm, earth on his hands. The sun was hot on his cheek, the pump water deliciously cold to arms and neck. His palate tingled for a glass of canary, his belly was eager for hot, plentiful food, his soul eager for the comfort of his wife's smile.

A woman worked in her kitchen, as she had done this quarter of a century; but now there was a purpose in it. It was Will's dinner she was preparing, *his* wine she was setting to cool in the still room.

The sun wandered about the sky rising, setting, dipping to the south, climbing up to the zenith. Moons came, and went, and came again. The leaves fell, the trees glistened in January rains, the buds of spring were a green haze. Ageing, dying, renewal. Only in man was there no renewal. Man had but one spring, his winter was everlasting. Anne, seeing the frost in her husband's beard, prayed: 'O God, let not our happy days end yet. Give us a few more days, Lord.' Knowing, in her humility, that a few more days was all she dare ask, for was not her sun almost at its setting?

Nor was she wholly at ease. For Will was back at his writing; and she equated writing with London – and loneliness. True, he seemed content enough. But if he was drawn away from her again – then, she knew, her heart would finally break. And the flames of Hell would be all about her.

Yes. He was doing what he had not thought to do again. He was writing. The power and the glory were once more flowing down his arm, into his fingers; his pen was feverishly scratching and carving them into the paper.

Why? he wondered. Strange imaginings the quiet of Stratford had brought him. An island, haunted by spirits, full of strange noises; a monster, got by the devil on a witch; a young innocent daughter, a testy old father; poetry drifting about the play like summer mists, an autumn poetry of dreams and sleep and insubstantial pageants; a play ripe and sweet as a September day; a play that took him back to that wet summer when he pored with Hamnet over his *Book of Wonders*.

He was not satisfied with it, of course. In fact, when he'd begun to write, he had feared his art was gone. The old father insisted on setting the scene with a long story that would have the groundlings yawning, the gallants at the side of the stage brawling and caterwauling. Why, even the character he had created knew he was being tedious, with his frequent demands of 'Dost thou attend me?' 'Dost thou hear?' 'Thou attend'st not.' He was worse than old Aegeon at the beginning of *The Comedy of Errors*.

But then, as always, the characters took over; and, in this case, so did his magical island. It would serve. But for the first time, he thought with a pang, there would be no, 'Say, Will, where do I enter?' 'Do I speak to him so? Or so?' It would not be a case of fetching Will from his writing to clear up a point. Will would be ninety miles away. A question could take a month an-answering. He must make all clear.

So, tiresomely, he had to put in stage directions, something he had never needed to trouble himself with before. 'Enter Ariel, invisible.' (How would Burbage deal with that, he wondered. Well, at least he wouldn't send to Stratford for guidance.) 'He vanishes in thunder; then, to soft music, enter the Shapes again, and dance with mocks and mows, and carry out the table.' Irritably, he sharpened his quill. Oh, how easy life had been when he could just show them what he wanted!

It was even worse with his next play. He, who had never before had time to write with any purpose save money-making and entertainment, now wanted to round off his history of this loved England. He had shown the bloodshed, the treachery, the long winter of discontent. Now he wanted to show the coming into calm waters. A fair-minded man, he wanted to show the blessings that Elizabeth, whom he had so disliked and feared in her lifetime, had brought to the kingdom. And, for the first time in his life, he would write with that definite purpose: not what Burbage wanted, not what the groundlings wanted, not what the King wanted; but what he, William Shakespeare, needed to do to give *some* shape to the hotch-potch of tragedy, comedy, history, pastoral, pastoral-comical with which he had kept London and the Court amused these twenty years.

But it needed pageantry. And he must write down what they had to do: 'Enter Cardinal Wolsey, the purse borne before him, certain of the Guard, and two Secretaries with papers. The Cardinal in his passage fixeth his eye on Buckingham, and Buckingham on him, both full of disdain.' 'Enter Trumpets, sounding; then two Aldermen, the Lord Mayor, Garter, Cranmer...' And so on. And so on. He was growing weary with this clerking. Poetry, conflict; words used as bludgeons, as rapiers, as sweetest lutes and viols: that was what *he* did with words. Why, he might as well become a clerk to the Lord Chamberlain.

But now, once again, he was writing to some purpose. It was grown late. Anne and Judith had been abed these three hours. But tonight he would finish the play. Then, tomorrow: an early rising, work in his garden, perhaps a stroll with John and Susanna in the Hall's Croft grounds, an evening of music or reading. Could life *really* be so pleasant? What had *he*, a botcher-up of plays, done to deserve so much? (Or was God waiting, as He had waited once before, like a tiger in the undergrowth?)

He had dismissed the servants. The candle burned with a steady flame. The fire was ashes. Silence. Only the quill, pecking angrily at the inkhorn, squeaking and snarling across the paper.

So it had been; always, it seemed, whether in the cottage in Chapel Lane, his London lodgings, the Globe, or New Place. The scratching of a pen. And his brain, curiously divided: a part in this comfortable room (did he not hear the cry of the night-owl, see the hearth, smell the candle?); a part in the King's Palace, or the Island. And which was the more real? He would never know. *This* pen would prick, Hamlet's rapier would not draw blood. His characters were like the spirits of the Island, such stuff as dreams are made on. Yet, to him, they were the only justification for his life.

ERIC MALPASS

Other men had made shoes, or doublets, fed the hungry, ruled a country. All he had done was create beings that melted into air, into thin air, the moment their pageant was ended. What a way to spend a life! Why, even the vintners, helping men to an insubstantial heaven, did better than he.

Yet, as he thought thus, he was still writing. *That* part of his brain stayed in the King's Palace, concentrated, involved utterly in a belated tribute to the Queen whose greatness he now saw. Archbishop Cranmer, holding the infant Elizabeth in his arms, was filled with prophecy:

> '...In her days every man shall eat in safety
> Under his own vine what he plants, and sing
> The merry songs of peace to all his neighbours.'

The merry songs of peace... The wheel had come full circle. These were, he suspected, some of the last words he would ever write. And they echoed some of the first words he had ever written, the words that had so moved Anne when they were young, long long ago, in the little cottage in Chapel Lane:

> 'Oh God! methinks it were a happy life,
> To be no better than a homely swain...'

The merry songs of peace. The life that could have been. Yet, even as he thought thus, he saw himself speaking the Epilogue he was now writing: the darkening Globe, the candles flickering on the stage, the smells, the hush, the magic. Oh, niggard God, to give a man so much: flowers, music, sunlight, love of women, poetry, work, friendship, the

166

swift joys of thought and movement – and but one brief life in which to taste them!

The play was finished. It went off to London – by the carrier.

The King's Men were delighted with it. They hadn't been too sure about *The Tempest*. Could it be that Will was getting fanciful in his old age, they wondered.

But *this* one: it had everything: old King Harry, already famous in folk history as tyrant and lecher; dukes, prelates, a noble Queen; hautboys, trumpets and – to complete the spectacle – let us fire off a few cannon. This will show the private theatres that the King's Men can still roar.

It did indeed.

But not yet. The King's Men were too busy to deal with old King Harry. Their own King James was demanding their attention. He had offered his lovely daughter, the Lady Elizabeth, to Frederick, Elector Palatine of the Rhine, and Frederick had come to claim his bride.

James was used to living at the centre of a maelstrom. He had a singular gift for infuriating everyone – Queen, Parliament, courtiers, bishops, people. But now, though he had infuriated his Queen who wanted her daughter to marry Philip of Spain, and his daughter, who at sixteen didn't want to marry anyone, yet he found, to his utter astonishment, that for the first time in his life he had done something immensely popular. Elizabeth was loved by all; she bore a hallowed name; marrying her to a Protestant was a splendid thing to do, said everyone except the Queen – and, perhaps, Elizabeth.

But, being James, he had to turn his lightening flash of popularity into a thunder roll of hatred. He spent more on the betrothal festivities than his predecessor had spent on settling the Armada. The revels lasted for six months, with a short hiatus caused by the inconvenient death of Henry, Prince of Wales, which closed the theatres indefinitely but did not for long deter the Court's merrymaking. And this came to a peak at Christmas, when six of Master Shakespeare's plays were put on, and in February when, to the accompaniment of fireworks, fireballs and river pageants, Elizabeth married her Frederick and set out upon her unhappy travels.

That was one more Christmas Will Shakespeare did not spend with his family. What? Six of his plays at Court, and him in Stratford! No. He was striving desperately to be a good husband, a good father; but he was only human.

Nevertheless, Court sickened him. Prince Henry, that bright star, dead and scarce mourned save by the common people. The fair Elizabeth sold to the German Protestants in return for their favour. Drunkenness, folly, silliness – and everywhere, and stronger now, that sweet, sickly smell of corruption. It was not as it had been in the old Queen's time. He was not sorry to come home.

CHAPTER 14

I COME NO MORE TO MAKE YOU LAUGH.

July was hot, that year, and dry. Stratford sweltered, from breakfast to sundown. Despite the wearing of straw bonnets by one and all, despite the eager search for shade, apoplexies were rife. Dogs ran mad, streams withered, it was said that in Hampton Lucy the cracks in the earth were so wide and deep that the stink of sulphur from the Pit rose from them.

In London, timbers warped and cracked, thatch was dry as tinder, the wells were drying up, but the heat did not prevent a full house for Master Shakespeare's new play, *All is True*. It sounded like comedy, and was said to be about King Harry VIII, and his wives. Well, if Will couldn't make a bawdy romp out of that story, he wasn't the man he used to be. They stood, smacking their lips, mopping away the sweat, packed cheek by jowl, eyes riveted on an empty stage.

Ah! Here came the prologue. They were prepared to titter already.

But the prologue's very first sentence took the smiles from their faces. 'I come no more to make you laugh.'

The groundlings looked solemn. The prologue told them plainly, they were more likely to weep than laugh. They resigned themselves to a hot, uncomfortable, tedious afternoon.

And, indeed, there was an unconscionable amount of talk. The merry wags at the side of the stage began pelting the actors with nuts, always a bad sign.

But now, fortunately, there was a change. Divers Lords, Ladies and Gentlewomen entered. There was movement, excitement, some bawdy conceits and quibbles. *This* was more the William Shakespeare they knew.

And here came Cardinal Wolsey. And then, with a suddenness that made the packed audience jump, a great uproar and clamour of drums and trumpets – and even, for good measure, the discharging of chambers!

The groundlings hugged themselves. You could always trust Master Shakespeare to get things moving.

And here, with more hautboys, a troop of masquers pouring on to the stage. One of whom, if they mistook not, would prove to be King Hal. Oh, this beat cockfighting!

But now something happened that Master Shakespeare, for all his careful stage directions, had not arranged. Out of the dim heights of the theatre, floating gentle as any snowflake, came a single, smouldering wisp of straw.

And another. And another.

Now the masquers were dancing with the ladies, but no one was paying attention to them any more. The snowflakes had become a blizzard. Angry little fires were beginning to spurt here and there. From above, in the roof thatch, came the sullen roar of flame.

John Heminge ran on to the stage, waved at the audience like a woman driving geese. 'Go. Go to your homes. Save yourselves,' he cried, emotion choking him.

They went. An hour later, the Globe was utterly destroyed. Yet the King's Men, with their usual efficiency, had got everyone away. One man had a fire start in his breeches. The King's Men put it out with bottled ale. No one was harmed. It was a miracle.

But the Globe was destroyed. It was the end of the world.

The carrier whipped his panting horse into the market place. Soon, now, the July day would give place to a stifling night. A few boys lolled by the stalls, hoping to earn a copper by carrying letters. The carter tossed a letter and a coin to one of them. 'Here, boy, carry this to Master Shakespeare, of New Place. And run before he opens it, if you would not be cuffed for bringing ill news.'

The boy caught letter and coin, dawdled off to New Place, knocked on the door. He heard footsteps coming along the hall...

Will had worked hard all day, trimming the hedges. Now, with a glass of canary, and his wife by his side, he sat, deliciously weary, awaiting supper.

He heard the knocking on the door. Doll Scattergood came into the room. He saw that she had a letter in her hand, and remembered it was Tuesday, the carrier's day.

He took the letter. 'To William Shakespeare, Gentleman, of New Place, Stratford upon Avon, in the County of Warwickshire.'

He broke the seal, read.

Anne watched him. And feared.

His fingers were trembling. He kept dashing the tears from his eyes, holding the long letter sideways above his face, the better to see through the tears. At last he said, 'It is not possible.' A long, shuddering sigh. 'No. It is not possible.' He looked at her as though begging her for confirmation.

At that moment, and for the first time, she saw him as an old man. He had the vague, lost air of the aged.

She said, gently, 'What is not possible, Will?'

He was silent, slumped in his chair, staring unseeing at the letter.

She said again, 'What is not possible?'

He said the words she had dreaded all her married life to hear. 'I must to London. At cockcrow.'

'But why, Will?'

Still he did not answer her. He *was* speaking, but to himself. 'That it should have been *my* play, my Harry the Eighth. But' – he looked suddenly angry – 'yes, I gave orders for chambers to be shot off. But not to fire the thatch withal. Drums, I said. Trumpets. Chambers. But – '

Anne could be patient so long. Then it was time for action. She crossed to Will, seized him by the shoulders. 'Husband! What, are you a dotard, to be so bemused by a letter?'

He looked up at her pitifully. 'To fire the thatch, with a stage cannon!'

She shook him. 'What – has – happened?'

'They have burnt down the Globe,' he said dully.

She laughed in her relief. She actually laughed. He could have struck her. She said gaily, 'Well, they can build it up again. They will not need you for that, Will.'

He said, 'I leave at cockcrow.'

She laughed no more. She was angry. He was like a child, with a broken toy. She said, 'Are you a carpenter, then? Are you turned mason, that you are needed to build theatres?'

He said sulkily, 'I leave at cockcrow.' The Globe burnt; his life, the lives of all of them, were in that loved building. *And* their livelihoods. Many of them were rich men, now; but they would be so no longer, when they had rebuilt a theatre, replaced costumes.

And all his wife had found to do was laugh!

His wife had laughed at him! If ever he had needed comfort it was now.

So he had gone off, cold and aggrieved, in that cold dawn light. It was all very well to say he owed Anne a life, but one did expect a little understanding. Oh, she was happy enough when he did what *she* wanted, but she had no conception –

He took the Oxford road. Men were already in the fields, he saw the chop of sickle, the sweep of scythe; heard, in imagination, the sweet hiss of the blade, smelt the new-cut grass. Men, working. The world, at work; this was something from which he had shut himself away. Oh, he had written a play or two, tended his gardens; but he had not worked *with* men – *that* was what was good. He urged on his horse when he thought of what they must do. Rebuild a theatre, recoup losses, replace costumes belike, hold the Company together. Men's work! There was no settled peace where women were. He could not live all his days in a house of women.

Yet he was soon back. By the time he reached London the King's Men had already drawn up plans for a new theatre (they were having *tiles* on the roof this time), the costumes had been saved almost intact, plays were going on at the Blackfriars. In fact, he couldn't escape the feeling that they rather wondered what old Will had come chasing up to London for. Nor could he escape the feeling that they held those damned cannon against him; just as *he* thought they should have been able to discharge a few chambers without burning the place down. It really wasn't a very satisfactory visit. They had managed without him! He hung about for a few days, and then, finding nothing to do, went back to Stratford.

Nevertheless, he did not come back empty-handed. He had brought work, the thought of which excited him strangely.

Burbage had said, 'Will, I have a tale will make you laugh. Do you know what that rogue Jonson is about?'

'No?' Will sipped his Rhenish. He did not feel like laughter. Here, he sat, as he had sat so often, with Dick and John and Harry, talking the endless theatre talk, discussing the London gossip, planning for the future. But this time the theatre was, for him, a tale that is told; the London gossip was already much about strangers; there *was* no future. So he sat, mumchance. What could he say? The price of beef is high in Stratford this month, gentlemen? The harvest is withered by the drought?

Nevertheless, he prepared to laugh. If any tale could amuse him, it would be one about the fiery, cantankerous Ben. He waited.

Burbage said, 'He is solemnly collecting all his poems and plays and masques. And he intends, God save the mark, to *publish* them.'

'Publish them?' Will was not so much amused as astonished. Collect and publish *plays*? It was unheard of. A play was to be spoken on the stage, with a copy for the bookholder, or prompter. And, if a play became popular, like his *Hamlet* or his *Love's Labour's Lost*, someone might publish it. But to publish a whole collection of them!

Burbage hadn't finished. 'And the monstrous conceited fellow vows he will call it, *The Works*.'

Now Will was really amused. What? Get together *Sejanus* and *Every Man in his Humour*, and a dozen masques, and call it *The Works of Ben Jonson*! He had always liked Ben; but Ben did come near to making a fool of himself at times. As soon collect all the plays *he* had written – how many? he wondered vaguely – and call them *The Works of William Shakespeare*. He chuckled happily.

But now, it seemed, an idea had struck John Heminge. He drained his cup, banged it down on the table, and said, 'Why not?'

They looked at him in amazement. Burbage said testily, 'Why *not*? Why, who would want to read all Ben's plays? Or' – he put a friendly hand on Will's shoulder – 'or even old Will's, come to that?'

'Who indeed? said Will, though it was a point he would have preferred to make himself, if it had to be made.

Heminge said gravely, 'When the Globe was burnt, I thought at the time: suppose all our bookholder's copies had been destroyed. What should we do for plays? There are not so many new authors coming along.'

Burbage looked impressed. 'Aye, we should be in a pickle, without Will's plays to fall back on.'

Harry Condell had another point. 'Besides, there is good stuff in Will's plays.' Will inclined to him courteously. 'I do not just mean catchpenny stuff, either. I mean thought, bits of poetry; things that one perhaps ought to do something to try to preserve a little.'

Burbage looked unimpressed. 'Voyages of discovery, eh, Will?' he said, remembering old conversations. 'But – no, Harry, not to be *read*. 'Twould be dull, tedious stuff.'

Without, he means, a Burbage to give it life, Will thought, modestly agreeing with every word. But Heminge said, 'I know I am right. The work should be put in hand. Then, if there were another fire, we should at least not be at the mercy of these new play writers.'

So, as often happened with the King's Men, a chance remark was seen to contain an idea. The idea was considered, discussed, analysed and then worked upon. Five minutes after Burbage had told his tale about Ben Johnson, they were deep in the problem of collecting and editing Will Shakespeare's plays; Will saying he would like to include *Venus and Adonis* and *The Rape of Lucrece*; the others really wanting only the plays, poems could be very tedious; Will saying he could not stomach re-reading those early plays, the *Comedy*, and, God ha' mercy, what was that one about two gentlemen of somewhere or other? Even *Romeo and Juliet*, he vowed, was no reading for a man of his age; Will saying that, whatever they decided to call it, he would not have a pompous title like *The Works of William Shakespeare*. Who did they think he was? Ben Jonson?

Nevertheless, when he rode back to Stratford, he had a mass of papers in his satchel: *All's Well that Ends Well*, *Othello*, *Macbeth*. Revising them would be a going back, and he had always gone forward, creating. Nevertheless, he was eager, and just a little flattered. *The Works of William Shakespeare*, now he was becoming used to the idea, had a certain ring about it. It went with New Place and a Grant of Arms. And, who knew? Some child, somewhere, might one day take such a book from the shelves, and blow off the dust, and read – his Caliban, his Ariel, his Titania. One day, long after he was dust, and Burbage and the new Globe were dust, a child might read, and stir, in an hour of wonder, before the book was replaced, and the words died on the air. A child, in some distant summer, spelling out a name no sooner read than forgotten. The name of William Shakespeare.

And so, once more, to Stratford. And the wonder of the changing seasons; and friends, and peace; Anne rejoicing in his presence; Susanna and John and the prattling grandchild.

And Judith. Oh, there was peace between them now; but no comfort. If he found himself alone in a room with her, they would smile at each other, with an uneasy brilliance, exchange a word or two, and then sit racking their brains for something to say. Both guilty. He because he had lacked understanding, she because she could not love her father, and so was damned for breaking the commandments. Both striving desperately to feel, and show, love; both wary, suspicious, prickly.

Anne knew that, with Judith in the house, the quiet happiness she had longed for with her Will could never be. If only Judith would marry; but the girl was nearly thirty. She was like the last bonnet left on the market stall, when the customers have all made their purchases and gone merrily home.

There were times when Will, keen business man though he was, would have paid a disproportionately large dowry to get the girl off his hands. But to whom? The young men of Stratford were wont to post to marriage-beds long before they reached Judith's age. Few were left: Richard Quiney's son Tom, who had the wizened, anxious face of a monkey, and was years younger than Judith anyway, and helped his mother in the tavern; Edward Reynolds who, it was said, had not two pennies to rub together, and anyway lacked a leg; James Walker, who was said to share some of his royal namesake's more unfortunate habits; these three misbegotten knaves were all he could call to mind. And he would not wish one of these on his daughter.

And Judith, with her nervous sensitivity, knew something of what her parents were feeling; and was wretched.

She did not see much of her father. Will had set up a writing-table in a small room overlooking the gardens, and a shelf for his few books. Here he settled down to revise his plays for publication.

He found such work tedious. *The Works of William Shakespeare!* Into those dusty pages you could not crowd the thunder of Burbage, the excitement of the groundlings, the wry laughter of Armin. As well hope to capture the flight of the swallow in a blown egg in a case, the dragon fly's flickering sheen in a pinned specimen.

Nevertheless, he persevered. And was, frankly, impressed. Harry Condell had been right. There were things here it were a pity to cast away. He might, he decided (if ever the book *were* published), give a copy to son-in-law John Hall. 'See, John. Oh, I make no claim; stuff for an idle afternoon. Yet, perchance, that last speech of Othello's. Or the murder of Duncan. If you did care to look sometime…' No one else would be interested; certainly not Anne and Judith, to whom an account from the butcher was reading enough. Susanna? No. Susanna was too busy with life to trouble herself with dusty words. But he persevered. Burbage and Heminge and Condell had asked him, and he had never failed them yet.

CHAPTER 15

...YOU ARE THE LORD OF DUTY –
I AM YOUR DAUGHTER; BUT HERE'S MY HUSBAND...

Every year, a blind man with a monkey visited Mop Fair.
Every year, when the lads of Stratford saw the dancing
monkey they were at once struck by its resemblance to Tom
Quiney, and did not hesitate to tell him so.

The monkey was one of the highlights of the Fair, and its
merry antics would still be discussed at Christmas. When it
was like to be forgotten, someone would see Tom Quiney's
face behind the tavern counter, and be reminded, and cry,
'Nay lads, do you remember that little ape at Mop Fair?
How a' would dance, ha!' And another would cry, 'Come,
Tom an I beat my tabor, wilt thou caper so?' It was generally
agreed among the tavern's customers that baiting Monkey
Quiney beat cockfighting.

Not that this ape ever harmed the mastiffs. Tom would
smile shyly, and keep his head down, and sometimes cast his
mother a beseeching look (not that she would lift a finger,
and might even join in the baiting. The Widow Quiney knew
what was good for trade). So Tom carried his cross; the only
happy moment of his day was when the last customer

179

staggered from the door, and he went up to his truckle bed under the eaves, and was alone.

one day, in the market, he met the daughter of his late father's friend, Will Shakespeare. She was four years older than Tom.

There were few people for whom Judith, the youngest and frailest of her circle, could feel pity, but Tom was one.

In the old days she had sat in her window and seen him running from the Grammar School. How the other boys push and jostle him, she had thought, longing to bring him in and soothe his bruises with unguents. And later, seeing him handling the heavy barrels outside the tavern, she had thought it too much for his puny strength. So she, whom so many pitied, knew pity herself, and found it a warm and comforting emotion.

But now, in the market, it flamed into a hot fire. For the women behind one of the stalls were crying, amid much laughter, 'Ho, monkey, let us sell thee to a fine lady, who will dress thee in silken breeches, and let thee sleep on her pillow.' Tom Quiney pretended not to hear.

Judith was shy; but she was a daughter of Anne Hathaway and a granddaughter of Mary Arden, and had inherited those two ladies' very different sorts of courage. She saw Quiney's distress. She called out to the women. 'Ladies, for shame! You do our sex much wrong with your roistering.'

But Judith, though nearing thirty, still spoke with her tongue rolled back in her throat. This tickled the market women mightily. They mimicked her speech, and mopped and mowed like dancing apes. Seldom were there such merry doings in Stratford market.

Judith flushed, and was near to tears, both of anger and shame. There was only one thing to do. She said, 'Sir, will you escort me to New Place?'

He bowed, humbly and gratefully. He was too bewildered to offer his arm, but she took it. They walked away, she hunched and quivering with fear and anger; he silent that she, the daughter of his father's friend, should have witnessed his shame.

When they came into the quiet of Chapel Street he stopped, and turned to face her, and said, 'Mistress Shakespeare, all Stratford mocks me because I am like the ape that danced at Mop Fair. So you will not wish me to escort you further.'

Her face was strangely sweet. He had never realised how sweet. She said, 'Master Quiney, I had a pet, a pretty marmoset. I called him my babe, and loved him dearly. And when he died, I was like to die.'

Her watched her face, so pale, the eyes so black and so kind, the hair straight and black. He thought he had never seen anything so beautiful. But her story puzzled him. 'So?' he said.

She too looked puzzled. What had she meant to say? She did not know. Only to offer comfort to this lad with the pleasant, anxious monkey-face. She said, 'He was so pretty. But you – you are a man, Master Quiney. You' – she touched him for a moment with her gloved hand – 'you must not dance for fools.'

She had touched him on the raw. 'I do not,' he said proudly, 'though all mock me.'

She said, smiling, 'I am sure you do not. And I shall be honoured if you will see me to my house, Master Quiney.'

This was the first time in her life that Judith had taken the lead in a conversation. She went home filled with happiness.

So, too, did Thomas Quiney. Gentlewomen had always been to him proud, mocking creatures. He had feared them, hated them, desired them. He had never before loved one of them. And now, he *was* in love with, so it seemed to him, a dark, lovely creature who had come between him and his tormentors once, and who might be prepared to do so throughout all the tribulations of his life.

So that Will, coming into the living-room from his writing, found an Anne strangely wrought up.

'Will, a young man has come courting our Judith.'

He looked up sharply. 'Who?'

Anne had considered well, and prepared her answer accordingly. Judith was nearly thirty, older in spinsterhood even that Anne had been, with a frail, quaint charm that would have no appeal for the robust, successful, Jacobean gentleman. So, if she was to marry, it would have to be to someone whose choice was also limited.

Like any mother, Anne wanted her daughter married. And she had other, less unselfish reasons. All her lonely life she had consoled herself with the thought that she and Will would have a few years together when they were old, for had not Will always promised her this?

Yet she had already learnt that, with Will and Judith in the same house, there would never be peace. The sweet, gentle Will she so loved became another person when Judith was present. He tried so hard. She saw him making tremendous efforts to be calm and loving. Judith, too, would be an obedient and biddable daughter. But, always, there would be something to destroy harmony.

So now she said, smiling: 'The son of an old and loving friend of yours, husband.'

Strange. He was already suspicious. Perhaps he knew that Judith was certain to choose someone of whom he would disapprove. 'Who?' he said again.

'Richard Quiney's son, Thomas.'

He said, quickly and harshly, 'Someone you yourself described the other day as a ne'er-do-well and a drunkard.' But in his heart he knew he was thinking, A vinter! A tavern-keeper, for the daughter of William Shakespeare, Gentleman. And was ashamed, and blamed Judith for giving him cause to feel ashamed.

Anne said coolly, 'But now I have met him, and found him pleasant and courteous. Oh, he is small, and ugly withal; yet his face is gentle, and in those wrinkles there lie much humour and kindness.'

It was not like Anne to be so analytical, he thought. He waited. She said, 'And the poor fool loves him, and he her, or I am no woman.'

He thought this over. 'Has he asked your permission to woo her?'

'Yes.'

'What did you tell him?'

'I said he must speak to you.'

So. The decision was his. Well, he would not have Judith a spinster all her life; and Richard Quiney had been a good friend, a Bailiff of the town, a man of substance. Why, Will's father and Richard's father had been friends; and both the families bore arms. So what more fitting than that these two sound and armigerous families should be united? But a tavern-keeper? The good Doctor Hall, MA Cantab., would look down his nose at such a brother-in-law. 'I will speak to Judith,' he said.

Anne rose, went out of the room.

Judith came in. She smiled and curtsied. She held herself straighter, seemed composed. More composed than her father, frankly. He rose, kissed her hand. 'Be seated, daughter.'

She sat down on a three-legged stool. He went back to his great chair. 'Your mother tells me you are being wooed?'

'Yes, Father.'

'By Thomas Quiney?'

Her face lit up at the name. 'Yes, Father.'

'Is it your wish that he should pay you his attentions?'

'Oh *yes*, Father.'

'And if I say no?'

She said piteously, 'Then I think I shall die.'

He said, 'You would not yet die, Judith. Men – or women – do not die for love. Yet you would be sad?'

'I should be sad.'

'But he is said to be a weakling, a ne'er-do-well?'

'He needs my strength. That is why I love him.'

'*Your* strength?' he could not help saying.

She astonished – and irritated – him by saying, 'I am an Arden. Besides, his need of my strength *gives* me strength.'

He was impressed. He rose, took her hands. 'All I want is your happiness, Judith. And yet – this fellow, four years your junior. Are you prepared to carry him through life?'

She said boldly, 'You are *eight* years mother's junior, sir. Yet I do not fancy she has carried you far.'

He laughed. He could never resist a quibble. 'Pert wench! Well, I will consider. But' – he was suddenly heavy – 'I could have wished a more acceptable son-in-law, daughter.'

She said quickly, 'Because he is a tavern-keeper?'

'No,' he replied hotly, 'because, as you have just reminded me, you are an Arden. And – as *I* will now remind *you* – a Shakespeare. Families of strength and character, whose daughters should bear noble sons.'

'And you think Tom will not give me noble sons? Well, Susanna has not brought forth much so far, despite her proud lord.'

'You go too far,' he said harshly. Susanna's lack of sons was a sorrow it hurt to probe.

Judith bobbed, all contrition. 'Forgive me, Father. It is that – for me this is life and death, and one's tongue becomes unruly.'

'I will consider,' he said again, waving her to the door.

She went, with a deep curtsey. Whatever had come over her, speaking so to Father? And in the hall she met Anne. 'Oh, Mother, I have angered him. I spoke back.'

Anne said, 'That will not affect you and Tom. Your father is a just man. He will do what he thinks right, whatever you say.'

And so poor Judith waited, and prayed, and watched her father as a storm-tossed mariner watches the weather-glass, and urged her lover to go and see her father. For soon she would be thirty; and she, resigned for so long to lifelong spinsterhood, was now desperate for a child in her womb, a babe at her breast, and Tom Quiney in her bed.

But Thomas was unable to work up enough courage to ask Master Shakespeare for permission to woo his daughter. So Will, seeing the misery and anxiety in his daughter's face, put on his hat and cloak, buckled on his sword, and went to the tavern.

He sat in a dark corner, his hat over his eyes. A serving woman brought him sack and sugar. He would see something of this Tom, weigh him in the balance, and then, if he thought fit, the mountain would approach Mahomet.

The young man behind the counter had sandy hair, a face brown and crumpled. The tavern was half full. The young man appeared courteous and efficient.

A voice called, 'Hey, Tom, hast forgotten how thou didst dance at Mop Fair?'

The young man looked shy and confused. The big man who had called out rose, came and banged down a large pot in front of Tom. 'Here, lad, drink. 'Twill aid thy dancing.'

Tom looked scared, and shook his head.

'Drink!' commanded the man.

Tom looked at him piteously, and took a small sip. Then another. Then as though his will power were gone, he emptied the pot greedily and quickly.

'Now thou shalt dance,' said the big man confidently.

Tom shook his head again, looked down shyly.

'Come, Master Quiney, a jig. Onto the counter with you,' the serving wench encouraged him.

Tom Quiney looked at her. And his look was no longer shy. It was drunken, foolish, and lascivious. He tried to hoist himself on to the counter, fell back, was pushed up by the men who had gathered round. The big man gave him another pot of ale. Tom drank it, standing on the counter. Then, as the drink worked into his brain, he began to jig and caper.

In his sleeveless leather jerkin, and with his creased face, his thin sand hair, he was a grotesque. And to Will, who had seen enough jigs in his time, and hated them all, this one was particularly painful. At least the jigs he knew had been done by professionals – men like Kempe and Tarleton. But this – done by a drunken tavern-keeper, by, God ha' mercy, a possible son-in-law – this made him feel physically sick. Besides, that glance between the serving wench and Tom; it was not the sort of glance that should pass between master and maid. It spoke of shared secrets, shared knowledge, understanding. He stormed out of the tavern, strode back to New Place. 'Send Judith to me,' he commanded his wife.

'But – but Will! She is abed.'

'Send her to me.' He flung himself into his chair, and waited. Soon Anne appeared, leading a terrified Judith in her night-rail. Anne was tight-lipped and silent.

Will forced himself to speak gently and with compassion. 'Judith, do not mention to me again the name of Thomas Quiney.'

The awful meaning of the words sank in. 'But why, Father?'

'Because the man is no more than a performing monkey. Let him earn pennies at the fairs; for certainly he shall have no dowry of yours.'

Judith gave a low moan. 'But he is kind, Father, and needs me. And, I think, loves me well.'

'As well be loved by a Barbary ape,' Will said scornfully.

Anne pushed a candle into Judith's hand, said, 'Go back to your bed, child.'

Judith crept away. Will had noted how straight she had come to hold herself; but now she was bent double, like an old woman.

Anne said sternly. 'Now, husband. What has happened?'

He told her: how a bully and a pot of ale had reduced Tom Quiney to a capering monkey; how he had obeyed a voice of command like the sorriest poltroon.

Anne said, 'Sit down, Will, and listen to me.'

Slowly, he sat down in his great chair. He watched Anne warily. She was going to read him a lecture, and in his own house. He ought not to allow it. He ought to be master. But – well, two heads were better than one. And – though he would not have admitted it even to himself – he could do with a little help. The sight of Judith carrying her candle, like an old woman, bedward, had been heartbreaking.

Anne said, 'All men speak well of you, husband. And rightly. You are a good man, an upright man.'

He waited. Anne wasn't one to flatter; there would be a sting in the tail.

There was. 'Only to your own, it seems, are you not perfect. I do not see you as the world sees you, Will. I know the flaws in the marble.'

He sat silent. He did not want to be told the flaws in the marble. *He* knew them. He knew several of which, he supposed, Anne knew nothing.

Anne said, 'You, I really believe, love all men, all creatures, all God's creation.'

It had never occurred to him; but it was true. He said, moved, 'With all my heart, Anne.'

'Yet you cannot love your own daughter. You can only cause her pain.'

This also was true. He said, groping for words, 'It is my duty, as her father, to stop her marrying that – that marmoset.'

She said, coolly, 'Or do you mean "that tavern-keeper"?'

He banged his fist down on the chair arm. 'Anne! That is unfair.'

'I do not see why. You have always climbed, and a tavern-keeper does not go with New Place and a Grant of Arms.'

He said angrily. 'It is *not* that. I saw the youth drunken and degraded.'

'And for that you would condemn your daughter to life-long spinsterhood and sorrow?'

He said, 'I would save her from her folly. Young Quiney will bring her only humiliation.'

They sat facing each other: tense, determined. Anne said quietly, 'Had I thought that you would bring me humiliation – as, indeed, you did on occasion, Will – I would still have married you. I would rather have hoped for a few months' happiness with you, than a lifetime of happiness with any other man.'

He watched her thoughtfully. She went on, 'Women are foolish creatures, and we sometimes love foolishly. But it is with our hearts. And if you say us nay, then our hearts break.'

He said, heavily, 'I have my duty as a father.'

She jumped to her feet, furious. 'Then do your duty as a father. Make your daughter happy.'

'That is not possible,' he said. 'Whatever we do, wife, Judith will root out unhappiness for herself as surely as a pig roots pit-nuts.'

With which unflattering simile he rose, took up a side candle, and went to bed, a sad and anxious man.

The father, the husband, the master of the house had spoken. And so it must be. Judith crept about, pale and unsmiling, Anne smouldered, Will was pompous and prickly as a porcupine. Was this the life for which he had given up the theatre, London, the love of friends?

Nevertheless, the garden drew him, that out-of-doors he so loved and of which he had seen so little. It had always been there, while he was immured in the Grammar School, the glover's workshop, the Globe, the Court. There had been bright mornings, and he had not seen them; the long, drowsy afternoons of summer, summer's eves, autumn's rich panoply, November mists and winter dusk, a great wind roaring in the trees. Now at last he had his fill of these, as the Gild Chapel clock ticked away his days and years, and brought him at last to 1616: a year in which, so he was told, he would take an unexpected journey...

CHAPTER 16

KNOCK, KNOCK, KNOCK! WHO'S THERE, I' TH' NAME
OF BEELZEBUB?

The twelfth day of Christmas. And, at New Place, the usual
revels.

But seemly, as befitted a family with an eminent and
Puritan son-in-law. A myriad candles, a great fire, wine, nuts,
kickshaws, Anne in her best blue gown, Will in russet and
gold, Judith in grey, plucking her lute, her thin, sweet voice
singing that melancholy piece of Ben's:

> *Have you seen but a bright lily grow,*
> *Before rude hands have touch'd it?*
> *Have you mark'd but the fall o' the snow*
> *Before the soil hath smutch'd it?*

Will listened, still, finger-tips together, moved as he so
often was by music, almost to tears. And now the song was
near its end. It had a dying fall. 'O so white! O so soft! O so
sweet – '

But Judith did not finish, her voice choked on tears. Will,
absorbed in the music, looked concerned but irritated. The
other guests, sister Joan Hart and her husband, the Walkers,

190

Hamnet and Judith Sadler, Francis Collins the solicitor, pretended not to notice. But Anne's arms were quickly about Judith. 'Daughter. What is it, child?'

Judith sobbed something through her tears. Only Anne understood it. 'I wish – I were dead, Mother.'

'Come, girl, into the kitchen with you. This is foolish and wicked talk. I will prepare you a posset, and you shall to bed straight.' But Anne whispered. The guests did not hear.

'Now! A round. "On the first day of Christmas",' cried Will, searching quickly through the sheets of music that littered the table. But at this moment a woman swept magnificently into the room. Her head and face were veiled. Her fingers were covered with enormous rings. She sat herself at a small table and cried, 'Now. I will read any gentleman's palm (or any lady's for that matter, if it be not too coarse with scrubbing). Provided only that the gentleman (or the lady, again for that matter) cross *my* palm with silver.'

There was much laughter. Judith was quite forgotten. Everyone loved this masked fooling. It was the highlight of any gathering. But a teller of fortunes! A gipsy! They felt a tingle of excitement, even though they all knew the gipsy was the fair Susanna.

Susanna looked at Will. 'You, sir. Are you the governor of the feast?'

Will bowed, his actor's bow. And smiled. But thought: oh, my two daughters. Was there something to be said, he wondered, for conception in the magic of a moon-drenched cornfield?

He went and sat down at the table, facing Susanna. She had grown, he thought, a noble woman; firm of shoulder, deep-breasted. She should, he thought less happily, have borne noble sons. He tossed her a silver shilling. 'What is my fortune, gipsy?'

She took his hand, peered. 'Sir, you are a joiner.'

There was much laughter. Will said, 'A joiner of what, mistress?'

'Of men and women. You are a priest.' She put her hands together in prayer. 'Whom God hath joined, let no man put asunder,' she intoned nasally.

Will said, 'So God too is a joiner? I am in good company, gipsy – '

But he saw two deep lines appear in John Hall's brow. And Anne, who had just come back into the room, also frowned.

Will wanted no accusations of blasphemy on this happy Twelfth Night. He said quickly, 'Tell me my fortune for this coming year, witch.'

She examined his palm. Her hands were soft, like a Court lady's. No scrubbing for Susanna. She said, 'You will meet joy and sorrow, success and failure, pain and happiness.'

He laughed. 'Faith, gipsy, so much? You are wise beyond your years.'

'You will meet a dark stranger. You will take an unexpected journey.'

'So. It grows more interesting. And what is the name of the stranger?'

'Death,' said a voice.

The room was still filled with laughter. Will, sitting forward over the table, whispered, '*What* did you say?'

'I said you would meet a dark stranger, and – '

'No! When I asked you the name of the stranger.'

She caught his seriousness. 'I – I said nothing. Father. I could think of no name.'

'You did not say – "Death"?'

'Father!' She pulled aside her veil. 'I would not. Even in jest. Surely – '

'Peace, girl,' he said, suddenly weary. Had it been a man's voice, or a woman's? He did not know. His own not inconsiderable imagination? But death had been far from his thoughts. An angel of the Lord? He had never much believed in such things. But he had to know.

He was never one to make a scene. He banged the table for silence. They looked at him in surprise. He said, in a level voice, 'When I asked, "What is the name of the stranger?" which man among you said, "Death"?'

They were silent, troubled.

'Which woman, then?'

Silence. John Hall said, 'We would not, sir. It would be an ill jest.'

'I see,' said Will. He put up a fist, rubbed it hard against his temple. Had he, or had he not, heard that voice? Yes, he had heard *a* voice. But whence did it come? From Heaven, or Hell, or from the echoing caverns of his own brain? He did not know. Well, he would not waste time on death. If it be now, 'tis not to come, he seemed to remember he had once written. If it be not now, yet it will come. He turned to Susanna. 'Now, gipsy, read me your Aunt Joan's fortune. There will be matter there, I am thinking.'

The evening went on: bright, friendly, cheerful. Only, every now and then, a glance stolen at Will. That had been a strange, uncomfortable moment. Will had not been fooling. Yet no one else had heard the dread word spoken. They were uneasy. It could mean many things for them all: plague, wars, civil strife.

At the beginning of a new year the future looks even more menacing than usual. Few can look a whole year in the face unflinching. So they wondered.

193

And Anne wondered most of all.

Even Will, who had vowed to have no truck with death, said to Francis Collins as he helped the solicitor into his cloak, 'Francis, something I have long thought to do, and now at last I have the time.'

'What is that?'

'Make my will, Francis.' He chuckled. 'It will be my best work since a piece I once wrote called *Hamlet*.'

As soon as they were in their bedroom, Anne said, 'Will, what ailed you?'

He laughed. 'Nothing, wife.'

'Yet you thought someone said the stranger's name was Death.'

'I imagined it.' He laughed, easily. 'Too much sherrissack, Anne.'

She was troubled. 'Susanna is a kind girl. She would not say such a thing.'

'It was not Susanna,' he said. 'And certainly not Judith. Why could she not finish her song?'

'You know why, Will.'

'Still on that tack?' He was sorry. But what could he do? Better a few tears now than a lifetime of misery.

Neither Will nor Anne slept much, that last night of the Christmas revels. Whence had come that name of Death, casting a long shadow over the New Year? And what would happen to poor Judith, who seemed destined for misery beyond human changing? Will, especially, was tormented by this. Was he right? Would it not be better to give the girl her chance of happiness? But had a father the right to let the inevitable suffering be on the girl's shoulders? On the other hand, had he the right to play God?

No, thought Will. He hadn't. And, being a man who always preferred being pleasant to being unpleasant, he made his decision. In the morning he would speak to Judith, tell her the knave could court her. He could hardly wait to see the happiness in her eyes.

He and Anne were still awake when something happened to rob them of both sleep and peace of mind.

At Quiney's tavern they were celebrating Twelfth Night in fine style.

Songs, catches, rounds, dancing, bawdry. Oh, it was a wonderful evening. Only one man was not enjoying it – Tom Quiney himself. He sat, slumped on a settle, thinking of Judith Shakespeare.

She had given him her father's message. And had said piteously, 'He is not a hard man, my father. If you were to go to him, and say – '

He said, 'What has me against me? My monkey face? My occupation? Yet my father was as good as he.'

'No,' she said quickly, taking his hand as they walked the muddy lane. 'It is not that, Tom.'

'Then what?'

She said, quietly, 'He saw you drunken. And dancing on the tavern counter.'

They came to a gate. He leaned on it, gazed at the bleak winter scene. 'He is right,' he said heavily. 'I am no husband for such as you.'

She was angry. Once let him get into this way of thinking and she was lost. She pulled him round to face her, kissed him desperately on the lips. 'Tom, do you love me?'

'Of course.'

'Then you must fight for me. A woman cannot fight. But *you* can. My father will listen to you, if you do but speak roundly.'

Fight? He had never fought in his life. And tonight, amid the revels, he thought of his weakness, his cowardice in his beloved's eyes, he thought of Judith, who seemed to him strong and decisive, and who could be his only if he too were strong and decisive, two things he could never be – if he were sober.

But tonight he was far from sober. Who *was*, in merry England, on Twelfth Night? He went and drew himself a cup of sack, drank it down.

It did him good. It put heart in him. But much more than that, it intensified all his emotions. His love for dear, sweet Judith overwhelmed him like a warm tide. A girl to slay dragons for, to scale battlements for. Had he *really* been afraid to visit her old father? He could not imagine it now. It was ridiculous. With *his* charm, *his* eloquence, he would win the old man over in ten minutes. Why, he and his lovely Judith might yet be married before Lent.

But very sensibly he reminded himself he had been drinking. Had the drink in any way affected his judgment?

He considered carefully. No, he decided. His brain was crystal-clear. And when he began to walk he found no difficulty. True, one of the settles had moved a few inches to the right, but this was a thing that did happen.

He found his hat, stepped out into the night. He did not think he had ever been so filled with happiness. A heavy drizzle made the black night wretched, but on Tom Quiney it fell like a summer fountain. How he loved this little town of Stratford, how he loved all men! And especially did he love this future father-in-law. He could not wait to throw an arm round the old man's shoulders, to cry, 'Sir, you love your daughter and I resp – respect you for it.' He giggled. It had never occurred to him before what a droll and difficult word 'respect' was. 'But, sir, even a fond father cannot love her as I love her. You need have no qu – qualms about me, sir.'

And then, Master Shakespeare, dabbing his eyes: 'Take her, Thomas. And may she make you as happy as you make her.'

He had made himself cry. So that when his foot slipped in some filth in the kennel, he was too overcome to save himself, and went down. But he was soon up, brushing himself down, and plodding gamely on. He was almost there.

New Place towered over him, stern and imposing in the darkness.

Not a light anywhere. They were abed. But a man on such a joyous errand *must* be well received. No one would be so churlish as to complain at being got out of bed for such a reason. He hammered cheerfully on the door.

Anne's heart nearly stopped. Though allayed, her fears that the story of the Devil's bastard might be abroad were still close to the surface. A mob of citizens, carrying torches, come to burn the witch? The Constable, bent on a quiet arrest to save Master Shakespeare embarrassment?

Will's fears were different. Robbers, murderers? But it was for the master of the house to answer the door at this hour. He leapt out of bed, went and peered out of the window, forgetting the shutters; cursed, found flint and steel and tinder, lit a candle. Meanwhile Anne had found his gown and was holding it for him. She pushed his sword into his hand.

The knocking continued. Will, crossing the landing, saw in the flickering candlelight a pale face in Judith's doorway. He signalled to her to go back into her room. Then, sword in one hand, candle in the other, he went down the stairs.

And found he was not alone. Some of the maids, coats pulled over their shifts, were crowding and twittering on the servants' stairs. Bates, James and Hubert were already standing by the door, cudgels in their hands. Watching from the balustrade of the landing were Anne and Judith, Susanna and John Hall (who were staying at New Place over the festivities). The knocking grew more peremptory.

A phrase was going round and round in his head. 'Wake Duncan with thy knocking. I would thou couldst.'

He could not conceive who would come knocking at this hour of the morning, but it could be nothing good. And suddenly he remembered the stranger. Suppose he opened the door to see – a scythe, glinting in the candlelight, gripped in skeleton fingers; a grinning death's head. Well, if that was that, the dramatist in him pointed out, it was a well-set scene: himself, centre-stage, the men flanking him with their cudgels, the maids grouped on the stairs, the watchers from the upper stage: with candle flames scattered about the stage like stars.

He drew the bolts, turned the great key, lifted the latch, opened the door a fraction, peered out.

It wasn't Death. It was a young man who bowed low, a little too low, recovered after a slight difficulty, and cried, 'Master Shakespeare, I come, a suppliant at your feet.'

The draught from the open door had blown out the candle. Will could see nothing. 'Who are you, sir?'

'Thomas Quiney, sir, at your service. I come to court your daughter, the Lady Judith.' Now he was in the house. He bowed even more deeply, but recovered well.

This was monstrous. There could hardly have been more witnesses in the noonday market. Will seized a candle from one of the servants, and cried out angrily, 'Back to your beds, all of you.' Then, civilly to Tom, 'Come this way, Master

Quiney.' He led him into the small room where he did his writing. He lit more candles, said, 'I think, Master Quiney, you had better sit down.'

Tom bowed again, sat down as though he had been given a sudden blow behind the knees. He was appalled to find that all the moving and eloquent things he had been about to say had fled. His jaw sagged.

Will looked at him with distaste, his ale bottle shoulders, his sad monkey features. And he stank of the kennel. To the fastidious Will, few men could have seemed less attractive. But he said gently, 'Have you any idea, Master Quiney, what o'clock it is?'

Tom pulled a watch from his pocket, focused on it carefully 'It is ten minutes after ten, Master Shakespeare.' He rose again and bowed. 'Forgive me, Father-in-law. I had no idea it was so late.'

'You are mistaken, Master Quincy. It is ten minutes to two. And why do you call me father-in-law?'

The boy looked hurt. 'May I not so? I would marry your daughter whom I love; and who loves me. And I love you, sir, dearly. I love – everybody…' He trailed off. He had the feeling he was not saying the splendid things he had prepared.

Will said, 'Tomorrow it will be all over Stratford that a drunken youth came to New Place at two in the morning, to court Judith. Now listen to me, sir. You have caused me much annoyance, and Judith some dishonour. I will not harp on that. But I do not wish to see you in my house again, Master Quiney. Nor do I wish you ever again to speak to my daughter.'

Tom looked unbelieving. 'But, sir, I *love* her.'

'If you loved her, you would not so have shamed her – and yourself.'

The door opened. Judith came in. 'Tom!' she cried piteously.

Will said, 'Judith, go back to your room. It is not seemly – '

'But, Father – ' She looked at Tom. 'He is not well. He needs me.' She stamped her foot. 'Can you not see he is not well, Father?'

'I see nothing the pump in the yard would not cure.' He had been very quiet, very gentle, hating what he had to do. Now he cried in sudden anger. '*Look* at him, daughter. Would you *really* want to marry *that*?'

'Oh, yes,' she cried. 'Can't you *see*? He *needs* me.' She added almost in a whisper. 'And God knows I need him.'

Oh, it was hateful. To hurt a woman so, and she your own daughter. But there was no help. He said, 'Now, Master Quiney, if you will kindly leave my house?' He saw him to the door. Judith reached out her arms to him, but Will held her gently yet firmly with an arm about her shoulders. Will shut and locked the door. He and Judith went upstairs. His arm was still about her shoulder. At her door, he kissed her with a new affection. Her cheek was cold. She said, 'I shall marry him, Father.'

He said, sadly, 'You cannot, child.'

She said, 'Do you know how old I am? Thirty-one. And do you still say I cannot?'

'I say you must not.' He went wearily back to his room.

Anne was sitting by the fire in their bedroom, waiting for him. 'Well, husband,' she said. 'You were right. Oh, the young fool!'

He sat down on the side of the bed. 'If only he had not come! I had decided that, in the morning, I would give my consent.'

CHAPTER 17

THIS ABOVE ALL: TO THINE OWN SELF BE TRUE.

Will Shakespeare, who so loved legal documents and legal quibbles, had a splendid time drafting his will. It took most of that black January. And Francis Collins' clerk, scratching away in a back room in Warwick, wrote everything out, three sheets of it, in a fair English hand, with a promise that, when it was ready for signing, Master Collins would bring it over to New Place for Will's perusal, and for his signature over a glass of canary.

Will was pleased with himself. He had remembered everybody, been fair to everybody: London friends, Stratford friends, relations. Most of his estate had to go to Susanna, that was only right; but he was particularly careful to show love and generosity to Judith – because he had condemned her to spinsterhood and, characteristically, because he had found her so difficult to love. Yes, Susanna and John Hall would be able to live in the style they deserved (and God might still send them a son). Anne would have her rights as dowager, and between John and Susanna and her was a great trust and affection. He need not fear that Anne would be neglected. And Judith – Judith would live her dim half-life at least in comfort.

So he thought, in the stone chill of Holy Trinity, while the crows shouted at the wind that tossed them about the churchyard limes, and the great east window gleamed in the January sunshine. But this morning, he also thought, he had seen the first snowdrops, the first winter aconites, in the New Place gardens. Spring! No time to think of death, and testaments, and a world in which *he* was not.

'Here endeth the second lesson.' The service was getting on. And the Vicar had a rheum, so he wasn't likely to preach for more than an hour. They should be out of church before they froze to death. And then: make up the fire, and settle down for a quiet day with his Anne; for Judith was away, staying with an Arden relation, and without her, poor child, New Place was very heaven.

Oh, he'd forgotten the banns. Well, there shouldn't be many of those. They would be into Lent soon, and who was going to the expense and trouble of the special licence required for a Lent marriage?

'Between Thomas Quiney, bachelor, and Judith Shakespeare, spinster, both of this parish. This is for the first time of asking. If any of you know cause…'

Anne put a restraining hand on his arm. He shook it off, glared furiously round the church. A few neighbours, catching his eye, smiled uncomfortably. But neither the widow Quiney nor her precious son were there. 'Let us pray,' said the Vicar. Will went down on his knees, fuming. *Cause or just impediment. He'd* give that Vicar cause or just impediment. *And* that sly, deceitful daughter. *And* that drunken weakling, who no doubt thought he was marrying an heiress…

As soon as the service was over, he made for the vestry. Anne seized his arm. 'Will, where are you going?'

'To see that parson. How dare – ?'

'Come home, husband. What, do you want the whole world – ? Besides, your behaviour is not seemly.'

She had sown a doubt. He went with her.

They walked home. Old friends, old neighbours crowded around. 'Will, this is happy news.' 'Blessings on your sweet daughter, goodwife.'

Will, bowing and smiling. 'Thank you, James. Thank you, neighbours.' Good actor though he was, his smile was forced.

Doll Scattergood opened the door to them, took Will's hat and cloak and gloves and stick while Anne went to her room. Then she followed Will into the living-room, straightened the cushions in his chair, poured him a glass of canary, withdrew.

He warmed his hands at the great log fire. Oh, life *could* be so pleasant. If only... But to be defied, by a drunken tavern-keeper and one's own daughter! And what good did they think they would do? They must realise he could, and would, forbid the banns.

Anne bustled in, flopped down into her chair. 'Is not this pleasant, husband? We will drink our wine, and then dinner will be ready. A boiled capon, with salted beef. And then – oh, we will sit and watch the daylight fade, two old folk – '

He said, 'Say, rather, we will visit Master Parson, and watch *him* fade. *And* that tavern-keeper Quiney.'

She said, laughing, 'Faith, you are like an ill-sitting hen.'

He flung himself into his chair, scowled.

She said quietly, 'Be yourself, Will.'

He went on scowling. 'What do you mean?'

'You have tried so hard to be kind and understanding with Judith. And you have succeeded, as a man like you must succeed in something so natural to him.'

He waited, suspicious. He had heard it said that men, some men, were susceptible to flattery; and that women, some women, took advantage oft hat fact. Well, he hoped his wife knew him better than that.

Anne said, 'And now this has happened. You think that, because you are a man, you must beat your chest and roar, whereas, if you would only listen to your own nature, you would make friends with both of them.' She added, 'You know that your whole nature cries out for friendship with all men.'

How right she was! He *would* like to be friendly, even with that absurd tavern-keeper; but things were not as simple as that. A woman, with her limited intelligence could see only a small part of any problem. He said, stiffly, 'I have my duty as her father.'

She said, 'Yes, and the marriage will not be perfect. But I believe that, for Judith, almost any marriage would be better than no marriage.'

He was silent. Doll Scattergood came and called them to dinner. Over the meal he was very thoughtful, and drank more canary than usual. Anne's 'listen to your own nature' had started echoes in his brain: Will, at the beginning of a promising career in London, had learnt that Anne, in Stratford, was pregnant – a moment of fearful decision – and his old friend, Richard Field, had said that if a man was true to himself he couldn't be *un*true to anyone else. It had impressed him – so much so that he'd used it in one of his plays. It had brought him back to Anne, and Stratford; and had helped him retain the self-respect without which he, however successful, could never have become the William Shakespeare, Gent, of New Place that he now was.

And here was Anne saying much the same: do what your own nature tells you to do.

His own nature told him to make friends, to forget the slight and the defiance of the young people. But he was still silent as Anne slipped her arm into his, and they strolled back into the living-room where more logs had been thrown on to the fire, and a few candles lit against the winter's dusk. Outside it was beginning, oh so softly to snow. Anne, too, was silent. Except to say, 'Is is not peaceful, and pleasant, husband, the two of us, alone?'

He remembered it now: *This above all: to thine own self be true. And it must follow, as the night the day, Thou canst not then be false to any man.* (Faith, it was true. And he, in his hurry and overwork, had put it in the mouth of a prating fool. When he revised his plays, he must give it to a more worthy character.) He said, 'I shall change my will. It is not meet that Quiney should drink the money you and I have saved, wife.'

'But you will not forbid the banns?'

There was a long silence. Then he said: 'No.'

The snow would come to nothing. The sky was already clearing to a pale whiteness, though a few flakes still fell, soft as sighs, more gentle than tears. The dusk was creeping into the room, accentuating the firelight, which played across Anne's face, brightening the eyes, deepening the wrinkles and the hollows. And it gave movement to her features as though she smiled. He sat for a long time in the gathering darkness, thinking, watching the firelight play on this old, simple, guileless wife of his, so different from his clever, quicksilver-minded lady mother. And at last he said, 'Anne?'

'Husband?'

'You *were*, I suppose, as ignorant as I that the banns were to be read? There was, I suppose, no connection between your sending Judith to her kinsfolk and the calling of the banns? There was, I suppose, no connection between my being cosseted with roast capon and canary, and the banns?'

'I am not one of your Court ladies, husband, I am but a simple countrywoman. I could not use such ploys.'

'No,' he said. And said nothing more. There was, for a man who was wise, a time to know, and a time to refrain from knowing.

Susanna had married in the sweet of the year. Judith married in February, at the beginning of Lent, the bleakest time of all.

Sunlight in all its brilliance had fallen on Susanna; sleet fell on Judith.

For Susanna, friends and relations came from miles around; but who was going to face the mud and the cold and the short days for a bride who insisted on marrying in February?

Everyone took it for granted that Judith was pregnant. Why else should anyone marry at such a time?

Judith could have recited every occasion in her life when either Mother or Father or fate or circumstance or the weather had favoured Susanna rather than herself.

But on her wedding day she seemed to cast of finally the jealousy and envy against which she had fought so bravely and so long. She was radiant. Her white dress gave her black hair and eyes a vivid intensity. The old, frightened stoop had gone. She stood tall, and proud. Will, standing beside her in the nave, marvelled at the fragility and delicacy of her beauty. The dry look of the spinster was gone. Here was a woman eager and ready for the turmoil of generation.

The bridegroom, too, in plum-coloured velvet, was a very different character from the Tom Quiney Will had known previously. He was sober, for one thing. And he too was radiant. When he and Judith led the procession back to New

Place, his wrinkled little face was alight with love and happiness. It was a wonder he and Judith found their way, so lovingly did they gaze into each other's eyes.

Will, following them, said, 'You were right, Anne. Those two have found something in each other of which the world had no inkling.'

Anne squeezed his arm, said nothing. He peered down at her. She was weeping. Then she smiled and said, 'Nay, husband. It may not always be thus with them. But – oh, Will, she is like a dusty cup that has been taken down from the shelf, and washed, and polished, so that it looks like new.'

The wedding breakfast was curiously happy. Less splendid than Susanna's, for was it not Lent? And, after all, there were only the Shakespeares and the Halls and the Widow Quiney and Joan Hart and her husband (who had not sold a single hat for *this* wedding) and their three sons. But it was one of those occasions when love affects every heart and every mind like a rare wine. Will (now that he was losing her) felt a new tenderness for his dark daughter. Judith thought what a fine, dignified man she had for a father, what a sweet and gentle woman for a mother, and even how much she loved her sister, now that the balance was redressed a little. Mistress Quiney had always been fond of Judith, and was delighted to have her for daughter-in-law. Doctor John Hall condescended to hold quite a long conversation with his new brother, and was civility itself. Joan Hart frothed and bubbled as delightfully as ever, though with many an anxious glance at her husband, who had been ailing since Christmas. But it was Judith and Thomas whose radiance lit the drab winter's day like summer sunshine. They smiled, they laughed, they whispered, as though enclosed in a

private bower of leaves, and the others warmed themselves
at such happiness as at a fire.

The Lenten feast was over. Time for the Halls to go back to
Hall's Croft, for Joan Hart to take her ailing husband back to
Henley Street, time for Thomas (still sober, thanks be to
God) to take his mother and the new Mistress Quiney back
to High Street.

At the front door, the servants sorting out cloaks and coats
and hats and sticks and gloves and lanterns. Judith giving her
bride-favour to Elizabeth (who would be eight in a few days)
to carry on her birthday. Laughter, chatter, a few April tears.

And then the lanterns bobbing away in the dusk. The door
shut, against the world. Anne and Will went back into the
living-room. Anne said, 'I never saw a happier bride.'

'Nor I,' said Will.

She said, 'And you are reconciled to it, husband?'

'Aye.'

He was standing with his back to the fire. She came and
stood before him, put her arms about his waist. 'And you will
not change your will?'

'Not if the knave treats her well.' He smiled down at her
fondly. Then, suddenly, he was enfolding her, and his face was
pressed against hers, and his tears were salt upon her face.

It was a strange thing. Five, six years ago he had come back
to Stratford to live, and it was only now that he felt it had
really happened. Always, before, there had been the sense of
something missing, of something incomplete. Not only for
himself, he suspected, but also for Anne. And now, suddenly,
it was as it should always have been. Complete. Rounded. He
had come home, to his Anne. It was perfection.

Despite the dreary weather, there were signs of spring.
The tree boles had lost their January deadness, the willows

were a green haze, the earth was beginning to breathe again. And he, with his poet's eye, could see the whole of the coming pageant: the daffodils, the glory of April skies, the hush of summer noon-tides, the golden mellowness of autumn. All this, with Anne, and the comfort and elegance of New Place, and the respect of Stratford. And now he wanted to prepare his plays for publication. He had been tardy. He would work – work at his plays, work in his garden. Work, for a man of energy like himself, was what gave life its zest; even though he was approaching his fifty-second birthday.

And so it was. It really did seem as though, with the departure of the shy and self-effacing Judith, a tension had gone out of the house. (Could it be, he wondered, that her brief dalliance with Satan *had* infected her?) Now between him and Anne arose a great sweetness. It was as though she could at last, and without reservation, enfold him with her love, and as though he could accept it freely. And one day, revising his plays, he came across some lines: *there is no living, none, If Bertram be away. 'Twere all one That I should love a bright particular star And think to wed it, he is so above me.*

It was like a revelation. This, he realised, was how Anne had thought of him. Him, with his indecisions and disloyalties and fears! *Him*, a bright particular star! It was absurd. And yet that was how Anne felt, he knew it. *There is no living, none, If Bertram be away.* And how much of her life had Bertram/William been away? Oh, earning a living, of course. But he could have earned a living in Stratford. And what else had he been doing, at these times when for Anne there had been no living? Whoring, playing the courtier, drinking in the applause of the groundlings: a tawdry Jupiter sniffing the incense of the people.

There is no living, none, If Bertram be away. Oh, what a wife he had! Was ever man so undeservedly, yet so faithfully and truly, loved? Was ever loyal wife so unappreciated, so neglected? From now on, he vowed, he would devote all his thought to making Anne happy. He had had *his* glory, a glory few men could attain. Now it was time to give Anne her little measure of content.

He rose, smiling. He would bid Anne put on her best, they would walk together in the brisk March weather. By Shottery, and the lanes of their youth, and the wind-fretted river.

He went into the kitchen. And found, not the bustling Anne he had expected, but a wife sitting at the table, facing a Judith who had her back to him, yet in whose very shoulders he read misery.

'Why, Judith,' he was about to cry. But Anne gave him a look so stern, so dismissive, that he crept away, closing the kitchen door silently behind him. Clearly, this was women's business.

He went back to his desk, troubled. He thought he knew what had happened. Like the rest of Stratford, he had wondered at Judith's hasty marriage in the Lenten season. And now, she had been married a few weeks. It was just about the time one would expect her to admit to her mother her pregnancy.

Well, neither he nor Anne were in a position to reproach her. But he was sorry. At fifty-one the demands of the flesh were less imperious than they had been at eighteen. It was hard to remember the cataract of emotion that had swept him and Anne away. Nevertheless, *peccavi. Et in Arcadia ego. He that is without sin among you, let him first cast a stone at her.*

With which pious thoughts he went back to his revision.

He was pleased when Anne came in alone. Though Judith's pregnancy would not have been a subject to be broached before her father, there would have been a certain tension after what he had seen in the kitchen. So he put down his pen, and smiled, and said, 'Well, wife, when is it to be?'

'What?' she looked bewildered.

'Our grandchild.'

She groped for a chair, still staring at him. 'What grandchild?' she asked stupidly.

He jumped to his feet, held the chair for her. 'I had imagined – Judith had come to tell you she was with child.'

'Will, she has been married but a few weeks.'

He began to realise he had put two and two together, and made six. He beat retreat. 'And Judith is well?'

'Well?' Anne cried bitterly. 'Well? She is excommunicated. And that precious husband of hers.'

'Excommunicated?' Will had little time for parsons, and the Church. There was enough interest in *this* world for one life, without concerning oneself about the next. But excommunicated! That was serious. 'Why?'

'Oh, my Lord Quiney could not be troubled to obtain the special licence for a Lenten marriage, and so was summoned to the Consistory Court at Worcester – *and* did not go. So he was fined, and excommunicated – and my poor Judith with him.'

He decided to look on the bright side. 'Well, excommunication will not stop him pouring ale, or her baking his bread or bearing his children.'

She looked at him with contempt. 'So far, I have told you nothing.'

He looked at her face. It was heavy with sorrow. He said, quietly, 'There is more?'

'Far more. Does the name of Margaret Wheelar mean anything to you?'

'Wheelar?' murmured Will, wrinkling his brow. 'Wheelar?' As to every man in Stratford, the name Margaret Wheelar meant to him bright eyes, a challenging glance that locked with that of every man she met, a flounce of skirt, a flash of ankle, a promise, if one were so inclined, which of course one was not, of easy conquest. It meant a girl who helped in the tavern, in the market, wherever there were men. It meant a girl that every married man, if directly questioned, would feign difficulty in placing. So Will said, 'Wheelar? Yes. I believe I do remember – '

'She is dead. In childbirth. And so is her bastard.'

Dead! A wanton; but lovely, lovely in her life as the wanton wind on wanton, sun-kissed leaves. But this would certainly not be Anne's view. He waited, warily.

'Thomas Quiney is to be brought to court, and will be charged with having had carnal intercourse with her. It is probable he will be made to do public penance.' And Anne, who so seldom wept, burst into tears.

'He *admits* it?'

Anne nodded, weeping wildly.

It was strange, thought Will. *He* had always been the one to set such store by the world's approval; yet this shame of his daughter's moved him little. But perhaps a woman felt these things in the core of her being, whereas to a man they were the small coin of life. A wanton, dead with her child. *There* was the shame, the tragedy, the pity of it. Did it so much matter who had lit the fuse?

Poor Judith; but she had made her choice with her eyes open, and in the face of plenty of good advice.

But now he was beginning to realise that Judith's reaction would affect him. These last few weeks, alone with Anne, had been very heaven. Yet if Judith left her husband? He said, 'Peace, wife. The gossips will have their day, but it will be forgot, by Mop Fair. What of Judith?'

'Oh, she defends her little marmoset. 'Twas entirely that Margaret Wheelar's fault, leading on a weak and amiable youth. And 'twas not adultery, why, at that time she scarce knew Tom, save as the son of her friend Mistress Quiney.'

'So she will stay with him?' Will sounded relieved

'Stay with him? She takes the view he needs her more than ever. Why, it will not surprise me if she tries to wrap herself in his penitential sheets.'

'Good girl,' he said, suddenly moved. Loyalty was one of the virtues he admired most. There was no doubt about it, the frail Judith, so tormented by devils from without and also by the devils of her own jealous nature, had conquered. She had defied her father and her mother to marry the man she loved, and now she would stand beside that man while all the world cast stones at him. Strength – the strength of the Ardens and the Shakespeares and the yeoman Hathaways – had flowed into her. He suddenly realised that he was perhaps more proud of his dark, frail Judith than he had been even of his loved Susanna.

Nevertheless, he sent for her. Admiration was one thing. Possessions were another.

She stood before him. He sat at his writing-table, holding a three-page document. He said, 'Judith, you have married a weakling.'

'Yes, Father.'

'And you have no regrets?'

'No, Father. He is the man I love.'

'Yet he was unfaithful to you, and caused the death of Margaret Wheelar and her child.'

'No. He was not unfaithful to *me*, who scarce knew him then. And he that gives his horse to a friend, and the friend is thrown thereby, should not be blamed for the death of the friend.'

Will smiled. 'A Daniel come to judgment.'

'Father?'

'Mere foolishness. But you have married a knave, Judith, and I will not give money to a knave. In my will I was generous to you; now I have changed that.'

'Very well, Father.'

'You do not reproach me?'

'I think you are wise, sir. It is for Tom to support me.'

He looked at her with compassion. 'And if he do not?'

'Then I shall be as poor as he. For truly, sir, Tom will always share what he has with me.'

'You are so sure, Judith?'

'We love one another, and always shall.'

The face, that had once been so tormented, was curiously serene. He said, almost gruffly, 'I have given you a hundred and fifty pounds, provided you fulfil certain conditions, and the interest on another hundred and fifty, given certain other conditions. Your husband is not to touch this money unless he settles land on you for the same sum.'

She said, with her first touch of spirit, 'There will be no haggling between Tom and me, sir.'

He said, 'And the broad silver-gilt bowl. I have seen you, at your embroidery – how often you have looked up to see the play of firelight on it.'

'Oh, Father.' She clasped her hands. 'The silver-gilt bowl! Oh, thank you.'

He rose. To Susanna, he had left almost everything; to Judith, a few pounds – and a silver bowl. And there were tears of gratitude in her eyes. And yet, a few years ago, she had been crazed with jealousy even if he talked and laughed with Susanna. He came round the table. He was proud of her. He took her hands. 'Do you think me a hard man, daughter?'

'No, sir. A wise and just one.'

He looked at her. Her serious face told him nothing. Smiling did not come easily to Judith. He put his hands on her shoulders, drew her to him, kissed her with great tenderness. 'God go with you, daughter. And with your rogue of a husband.'

'And with you, Father.' She bobbed, and was gone. It was the last time they were alone together.

The next day he signed his will. Fancis Collins rode over from Warwick, and Will's friends Julyus Shawe, John Robinson, Hamnet Sadler and Robert Whatcott came in to drink a glass of Rhenish and do a little witnessing. There were three pages, each of which Solicitor Collins insisted on everyone signing. Writing was a slow and deliberate business; it all took a long time and quantities of Rhenish, before the work was finished to Master Collins' satisfaction. But in the end everyone felt, individually and collectively, that they had done a splendid day's work, and they sang a few catches to express their satisfaction.

And Anne, sitting in the kitchen, and knowing what was toward, fell to weeping. A man is no more like to die because he has signed his will; nevertheless, he has packed his belongings, and is now ready for the journey.

That was on 25 March. The next day was less pleasant. Will, Anne and Judith sat in court, and heard Tom confess his nine-month-old sin, heard the Justices' cries of horror and indignation, heard him sentenced to appear at church dressed in a white penitential sheet on the next three Sundays, to be publicly denounced.

During the solemn sentencing, Will watched the white face of Judith, who seemed near to fainting. He watched the sad, wistful little face of Tom Quiney. He watched the relish on the faces of the Justices as they savoured that warm, satisfying emotion, righteous indignation. What? Were there no adulterers in Stratford save this poor monkey? Why, he himself was indifferent honest. Yet he – Oh, it was monstrous.

Later, and without a word to anyone, he went to see one of the Justices. He went as that rich landowner, William Shakespeare, Gent., of New Place. His conversation was cordial, and friendly, and included several droll stories of life at Court, and even a passing reference to his friend the King. Soon afterwards, Tom's sentence was unaccountably reduced to a five shilling fine. Since no one wanted to drink at the tavern kept by an adulterer, Tom was hard put to it to find the five shillings. But he did. And since a man needs his ale, and since Tom was not overstrict about swearing and tippling in his house, the customers soon came back.

And Judith guarded her husband with a strange, protective love. Watching his little, crumpled face, she could have wept with love and compassion. He was her husband, child, babe. Her love enfolded him utterly.

CHAPTER 18

NOW CRACKS A NOBLE HEART.

What an April that was!

A sun that darted in and out of clouds like a merry child; warm, beneficent showers; and, after the showers, the earth sparkling as though it had rained diamonds. Flowers, leaves, birdsong, sunlight, in an explosion of life and joy and colour!

And New Place seemed to glow and sparkle with happiness. Judith would call, and stand in the kitchen, helping herself to raisins and apple-slices, and chatter to her mother while she worked. Judith, married and knowing herself now (virtuously) pregnant, was completely fulfilled. Something had happened that she had never thought *could* happen, that her father and her mother had both thought impossible. She had caught (even if it were for only a year, a month, a few days) the sweet bird of contentment.

And John and Susanna would come and stroll in the garden on sunny Sunday afternoons, and little Elizabeth would gather the daisies that starred the lawns, but not the daffodils. Her grandfather prefers his flowers to his grand-daughter, Susanna would say, with a smile at the old man that reminded him of his mother's. John and Will would discuss the garden herbs, and the human condition, and the

217

state of the country, and Doctor Harvey's strange discoveries. Anne and Susanna would discuss Elizabeth, and Judith and Tom Quiney's shame, and Elizabeth, and their menfolk and the price of things, and Elizabeth.

Will would be happy to see the Hall's Croft people arrive, and just as happy to see them go. For then there would be the long evening with Anne, with little said between them, but she content that he was there, and he lapped in her warm contentment.

And Anne? For Anne, it was heaven on earth. Will in Stratford, and settled now. That last visit, she felt, had cured him of London, she would never know why. Her family about her, Will and Judith no longer forever jarring. Her own inferiority no longer a burden, for she knew she had served her husband well; if he had grown, then so had she, in her fashion. And she also knew, in her heart, that she had sacrificed her life to his ambition. He, despite his occasional protestations, would never know it. She scarcely acknowledged it herself; but it was there. Had she not been loving, amenable Anne Hathaway, Will could never have been William Shakespeare.

If he had grown... She remembered the braggart youth, striving so desperately to be a poet, to be a gentleman, who unaccountably had fallen in love with Anne Hathaway, very much a spinster of this parish. Why had he? She had no illusions. She imagined, in her country wisdom, that there comes a moment in the development of a boy when he must fall in love. And then he will fall in love with the first girl his eyes fall upon.

So it had been, she thought, in Will's case; it was thanks to his honour and his loyalty, and her unfailing love, that they were still together. For his love was not strong. There were many women, she thought, whom William

Shakespeare could have loved and worshipped; clever, beautiful, witty creatures. Yet he had come back, at the end of life, to simple country Anne: thanks to her love; thanks to his honour.

Then, like a lightening flash from those April skies, the blow fell. Her sister-in-law, Joan Hart, was in the New Place kitchen. Weeping. 'Anne, it's Will. He's — he's dead.'

It was as though a great fist had struck Anne violently in the chest. She collapsed on to a chair. And then, suddenly, she wanted to laugh and sing, because she realised that Joan spoke of *her* husband Will, not of Anne's.

She rose, went and embraced her sister-in-law desperately. She had known, for a brief second, Joan's sorrow. And it had nearly killed her. Joan would carry that agony to the grave. 'Oh, Joan, my dear!' She sought for words of comfort, where there were no words, no comfort. And knew that she too had something to carry to the grave: the shame at her own ecstasy of joy when she discovered that this sorrow was not hers, but another's.

The funeral was on 17 April, a day of high, windy splendour, not a day on which to be committed to the dank earth, thought Will Shakespeare. He did not return home with the gentlemen mourners, but prowled about the churchyard, his thoughts for once on death.

For next week, he had suddenly realised, would be his birthday. He would be fifty-two, a good age; death, who had taken Augustine Phillips, and sweet Armin, and little Hamnet, and these friends and fellow citizens who lay all about him, grinning up at his shoe soles, death would not refuse an ageing poet:

Sen he has all my brether tane,
He will naught let me live alane;
Of fouce I man his next prey be: –
Timor Mortis conturbat me.

And William Dunbar had been quite right, he thought, to be troubled by the fear of death. Death *had* come; the old Scotsman had lain in the earth these hundred years.

Yes. He has taken Augustine and Robert of the King's Men. Who will be next? I am older than Burbage, older than Heminge:

He has tane Rowll of Aberderne,
And gentill Rowll of Corstorphine;
Two better fallowis did no man see: –
Timor Mortis conturbat me.

He prowled, filled with a strange, sweet sorrow, a little drunk with Dunbar's melancholy lines, shocked by the sight of an open grave under this rumbustious heaven.

There was, he remembered, a charnel-house in the churchyard. It had frightened him as a boy, but now he would not be afraid. He found the entrance, and went inside.

It stank. The smell of corruption affronted his nostrils. And here was a great pyramid of skulls and bones: lovely women; wise, honourable men; knaves and fools. All the richness of living and loving and learning come to this? Lord, he thought wryly. There will be a fine jarring and jostling in here on Resurrection Morn. 'My skull, sir, if you will allow me.' 'My thighbone, mistress.'

He was revolted. When a man was laid in the earth, he should be allowed to stay there. He had earned his rest. He should not be dug up after a few years, and his parts flung in here, to make room for Sir This or Lord That. William Shakespeare should not, anyway. He had always, even on tour, maintained a certain detachment. Much as he loved humanity, he refused to be a part of it, even in death. He came outside, and took great gulps of the clean spring air. He walked home. *He has done petuously devour The noble Chuucer, of makaris flour...* There was no time to lose. He sat down at his writing table, took up his pen. What? *Odi profanum vulgus et arceo?* No. They needed something more direct. He would see that he slept in peace, in gentlemanly seclusion, not with the common sort:

> *Good frend for Jesus sake forebeare*
> *To digg the dust encloased heare!*
> *Bleste be the man that spares thes stones*
> *And curst be he that moves my bones.*

He read it through, sanded it. He'd written better in his time, he thought. But 'twould serve. He'd said what he had to say. He took the paper, went along to see Jowett the stonemason, and gave his orders. Then he felt better. The fear of death troubled him less. He would rest in peace.

And so he did. Six days later Anne found him sitting in his garden, as he had so often sat, staring at the wonder of sun and wind on leaves as though he could never see enough of such beauty. But his eyes had no sight. The brain that had given life to a thousand characters was empty, empty of all thought. To him, the eager birdsong was a silence, merged with a greater silence. The earth, whose beauty he had loved more than did all his fellows, would now serve for a winding sheet. A handful of his loved flowers would deck a grave.

'What is the name of the stranger?' he had asked, laughing.

And a voice had replied: 'Death.'

So. Her Will-o'-the-Wisp had fled, as so often before. But this time – ? No longer need she wonder, with a leaping heart, 'Who knocks at the door? Is it Will?' Whoever came knocking, it would not be Will.

They buried him as befitted a gentleman of worship. The Bailiff and several Aldermen attended the service; and he, who so loved sun, moon and stars, the wind and the rain, was nevertheless buried in the chancel, in a place of honour. And he, who also loved honour, and pride of place, would no doubt have preferred it this way. And the Vicar preached a homily, explaining that though our late brother in Christ had had to do with those schools of filthy lusts and whoredom, the theatres, he had since redeemed himself by living in style and Christian piety in the finest house in Stratford, and giving adequately to church expenses. And they put up a monument, showing him as the fine, well-fed, complacent Stratford burgher they wanted to remember him as having been, though they did think to put a pen in his hand.

And then, very properly, and naturally, they forgot him.

But there was one who did not forget him. It had been his birthday, and he and Anne had sat in the warm sunshine, talking, smiling, bound close by a love and friendship that seemed to deepen and strengthen every day. And John and Susanna and Judith were to come for supper, bringing presents. And, after that, a few neighbours for the sort of musical evening he so loved.

She had risen, saying she must go and prepare the supper table. He too had risen, and had kissed her hand, smiling; he would sit a little longer, he had said, and then go weed the borders.

But he had sat longer than he thought: still and silent; while the bustle and tumult of an English spring went on without a moment's check: the birds building their nests, the ants and spiders toiling, the bees foraging, the flowers opening to the sun. And the borders stayed unweeded.

But oh, it was unjust. To visit that garden; and, leaving the blackbird and the wren and the bustling spider to go about their business, to take only William Shakespeare! And it was cruel. Judith was wed, Anne and Will were alone, as he had always promised, as she had always prayed for – together, wrapped in an ever-flowering love. And now, after a few days, a few weeks – farewell, my Will-o'-the-Wisp, my only love…

CHAPTER 19

FEAR NO MORE THE FROWN O' THE GREAT...

At the rebuilt Globe, they were doing *Cymbeline*.

The last groundling had been packed in, John Heminge was already counting the money, the opening trumpet had sounded from the roof. Burbage, ancient and fierce as Cymbeline, waited in the tiring-room.

To him came Condell, bewildered and forlorn. 'Dick, I have heavy news. Will Shakespeare's dead.'

Burbage did not say a word. But he seemed to lose stature. At last he said, 'Will? The best of us all, Harry. When *he* left, something went out of us.'

'And now. Something has gone out of the world.'

'Nay, Harry. One man's going cannot affect the world, except he be a king, or emperor.' Burbage would be generous, but he would always keep his feet on the earth. Will had been good as an actor, better as a play writer, best of all as a friend. But he was only – what was Will's own phrase? – a poor player, who had strutted and fretted his hour upon the stage, and now would be heard no more. Besides, Burbage had a company to keep together, a performance to see through. He did not want any emotional outbursts at present. He said, 'How do you know this? About Will?'

'Richard Field brought the news.'

'Tell no one, till after the performance.'

Condell withdrew, thinking it unnecessary to tell Burbage that most of the actors knew already. But it did not harm the performance. In fact, that afternoon was one they would all remember. The play had a magic intensity that held the audience in rapt silence. The whisper had gone round the players: 'Will Shakespeare is dead.' Will Shakespeare, from whose brain had sprung the words they were now speaking, the characters they were now playing. Each man that day paid his own tribute to Will by playing as he had never played before. They were inspired. It was only when they came to the fourth act that voices faltered:

> Fear no more the frown o' the great,
> Thou art past the tyrant's stroke;
> Care no more to clothe and eat;
> To thee the reed is as the oak:
> The sceptre, learning, physic, must
> All follow this, and come to dust.

It was too near the bone. The young actor who played Arviragus remembered Will's kindness to him when he had been but a lad playing wenches' parts. But he got through; the King's Men were professionals to their finger-tips:

> Quiet consummation have;
> And renownéd be thy grave!

His memorial had been spoken. In love and kindness and sorrow. And the groundlings, did they but know it, had paid their pennies to hear it. It would have pleased him.

It was Heminge and Condell who rode north to pay their respects to the widow, to lay flowers on the grave, and to try to get back the plays Will had taken to Stratford for revision. They found a woman composed, kindly and simple as ever, but old even beyond her sixty years, old and stricken. They found a grave from which a mason had shoved aside the June roses to carve some doggerel. They found the plays. Will had done some work on them. There was more to do.

They took their leave, with great courtesy. Both men of kindness and compassion, they yearned to do, say, something comforting. But they could find nothing. Anne's grief wrapped her like a shroud. Though she walked with them to the stables, and talked, and even smiled, they knew their visit, their longing to help, did not touch her. Nothing could touch her, for she could not feel. And if she *did* feel, then she would die.

'Oh, and your Majesty, one of the King's Men is dead. Shakespeare. His name has been struck from the lists.'

Shakespeare? An importunate fellow. And James always suspected that he could write as well as his king. Aye, well. The knave had had some pretty conceits, but his 'Banquo' had been a sair disappointment. If only he had had the wit to stick to comedy. He might have made a name for himself.

'The man Shakespeare is dead, Southampton.'

So. *The love I dedicate to your lordship is without end; etcetera, etcetera, etcetera. Your lordship's in all duty. William*

Shakespeare. Yes, he had been quite fond of Shakespeare in his youth. Until, when it came to the test, Shakespeare had failed both him and Essex. But what could you expect? It was fatal to try to be friendly with the common sort.

'Will Shakespeare's dead.'

A dark woman in Southampton's household, black hair, now streaked with grey, smiled, catlike. Dead, was he? God, he and she had danced a savage measure. And now? She wept. Not for Will, but for the young men who came no longer at her call; for her own fading beauty, and the end of loving.

No man is an island…therefore never send to know for whom the bell tolls; it tolls for thee, thought Edward Alleyn uncomfortably. His future father-in-law's words had always impressed him. And now, whenever an acquaintance died (as was happening more and more often) he remembered them. And Will Shakespeare was only two years older than he.

'Will Shakespeare?' mumbled Philip Henslowe. Well, *there* was a soul gone to perdition, if ever there was one. For Philip, who never forgot anything discreditable about anyone, remembered that young Will had not only got a girl into trouble but, even worse, if possible, had left Philip in the lurch in order to bolt home and marry her. He shook his head mournfully. But cheered up a little as he thought of the goodness and justice of God, and the heated pincers, and the devils skilled in torment.

CHAPTER 20

...THE LONG DAY'S TASK IS DONE
AND WE MUST SLEEP

Judith bore her child in November; the grandson for which her father had so longed.

The birth was long, and painful. Physically, she was worn out. Yet, lying with the babe on her breast, she was filled with peace and joy. Her husband was already proving neglectful, her mother was detached, wrapped in a shroud of misery, her father dead. But now, she had her own companion, moulded of her flesh, someone to whom she, and she alone, was *everything*: food, warmth, comfort, companionship. What the wide world was to other men, so was she to this morsel, this dear scrap.

'What will you call him?' asked Anne, not caring, but a grandmother must ask these things, even though the world has ended; she was thinking, though without much hope, that she would like Judith to say, 'William.'

'Shakespeare,' Judith said astonishingly.

'Shakespeare?' Anne was horrified. 'But that is not a Christian name.'

Judith's eyes shone. 'I shall call him Shakespeare in honour of my father.' For a strange thing had happened.

Although her father had always been a frightening companion, in whose presence was neither comfort nor peace, his death had moved her deeply. She had mourned for him more profoundly than had his favourite Susanna. Now, in death, he was all that was strong and noble. If only – if only she could but see him, once, to fall at his feet and tell him of her love!

And she would name her dear scrap after him. Not William. There were too many Williams. But Shakespeare. Shakespeare Quiney. And whenever she called the child she would think of that strange and remarkable man, her father. Shakespeare.

But, alas! Shakespeare Quiney, born in an English November, lived through an English winter and died in an English May. Poor judgment, to come into a November world, and depart on a May morning; but when one lives only to six months, one has little time for forming judgment. So little Shakespeare Quiney went his lonely way. One peep into a lighted room and he was back in the dark, leaving his mother comfortless.

But then, the next year came Richard. And two years later Thomas. Cruel births, both of them, but Judith suffered all that, and gladly, to have again someone to whom she would be everything. For to her husband she was everything only when he was in trouble and needed her strength, which, thanks to her, was becoming less often.

So the years passed, for little Stratford, in birth and begetting, in seedtime and harvest, in milking and hedging and ditching, in buying and selling. And in great London, Philip Henslowe died, and went confidently to meet his business partner, God. And Richard Burbage died (and, with him, so it was said, 'young Hamlett, ould Heironymoe, Kind Leer, the greued Moore, and more beside, that liued in him, haue now for ever dy'de.' An unnecessarily pessimistic statement, as it turned out).

Yes. Exit Burbage, leaving Heminge and Condell to work alone at collecting, editing and publishing those plays, written by one of their Company, that had served them so well. It was a long and heavy task; they finished it in 1623. And, as they worked, they came more and more under the spell of their old friend. In life he had been pleasant, gentle Will, a reliable and popular member of a team; now they began to see more. There were riches here that, in the hurly-burly of production, no one had noticed: breath-catching poetry, thoughts that lit up the dark business of living like flashes of lightning. When they had done, Condell said, 'John, this work has taught me more about what it means to be a man, and inhabit the earth, than all my years of living.'

The two men sat silent for a long time. Then: 'Yes,' said Heminge. Another silence. 'Such pity, that we cannot tell him so.'

She was sixty-seven. There could not be much of life left to her. Not that she wanted it. There was no living without her sweet Will-o'-the-Wisp. But, after life – ? 'Sir, I am greatly troubled. In my youth, I committed mortal sin. And now, I am old, and the flames of Hell reach out for me.'

'Let not your heart be troubled, daughter. Is it not said that the tears of repentance will quench the very fires of Hell?'

She was silent. Then she said piteously. 'But, sir, I cannot repent.' The priest's eyebrows rose. 'What I did, I did in love and tenderness and compassion. And yet – the sin was mortal.'

He said, gently, 'Without repentance there can be no salvation. What was your sin, daughter?'

'I lay with my husband, before he was my husband.'

He said nothing, waiting; but it seemed to Anne there was nothing further to be said on this subject. The laws of God were fixed, and immutable. This priest could not change them.

But there was something he *could* do. After a time she said, 'And now, sir, I would lie in my husband's grave. Will you remember?' She gave a fleeting, sad smile. 'I shall not be long.'

'But that cannot be,' he said quickly.

'Cannot? Why?'

'Your husband gave orders that his grave was not to be disturbed.' The Vicar of Holy Trinity was looking alarmed. 'More, he laid a solemn curse on any who did so. As you yourself well know, madam.'

'But *that* is not what he meant. He meant he did not want his bones thrown into the charnel house.' She shuddered.

'That is not what he said, mistress.'

She cried aloud, 'Sir, am I to have *no* rest, either of body or soul?'

He said, 'As to your soul, daughter, you know the remedy. As to the other, if you are prepared to flout such a curse, I am not. Nor are my gravediggers, who are pious and god-fearing men.'

She walked back, under the cool churchyard limes, rebuffed, weary, oppressed. Life was an emptiness, death a terror. She plodded on. New Place would be lonely and empty, for Doctor Hall would be on his rounds, and Susanna and Elizabeth, she knew, were out visiting. But at least it would be cool.

Doll Scattergood met her at the door. 'Oh, mistress, two gentlemen have arrived, wishing to see you. I put them in your little room, mistress.' The maid was clearly excited. 'Two proper gentlemen, come from London, they say.'

'Thank you, Doll.' She was in no mood for visitors, today of all days. Besides, she was growing old, and company bewildered her.

She went into the small sitting-room where, nowadays, she spent more and more of her time. As her own private withdrawing room, it had fewer reminders of happiness. And they would be undisturbed.

The two gentlemen rose, bowed very low.

She was reminded of a black spade beard, a black cap of hair. Now beard and hair were white, but there was the same courtesy. Delightedly she held out her hand to be kissed. 'Master Heminge. You are very welcome, sir.'

'Thank you. You remember my friend, your husband's friend, Harry Condell?'

'You are both welcome. Pray sit down, gentlemen. Now. A glass of canary.' She rang a bell. It was as though, for the moment at least, she had cast off twenty years. 'You are from London, I hear.'

'Yes.'

Doll Scattergood bustled in with the wine. Condell said, 'You are well, madam?'

'Indifferent well. This world is become a burden. I would fain be away. And yet – ?' She shivered.

'The fear of something after death – ? Nay, mistress. Be like your husband. And me. *He* did not believe that a loving God would burn men in Hell. And nor do I.'

Her spirits rose. Put like that – She turned to Condell. 'And you, Master Condell?'

He shrugged. 'Madam, I am but a poor player. My opinion is worth nothing. Yet, when I look upon the tortured face of Christ, I cannot believe He would have us suffer so.'

She sat back in her chair. Oh, these gentlemen had made her feel like Mistress Shakespeare again; she no longer felt like some old witch being sentenced to the fire. Well, it would not last, she knew. But it would help her on her way. She lifted her glass. 'Your very good healths, gentlemen.'

They responded. Then Heminge said, 'Mistress Shakespeare, Harry and I have gathered together all your husband's plays. They are to be published' – he saw her look of incomprehension – 'made into a book. The printing is not yet done. But – we found so much in these plays, so much humanity and laughter and poetry – that we wanted to tell Will, for we are sure he did not realise all he had put into them.'

'And since,' said Condell, smiling, 'we *could* not tell Will, we decided to come north and tell you, Mistress Shakespeare.'

She did not quite grasp all this. But she did know they were being immensely kind; and that they had ridden ninety miles in a summer's heat to be kind. She leaned forward, pressed their hands, smiled in gratitude.

Heminge picked up the great file of papers. 'Tonight we lie at the inn. Tomorrow we must return to London. But we will leave the plays with you tonight, so that you may peruse them.'

She said nervously, 'Sirs, I am no reader. But I am most grateful.'

They smiled, as at a joke. The wife of William Shakespeare, no reader? Heminge said, 'See, madam, in our preface we say, what in God's name is true, that we have done this work without ambition for profit or fame but "to keep the memory of so worthy a friend and fellow alive, as was our Shakespeare".'

She was an old woman, and tired. Things were suddenly becoming blurred and jumbled. She only knew that these men were kind, and were Will's friends, and were saying pleasant things about Will. And that, in some way she did not quite understand, this great volume of papers was what Will had written. A tear crept down her cheek.

She sat in her high-backed chair, the *Works of William Shakespeare* in her lap. Her old, parchment-like fingers played nervously with the pages. Sometimes her faded-blue eyes would look at her two visitors in bewilderment, dart away, come back to smile in recognition. Sometimes they would look down at the book, without understanding, and the fingers would jerk and pluck again at the pages.

They waited, eager for her to begin reading, yet knowing they must wait. And at last she opened the book, and bent low over it, peering at the words and shaking her head. For it meant little to her.

But now her old mind was back in a cottage in Chapel Lane. And a young poet was reading a passage to his young wife, beside the fire, in the days before her world was threatened and riven. Without looking up she said, 'Will wrote about a sad king, who wanted to be a shepherd. And could not.'

Heminge and Condell looked at each other. Anne said, 'It was about contentment, and peace.'

'Ah,' said Condell. He took the book, turned the pages. 'Is this it?' He began to read. '*O God! Methinks it were a happy life…*'

'Yes. Oh, yes,' cried Anne. She listened, rapt. When he had finished she said, almost to herself, 'That could have been my life, and Will's. Only – it was not to be.'

When they had gone – each hoping, though not saying, that the old lady would not use her husband's plays to light the fire, and that New Place would survive the perils and dangers of the night – she sat there, the book open before her, painfully spelling out the words her husband had written so long ago: *O God! Methinks it were a happy life, To be no better than a homely swain; To sit upon a hill, as I do now –*

She could not read it all. She was too tired, and reading did not come easy. But she found another line in the same passage: *Ah! what a life were this; how sweet! how lovely!*

She wept a little, and closed the book on a finger. So William Shakespeare's widow sat, while a summer's evening passed; with his plays, which she could not read, on her lap. Sweet Will, sweet Will-o'-the-Wisp, of whom she had known so little in life, and whom they would not even let her join in death.

Nor did they. For while Heminge and Condell were riding quietly back to London, with a sense of a kindly act well done, and an undefined feeling that they were about to be responsible for a resurrection, a second coming, Anne was being laid in Trinity chancel, not with, but beside her husband.

And there they would sleep; while springs and winters passed them by; and the rose bloomed and the rose faded, bloomed and faded; and the earth wheeled into the sunlight of far distant summers, into centuries yet unknown.

Quiet consummation have;
And renownéd be thy grave.

Eric Malpass

The Lamplight and the Stars

Nathan Cranswick's third child comes into the world on the day of Queen Victoria's Diamond Jubilee. Whilst the Empire celebrates, Nathan's concerns are about his family's future. A gentle and wise preacher, he gratefully accepts the chance to move from the dingy, cramped house in Ingerby to the village of Moreland when he is offered a job on the splendid Heron estate. Anticipating peace and tranquillity for his wife and young family, his hopes are cruelly dashed when their new life is beset by problems from the beginning. A family scandal and the Boer War menace their whole future, but finally it is the agonising choice facing his gentle daughter which threatens to tear the family apart...

Morning's at Seven

Three generations of the Pentecost family live in a state of permanent disarray in a huge, sprawling farmhouse. Seven-year-old Gaylord Pentecost is the innocent hero who observes the lives of the adults – Grandpa, Momma and Poppa and two aunties – with amusement and incredulity.

Through Gaylord's eyes, we witness the heartache suffered by Auntie Rose as the exquisite Auntie Becky makes a play for her gentleman friend, while Gaylord unwittingly makes the situation far worse.

Mayhem and madness reign in this zestful account of the lives and loves of the outrageous Pentecosts.

Eric Malpass

Of Human Frailty
A biographical novel of Thomas Cranmer

Thomas Cranmer is a gentle, unassuming scholar when a chance meeting sweeps him away from the security and tranquillity of Cambridge to the harsh magnificence of Henry VIII's court. As a supporter of Henry he soon rises to prominence as Archbishop of Canterbury.

Eric Malpass paints a fascinating picture of Reformation England and its prominent figures: the brilliant, charismatic but utterly ruthless Henry VIII, the exquisite but scheming Anne Boleyn and the fanatical Mary Tudor.

But it is the paradoxical Thomas Cranmer who dominates the story. A tormented man, he is torn between valour and cowardice; a man with a loving heart who finds himself hated by many; and a man of God who makes the terrifying discovery that he must suffer and die for his beliefs. Thomas Cranmer is a man of simple virtue, whose only fault is his all too human frailty.

Eric Malpass

The Raising of Lazarus Pike

Lazarus Pike (1820–1899), author of *Lady Emily's Decision*, lies buried in the churchyard of Ill Boding. And there he would have remained, in obscurity and undisturbed, had it not been for a series of remarkable coincidences. A discovery sets in motion a campaign to republish his works and to reinstate Lazarus Pike as a giant of Victorian literature. This is a cause of bitter wrangling between the two factions that emerge. For some, Lazarus is a simple schoolmaster, devoted to his beautiful wife, Corinda. For others, who think his reputation needs a sexy, contemporary twist, he is a wife murderer with a deeply flawed character. What follows is a knowing and wry look at the world of literary make-overs and the heritage industry in a hilarious story that brings fame and tragedy to an unsuspecting moorland village.

Sweet Will

William Shakespeare is just eighteen when he marries Anne Hathaway, eight years his senior. Anne, who bears a son soon after the marriage, is plain and not particularly bright – but her love for Will is undeniable. Talented and fiercely ambitious, Will's scintillating genius soon makes him the toast of Elizabethan London. While he basks in the flattery his great reputation affords him, Anne lives a lonely life in Stratford, far away from the glittering world of her husband.

This highly evocative account of the life of the young William Shakespeare begins the trilogy which continues with *The Cleopatra Boy* and concludes with *A House of Women*.

ERIC MALPASS

THE WIND BRINGS UP THE RAIN

It is a perfect summer's day in August 1914. Yet even as Nell and her friends enjoy a blissful picnic by the river, the storm clouds of war are gathering over Europe. Very soon this idyll is to be swept away by the conflict that will take millions of men to their deaths.

After the war, the widowed Nell leads a wretched existence, caring for her husband's elderly, ungrateful parents, with only her son, Benbow, for companionship and support. But Nell is a passionate woman and wants to share her life with a man who will return her love. Meanwhile, Benbow falls in love with a German girl, Ulrike – until she is enticed home by the resurgent Germany.

This moving story of a Midlands family in the inter-war years is a compelling tale of personal triumph and disappointment, set against the background of the hideous destruction of war.

TITLES BY ERIC MALPASS AVAILABLE DIRECT
FROM HOUSE OF STRATUS

Quantity		£	$(US)	$(CAN)	€
☐	AT THE HEIGHT OF THE MOON	6.99	11.50	15.99	11.50
☐	BEEFY JONES	6.99	11.50	15.99	11.50
☐	THE CLEOPATRA BOY	6.99	11.50	15.99	11.50
☐	FORTINBRAS HAS ESCAPED	6.99	11.50	15.99	11.50
☐	THE LAMPLIGHT AND THE STARS	6.99	11.50	15.99	11.50
☐	THE LONG LONG DANCES	6.99	11.50	15.99	11.50
☐	MORNING'S AT SEVEN	6.99	11.50	15.99	11.50
☐	OF HUMAN FRAILTY	6.99	11.50	15.99	11.50
☐	OH, MY DARLING DAUGHTER	6.99	11.50	15.99	11.50
☐	PIG-IN-THE-MIDDLE	6.99	11.50	15.99	11.50
☐	THE RAISING OF LAZARUS PIKE	6.99	11.50	15.99	11.50
☐	SUMMER AWAKENING	6.99	11.50	15.99	11.50
☐	SWEET WILL	6.99	11.50	15.99	11.50
☐	THE WIND BRINGS UP THE RAIN	6.99	11.50	15.99	11.50

ALL HOUSE OF STRATUS BOOKS ARE AVAILABLE FROM GOOD BOOKSHOPS
OR DIRECT FROM THE PUBLISHER:

Internet: www.houseofstratus.com including author interviews, reviews, features.

Email: sales@houseofstratus.com please quote author, title and credit card details.

Order Line: UK: 0800 169 1780,
            USA: 1 800 509 9942
            INTERNATIONAL: +44 (0) 20 7494 6400 (UK)
                      or +01 212 218 7649
            (please quote author, title, and credit card details.)

Send to: House of Stratus Sales Department   House of Stratus Inc.
            24c Old Burlington Street   Suite 210
            London   1270 Avenue of the Americas
            W1X 1RL   New York • NY 10020
            UK   USA

PAYMENT

Please tick currency you wish to use:

☐ £ (Sterling)   ☐ $ (US)   ☐ $ (CAN)   ☐ € (Euros)

Allow for shipping costs charged per order plus an amount per book as set out in the tables below:

CURRENCY/DESTINATION

	£(Sterling)	$(US)	$(CAN)	€(Euros)
Cost per order				
UK	1.50	2.25	3.50	2.50
Europe	3.00	4.50	6.75	5.00
North America	3.00	3.50	5.25	5.00
Rest of World	3.00	4.50	6.75	5.00
Additional cost per book				
UK	0.50	0.75	1.15	0.85
Europe	1.00	1.50	2.25	1.70
North America	1.00	1.00	1.50	1.70
Rest of World	1.50	2.25	3.50	3.00

PLEASE SEND CHEQUE OR INTERNATIONAL MONEY ORDER.
payable to: STRATUS HOLDINGS plc or HOUSE OF STRATUS INC. or card payment as indicated

STERLING EXAMPLE

Cost of book(s):..................... Example: 3 x books at £6.99 each: £20.97

Cost of order: .... Example: £1.50 (Delivery to UK address)

Additional cost per book:.............. Example: 3 x £0.50: £1.50

Order total including shipping:.......... Example: £23.97

VISA, MASTERCARD, SWITCH, AMEX:

☐ ☐ ☐ ☐ ☐ ☐ ☐ ☐ ☐ ☐ ☐ ☐ ☐ ☐ ☐ ☐ ☐ ☐ ☐ ☐

Issue number (Switch only):

☐ ☐ ☐

Start Date: **Expiry Date:**

☐ ☐ / ☐ ☐   ☐ ☐ / ☐ ☐

Signature: _____

NAME: _____

ADDRESS: _____

COUNTRY: _____

ZIP/POSTCODE: _____

Please allow 28 days for delivery. Despatch normally within 48 hours.

ices subject to change without notice.
se tick box if you do not wish to receive any additional information. ☐

e of Stratus publishes many other titles in this genre; please check our website (**www.houseofstratus.com**) for more details.